LOVELY WICKED THINGS

HOLLOW'S ROW
BOOK THREE

TRISHA WOLFE

TRISHA WOLFE
LOCK KEY PRESS

Spotify Playlist

Media Vita in Morte Sumus – Notker
Dark Signs – Sleep Token
A Girl Like You – Machine Gun Kelly
I Wanna Dance With Somebody – Sleep Token
High – Stephen Sanchez
Sugar – Sleep Token
Way Down We Go – Taylah Withers
Villain – MISSIO
Time is Running Out – Muse
Got You (Where I Want You) – The Flys
Alkaline – Sleep Token
Rain – Sleep Token
10,000 Emerald Pools – Borns
Breath – Breaking Benjamin
The Wolf – Fever Ray
Nights in White Satin – Oceans of Slumber
Bad Things – Summer Kennedy
Blood Sport – Sleep Token
Time After Time – Cyndi Lauper

"It is not enough to conquer; one must learn to seduce."

— VOLTAIRE

HARBINGER KILLER LETTERS

FIRST HARBINGER CRIME SCENE: OXFORD, ME CASINO LOCATION

A flutter is a risk, no matter the wager.
One taken to fill the lungs.
I am the Harbinger of the endless.

SECOND HARBINGER CRIME SCENE: NEW HAVEN, CT RECOVERY CENTER LOCATION

Omens in the eyes divine of doom.
Two taken to save humanity.
I am the Harbinger of time.

THIRD HARBINGER CRIME SCENE: MEDFORD, MA UNIVERSITY LOCATION

Deny death, heed the warning.
Three taken is the gift.
I am the Harbinger of fate.

SIGIL

KALLUM: SIX MONTHS AGO

M*edia vita in morte sumus.*

In the midst of life we are in death.

The Latin antiphon composed by Notker was conceived by the Benedictine monk amid a chasm, where the erection of a bridge over a yawning abyss stirred his soul in such a way, the product of which was his immortalized art born the same year he died.

The chorus of the hymn became a medieval battle cry as it branched out beyond its Catholic roots. It became more than a philosophical question, Notker's vision evoked to move us in its melancholic embrace through every new rendition.

His moment of enlightenment, a voice through the ages.

As for me, standing at the precipice of my abyss, my moment feels like a heart attack.

The muscle squeezed in a ruthless, unforgiving vise.

Breath hung on a searing ache that sets my damned soul aflame. Arteries constricting. Pulse slamming vein walls. A slice of white-hot pain through the sternum.

A pain so euphoric I'm nearly brought to my knees.

But I'm not dying.

I'm being brought to life.

The moment I see her, I'm strangled by melancholy steeped in honeysuckle and clove. I'm ensnared by the Grim Reaper's clutch while angels intone the heavenly chorus, my acute existential crisis all but expelled from the bowels of despair.

It's impossible to describe something so ineffable.

For the desensitized, to feel alive, we perpetually balance on the brink of death. That dare to take a step off the edge an electric chord zipping through our veins, the taunt whispered in our ears and prickling our skin with the challenge.

Yet it's only ever a weak simulation of what lies just beyond our reach.

Then without warning, *she* crashes into me—this exquisitely beautiful creature—and I'm not simply inspired to take a step, I leap right off the edge.

She's the mirror flame of my own, yet it's her fire that makes me feel.

Bringing my hand to my chest, I touch the mark carved into my pectoral as it flares with renewed heat, the rough edges of the sigil felt beneath the fabric of my shirt.

Because we harbor even a kernel of the infinite within us, we are painfully aware of our limitation, of the absence of divinity. We are temporary. This is our great existential wound. By slicing my flesh, I have merely scraped mine open to expose where she has always belonged.

A bruised night hangs over the campus, and I move from under the shelter of the eaves. I am suddenly symptomatic, made acutely aware of my gaping hole, my torn flesh, of my missing half rend from my being.

I summoned her. I brought her here. I follow her now, tethered to her like an echo of her movements, a shadow stalking her like a demon across the university grounds.

As if she senses me, she looks around warily. I only hang back for a moment—but that's all it takes, one short moment in time to forever alter our course.

The attack happens suddenly, barely giving me time to identify the wrath singeing my insides before the altercation has escalated.

She's dragged to the asphalt. Wellington hovers on top of her and his filthy hands wrap her neck. And a single thought invades my mind, that I'm going to end him. *Brutally*.

As if reflected in a dark mirror, this thought instantly manifests when she sinks her thumbs into the sockets of his eyes. He belts out a drunken wail, allowing her to escape and seize the discarded tool.

Her mounting fury snaps like a crack of thunder, and I'm grounded where I stand, entranced, enamored, a lightning rod inviting her strike. As she rises to face her attacker, the soft white light of the moon highlights her beautiful features, the pale vein streaked through her hair.

A heartbeat suspends us, waiting for a solitary breath to unleash the torrent.

3

The pulse of a drum resounds from the depths, intensifying. Time stills, torturously slow.

The weapon slices the air.

The lug wrench draws blood at the point of contact. Dark red mists the night, coating the fabric of time in a thick, cloying film and scenting the air with iron and violence.

Wellington stumbles off-kilter and touches his temple before he goes down.

Against the darkened backdrop of the lot, a cosmic divide between heaven and hell ripples at the seams, painting the canvas of this plane with impassioned strokes of hematic red.

Her strangled cry splits the ozone to propel me forward, and when I finally reach her, I drop to my knees.

Racked with tremors, she grips the lug wrench as she struggles to heave in a breath, her light hazel eyes unblinkingly lost at the damage spread on the ground before her. Her hair is wild and escapes the band holding it back. Flecks of blood spatter her face like the curry I can taste imbuing the air between us.

I dare to take her face between my palms. My entire body pulses, lit with the electric current of the sun from this first touch. I turn her unseeing gaze on me.

Her pupils are blown, shock and panic coursing through her system as her pulse fires against my fingers.

"*Breathe*," I command, and her mouth parts as she gasps air into her lungs. "That's it, come back to me. Come back to me."

She locks on to my gaze, staring almost through me, but a sliver of lucidity begins to crest in her shimmering eyes. The hazy lampposts cast the scene in a sickly orange, making the moment feel surreal, outside of us, yet I know neither of us have ever been more present.

She drags in another unsteady breath, my touch anchoring her to me, as I shift my gaze to the body sprawled on the greenery of the parking lot. A ridge of thick shrubbery conceals us from the media building. The conference ended hours ago, leaving the university grounds empty, but we won't be cloaked for long.

A fierce desire to protect her from what's coming wars with my raging sense of self-preservation. I've never experienced a desire more demanding. It's pure fucking torture.

It's goddamn bliss.

In the midst of life we are in death.

"*Media vita in morte sumus,*" I murmur, my tone as fragile as this moment woven between us by Athena herself.

She still hasn't spoken a word, yet I read every raging emotion in her eyes. I've never feared anything, not even my own sadistic father, but confronted with the threat of losing her, I'm fucking terrified.

As I reluctantly release her, I take in the blood staining my palms. Her sin made mine. Her eyes absorb the sight, and she shivers. I quickly remove my suit jacket and drape it around her trembling shoulders. As if coming out of a trance, she pulls the lapels tight, her delicate fingers depositing blood on the fabric, and I think about how those same delicate hands just caved Wellington's temporal bone.

A groan disturbs our solitude. Of course, Wellington is

much too insolent, demanding attention even in death. He can't simply die in peace. Ironic, seeing as how he constantly lectured on the subject.

Kneeling in front of me, she startles, thrust into the present. "He's alive."

"But should he be?"

The thought leaves my mouth unfiltered. Her fine eyebrows draw together as if she's sorting and weighing the answer to that question within herself.

"Here," I say, snapping up his wrist. "Grab his other arm. He can't be left here."

A few seconds of hesitation pass before she says, "We shouldn't move him." She glances around the deepening night. "I have to call this in."

Operating on instinct, she pushes to her feet, her movements shaky. I still have Wellington's limp wrist clutched in my hand, his pulse unsteady beneath my fingers, as I watch her drive her fingers into her dark hair. The unruly streak of white becomes tinged with red. It falls across her eye, lodging a fierce need in me to sweep the length behind her ear.

Much too large for her, my jacket hangs on her shoulders. She holds the collar so she can grab a phone from her back pocket, but she only stares at the dark screen. Then she begins to search the ground.

"Shit," she mutters as her search becomes frantic.

I'm in no rush to get Wellington help. I could watch this goddess all night, listen to her softly muttered curses and desperate gasps for breath until the end of time, but there's a man bleeding out on the ground, and soon someone *will* call for help.

I glance at the bastard near my feet. "Plans change, Percy." As cautiously as I can, I stand and approach her. "We need to move him."

"No, I need to find it," she says, her voice raspy and broken, which reminds me of his hands around her throat.

Reflexively, my hand clenches into a fist. I'm a volatile substance heated too quickly as I search the ground and swipe up a ring of keys.

"Here." I tuck the keys in her palm, closing her fingers around the solid objects.

She stares vacantly at our clasped hands, then finally removes hers from mine to slip the keys into the bag at her hip. "Thank you."

I trap her face between my palms again, flames licking my viscera at the feel of her soft skin. "We have to move him," I say. "Now."

She stares back at me, long lashes framing her light eyes that reflect the stars, and I swear if she asked me to light myself on fire right now, I'd strike a match.

Mercifully, she nods against my hold. No other words are spoken as I reluctantly release her and we heft the drunk and battered professor and lug him across the shadows of the campus.

I make sure to grab the weapon.

My thoughts are a snarl of hypotheticals, an infinite number of paths stretched before us, each one littered with too many unknown variables. Forced to select one, I take the path which leads us into the dim interior of Wellington's lecture hall, where I let him drop to the lacquered hardwood.

Despite the dire circumstance, a fiendish smile tips my

mouth. Wellington's insult to me during his speech now feels more like a trivial afterthought. Casting a critical look down on his bloodied face, I no longer see a rival, if he ever was much of one from the start.

"Who's the washed-up charlatan now?"

"You know him," she says to me, and I note an undercurrent of accusation layered beneath.

I sink my hands into the depths of my pockets. The subtle glow of bookcase lamps is the only source of light, casting the classroom like a darkened stage.

"Unfortunately," I tell her honestly. "He's a professor of philosophy here, but more of a hack."

She paces a few steps, then turns to face me. "Who are you?" she demands.

I lift my chin, the weight of her question met with a host of conflict and friction.

The only certainty I know is, since my first touch, I won't be able to keep my hands off her. I've never felt such a compulsion to enmesh myself in another person. She's become a part of my state of being. Entanglement theory on a cellular level, entwining us with an epic origin story.

Plato's *Symposium* states humans were once whole beings that, due to the gods' fear and envy, were severed in half. One made two.

When one finds their soul mate, they will cleave to them, will abandon all else to be with their other half. Where, in the throes of passion, their need to satiate an endless desire, they will starve and wither in each other's embrace.

Stale philosophers can argue whether or not Plato

actually believed in the concept of soul mates, or if the myth was delivered by a comic as satire.

I'd vainly argue that no one spouts such passion, such fervor, only to dismissively sweep it aside. If Plato ever entertained this belief, then the proof may lie in such a verse:

He whom love touches not walks in darkness.

Daringly, I free my hands and devour the distance between us to capture her wrists. Her gaze lowers to the inked sigils on my fingers as my thumb purposely strokes her skin. The staccato beat of her pulse accelerates under my touch.

"I'm the man who's been waiting for you," I confess, the raw honesty flayed from my dingy soul.

She momentarily forgets about her questions and the bastard bleeding out on the floor as her gaze connects with mine, a heated swirl of curiosity and fear and recognition all banked behind those alarmingly expressive eyes.

I tilt my head and nod down to Wellington. "What happened with him?"

She blinks. "He's a killer."

Those three words punctuate the atmosphere with damning conviction. The silence of the hall insulates us, fueling the burning ache in my chest as I study the unearthly woman in my grasp.

Her intoxicating fragrance of lily of the valley and ylang-ylang infuses the enclosed space, damn near drugging me. "How do you know that."

Her teeth sink into her bottom lip, my suit jacket swallowing her. And goddamn, that's such a tempting thought. How I could swallow her down my gullet this instant.

She shakes her head tentatively. "I don't know. I lost something," she says on a shaky breath.

The powerlessness I feel watching her descend further into a state of shock spears my rib cage. The fear of losing her is tangible—a loss so debilitating, it reaches sharp claws down my throat to scrape at my insides.

Delicately, I tow the band down the length of her hair, bringing her dark layers over her shoulders. The air between us crackles as my gaze travels to the base of her throat where a teardrop diamond rests. My movements slow and cautious, still securing her wrist in one hand, I lift the pendant with the finger of my other.

"Maybe you wanted it to be lost," I say.

For three solid heartbeats, she doesn't blink, doesn't breathe. Her gaze fuses to mine, a lifetime and even perhaps a hundred lifetimes held in the pools of her stormy irises.

My breath lodges in my throat as I release the necklace and turn my bloodstained palm up to her, an appeal issued in the dark encasing us.

Her gaze drops to my hand before meeting my eyes. "I don't know you—"

"You do."

"How can I trust you?"

"You can trust that I've never been more selfless than I am right now," I say. "Trust my intent. I want to protect you."

She stares at my palm, her features softening as her hesitancy falls away.

Then she takes my hand.

Satisfaction flares in my veins. My long fingers entwine around her slender ones, and I know in the hollow space beneath bone and cartilage I will never be able to let her go.

Wellington stirs on the floor. "Fuck...mother fucking hell."

The disruption initiates the next sequence of events.

She releases my hand as Wellington rolls over, one side of his face caked in layers of blood. He rubs his bruised eyes before his bleary gaze darts up to her.

"You fucking cunt," he seethes around a wet croak. Movements clumsy, he digs out his phone from the inseam of his tweed blazer. "My lawyer is going to sue—"

I kick the phone from his hand. Crush it under my combat boot.

The reverberating *crack* of the screen beneath my heel shatters more than his device.

Our state in this moment is unstable, fragile and volatile, and her eyes are on me, a fire ignited behind her caution and fear. I want to fan the flames, to see the world burn to cinder with her.

Make it our own.

Wellington touches his temple with a hiss. He looks at the bright-red blood on his fingers, then his smashed phone. "You're the goddamn devil, Locke. You're finished," he threatens as he heaves himself up onto his side. "Your career is scorched earth."

My nostrils flare, and I breathe in the scent of blood lingering beneath the faint honeysuckle.

From my periphery, I see her lower and take the lug

wrench in her hand. She holds it out toward him in warning. "Just…don't move. I need to think."

Momentarily halted, Wellington glares up at her. "You're fucking insane. You both are." His obnoxious chuckle echos against the wood surfaces of the hall, a sick, menacing sound that triggers a dark rage.

I'm a bystander on the edge of this production. The stage is so beautifully set, the script poetry waiting to unfold.

All we need is a catalyst.

And Percy Wellington is nothing if not giving of his efforts.

He spits a trail of blood at the floor. "Seeing how my face bears the proof of your assault, even your pretty little head is quick enough to figure out how this will end, sweetheart."

As if the endearment triggers her, she tightens her hold on the weapon, her chest rising and falling with quick inhalations as she disappears somewhere within herself. "He's right."

The resulting pain that blazes to life within her almost knocks me to the floor. Her state of shock offered her a reprieve, but now, like a dam cracking, that heartache comes flooding back.

I'm hit with the intensity of her anguish so hard, I suffocate under the resounding swell of it.

"He's right," she says again, a distant look glazing her eyes.

Wellington struggles to crawl an inch forward. Disoriented, he slaps at the wood floor, pulling his body toward the exit of his lecture hall.

She pushes my suit jacket off her shoulders, tows the strap over her head and sets the bag aside, then grips the tire iron with both hands, her movements methodical. "He'll get away with everything," she says, a gentle whisper beneath her rising fury. "Because of me, he'll walk."

"Don't let him."

Our eyes clash, a charged current dangerously strong snaps between us. If she wielded that weapon against me, I'd welcome her lovely death. I'm almost envious of that undeserving bastard.

She angles toward the broken man slithering along the floor and the drums surge. The beat pounds harder, faster, and I can feel the fire, hot flames licking my flesh as she takes one determined step after another in his direction. Adrenaline scorches the chambers of my heart when she blocks his path.

A change has overtaken her, and I'm not the only one who witnesses the transformation. Wellington's smug expression falls. Real fear blanches his skin as he holds up a hand in useless protest.

"I can't let the killer get away," she whispers.

Darkness has many names, takes many forms. In this moment, she gives it vengeance.

The weapon arcs downward.

His disembodied cry is soon silenced as the sharp end of the tire iron clips his jaw. Beautiful eyes flared wide, mouth parted, she flips the weapon around and brings the bulk of the thick wrench down on his face.

My heart drums to the climbing rhythm. I feel the next

13

strike as much as hear it, the wet smack that rends the air, and the sickening crunch that follows.

Three perfect strikes to deliver his death.

The display is brutal, and passionate, and horrifying.

For a few prolonged seconds, she revels in the delivery of her pain. Taking life, stealing catharsis. She unleashes a punishment to the fucking universe for the loss I still feel bleeding from her soul.

Blood is splashed across her face and clothes, her fury a work of art. Savage lust fires through my blood, blistering my arteries. Her violence is intoxicating. Every visceral emotion harnessed within her, I feel inside me, damn near overloading my senses. Pure adrenaline ravishes my veins until I'm vibrating with an electric current, a monster brought to life.

Silence rings in the air at a deafening octave as chaos bathes the aftermath.

I've stepped closer to her. She's shaking, muscles trembling from adrenaline and exertion. I wrap my hand around hers and take the weapon.

We stare down at the body, the carnage. Wellington's jaw has been dislodged, the lower half of his face torn off. Blood pools black on the lacquered floor. She doesn't turn away.

And amid the destruction, I have never been more inspired. I look at her, my dark little muse sent to stir my soul. She is so much more than I envisioned.

She swipes her bloodstained hair from her face, her chest heaving. "I'll wait here while you make the call."

Lungs gripped in a vise, I step toward her. This

moment is fragile, and I can't scare her, or else she'll slip right through my fingers. "*Ut operaretur eum.*"

Her gaze traps mine. "I don't understand," she says, her voice quivering.

"Let us work without reasoning." I sweep a hand to encompass the body, blood, mayhem. Voltaire's words have never held more meaning for me than in this very moment.

A light flickers in the depth, a single ray of connection where her soul recognizes mine. Gingerly, she touches her forearm, her thoughts drifting to some other subspace.

"One must cultivate one's own garden," I say.

Her eyebrows pinch together as distress crests within her. "Why do I know that?"

A requirement of any college literature course, she's likely read the text, but I'd rather believe in the predestination of us.

"It's the only way to make life endurable." My smile is morose as I deliver the words, marveling at the shiny wet tears clinging to her dark eyelashes.

A broken sob is torn from her chest. "Nothing has been endurable."

As her body succumbs to exhaustion, she collapses. I catch her as her chest crashes into mine, enfolding her into me as I wrap my arms around her trembling body to weld us closer.

My heart beats in perfectly timed choreography with hers. The pure serenity I feel will be my undoing.

I release the weapon and run my hand down the cool strands of her hair. "Tell me what to do."

Tilting her face up, she swallows, her eyes pierce mine with conviction. "Sever the head."

An erotic buzz ignites my blood. I've never felt anything so intoxicating, and I would become a slave to this feeling in due course.

From here, we work together in tandem. Admittedly, it's not an easy task. I wasn't prepared for this outcome. What bone I can't saw must be broken. Every move that follows is meticulous, every act painstakingly analyzed, but my lovely little sprite directs the assembly.

Where the violence was beautifully reckless, our staging is carefully constructed. A union of chaos and logic that is flawlessly harmonized.

I stand back and admire her work. "A masterpiece."

Countermeasures have to be taken, of course. But the university is no Fort Knox. Any security footage that might need to be addressed is easily attained. All evidence tied back to Wellington's own lecture hall.

The secluded corner of the quad is dark and peaceful where we stand beside each other. The arousing jolt at her nearness urges me to reach out and take her hand in mine. Without words, I turn toward her and draw her close. Traces of dark red cover her clothes, still speckle her face. As her gaze lifts to touch mine, I track my thumb across her lips, smearing the blood. It's stained in the fine fissures of her skin.

I'm possessed by the desire to taste her, indulge in her and feast on her until I'm delirious from gluttony.

My mouth hovers close to hers, a dare, a promise.

A goddamn inevitability.

"Are you insane?" she asks me suddenly, but there's no derision or judgment in her tone.

"By now, most likely," I admit, though I've never thought of it in a clinical sense. I don't see the world in three dimensions, a spiral through quantum theory that altered more than my perception.

I have desired my muse for so long, I've stretched the bounds of sanity.

Before exhaustion completely claims her, she says, "I think I might be."

I caress the back of her hand with my thumb. "What you are, to me, is so fucking lovely, sweetness."

With the final addition to set the scene and tell the story, I place the wiped-down tool in the backseat of Wellington's car. Then I take her to my townhouse near the university, where I leave her in the bedroom shower.

I listen to the water rain down on the marble as I build a fire. After which I toss her bloodstained jeans into the flames. As I hold the shirt, my fingers tracing the rusty splotches of blood, precaution urges me to tuck the garment away in my closet.

The shower cuts off, then I hear the soft pad of her feet behind me. I turn to see her dressed in my sweatshirt, and the sight of her there, wearing my clothes, robs me of all reason.

"I don't regret what I did," she says, her voice weak, "but I can't live with it, either."

Her despondence trips my pulse. Despite all my tireless efforts, nothing has changed. I can feel her descent, know what she's contemplating, and a flame of rage ignites beneath my sternum.

"I need the blade you used." She rings a hand down her damp hair. "I'll turn myself in. I'll never mention you." She releases a derisive breath. "God, I haven't slept in days. I don't know who you are. I can't even remember how I got here." She begins to pace, pulling at the hem of the sweatshirt. "Is any of this real?"

Her spiral grips her fast and fierce. She's going into shock again, panic infusing my bedroom with a crackling intensity.

Tomorrow, or maybe even the day after, when the shock has faded, her conscience will tear her apart. She'll ruin herself. She'll ruin us.

I can't let her.

"Come here." My sure tone snaps the connection between us taut.

When she crosses toward me, I expel the tension from my chest. The rising flames cast her features in a soft glow. My nostrils flare as her scent invades my system like the most potent aphrodisiac.

I swallow. "Tell me what you need."

A desperate laugh slips past her lips. "Can you make me forget?"

Without hesitation, I say, "Yes."

She studies my eyes, searching me for the truth.

"I can make us both forget," I say, banishing the doubt from my thoughts. "But you have to trust me."

I undo the buttons along the placket of my black shirt, then wrench my arms from the sleeves and toss the balled garment into the fire. Gaze transfixed, she sweeps the sculpted reliefs of my chest, examining the dark ink and markings.

Her touch damn near sends me to my knees. I'm so awestruck by her, so desperate to keep her, I'm torn over whether I should steal her and lock her away in my mountain home.

"I know who you are," she says, a little shiver clinging to her shoulders. "I've read your papers."

Her eyes latch on to mine, and I admit, my ego soars. The desire to make her know exactly who I am is a depraved demon clawing from the inside.

"Do it," she says, her demand every bit a plea.

A lifetime of study into the hidden wisdoms of the world has either given me an advantage, or made me delusional. Either way, it's prepared me for this moment in time. If sanity means returning to my uninspired life before her, then I'll readily descend right into the maddening abyss.

I retrieve my ritual blade and bring it between us. There's no fear detected in her features, though there absolutely should be.

Do I believe this will work? For her, to keep her from self-destructing, I have no other choice. And if it fails, if her mind shatters…

Clasping her neck, I thread my fingers into her hair and tilt her face up to me. "Even in the darkest chasm, the deepest crags of hell, I will find you. I won't leave you in the dark."

With a reverent touch, she places her hand over the sigil scored into my chest. "But I don't believe in any of this."

"I'll believe for the both of us." A practitioner of the

dark arts, my conviction in chaos magick is more than a belief system, it's coded in my DNA.

I was born to raise fucking hell.

She lowers her hand. "I trust you."

And I'm drowning in her.

While my selfish nature demands to keep her for myself, this beautiful, exquisite woman and her heartsickness that breathes life into my decaying soul, I can't bear to feel her suffer.

So I do the humane thing and make her forget.

Not because I'm virtuous. The simple truth is I can't deny her, because I can't deny myself. Blood of my blood, flesh of my flesh, marrow of my bone.

I trap the lock of white framing her face, caressing the damp strands. "You have my word," I swear to her.

Not a promise.

A threat.

Nothing and no one will come between us.

She stands before the fire, her back to the crackling flames. A deity amid the light, a beautiful force destined to annihilate me.

With pained regret, I tug the sweatshirt down her shoulder and expose her soft skin.

I kiss her shoulder worshipfully, my mouth lingering, breathing her into my lungs to memorize the fiery ache. Then, as I pull away, I puncture my finger with the blade. As I trace the sigil along the delicate joint of her neck and shoulder, the chorus of the hymn stirs my soul.

In the midst of life we are in death.

Could any philosopher deny the soul has a mate when staring into their twin flame?

He whom love touches not walks in darkness.

I'll always find her, no matter how dark her mind goes.

I rest my forehead to hers as I continue to trace the symbol over her skin, our breath mingling, our emotions a tangle of heat and want and heartache.

Then I capture her lips with mine in a decimating kiss to chase back her pain. Fuck, I eat her pain like a goddamn fiend. I take it for her, every morsel of anguish and fear and sickness. I kiss her with a desperation my soul has never known.

When her mouth closes against mine, kissing me back with equal hunger, I tremble under the annihilating force, the tender feel of her tongue meeting mine with demanding need.

Sheltered in this moment, time stalls for us, and I covet every second.

"Stay," I whisper over her lips.

Her breath shudders hot across my mouth.

"Stay with me," I plead.

She blinks up at me. "I'll stay with you."

At her concession, I scoop her lithe body into my arms, relishing the feel of her palms braced on my bare chest as I carry her toward my bed. Before I even draw the covers over her, her eyes are closed, her body fighting against the sleep pulling her under.

I place a gentle kiss to her forehead, then step back and check the time on my watch, already dreading the loss of it. But there is still a lecture hall that needs to be cleaned, evidence destroyed, and surveillance to alter.

By the time the sun breaks the sky and I reenter my

townhouse, I know the fallout before I cross the threshold into my room.

Her bag is gone, and so is she.

A hollowness takes up residency inside my chest as I stare at the dimmed embers in the fireplace. Like the dying light of the fire, the coals growing dull, my inspiration is fading without her.

Before my muse crashed my life, I inked a sigil in my chest. As my obsessive desire all but consumed me, I carved into that mark tonight. I made a demand of the universe, I opened the wound and let the blood flow. And now that I've tasted my muse, I know it will be a vain and futile attempt to try to forget her.

I can no more purge her from my thoughts than I can tear my soul mate from my sternum.

She is the bridge erected over my abyss. She is life sparked amid my death.

My desire was born in those hauntingly beautiful hazel orbs that are cast with silvery storm clouds.

I lower to my haunches and reach into the fireplace, scraping aside ash as I take the tiny object between my fingers. I twirl the shiny gold piece as I stare at the initials.

The object that brought her here, the token she's searching for.

Time and tide wait for no man.

My muse will return to me.

2

MUSE

HALEN: NOW

There are as many conflicting tales around the muses as there are the gods themselves. Their origin, their number. Whether they were deities or forces.

One myth says the goddess of memory birthed the muses, and that they were then given to Apollo to raise. Hence their devotion, love, and aptitude for the arts and science.

The irony doesn't escape me—as I'm sure it hasn't escaped Kallum—that memory and logic presided over the muses. Two connections to me. A wink from the universe, a jab of cosmic synchronicity as my memory returns with a vengeful force.

Yet the one aspect all the poems agree on is that the muses were a source of creative inspiration, existing merely to inspire hungry souls.

Six months ago, with one violent act, I was claimed by one such ravenous soul.

I stand at the entrance of the storage unit, my hand gripped to the halfway drawn roll door, a shaft of evening sunlight slashed across dingy concrete.

A file box sits in the corner of the unit. I haven't opened that box since I sealed it closed in the early morning hours, where the sky was still black, a blank canvas awaiting a new start.

My gaze drifts across the discolored blots on the floor, my vision unfocused, and suddenly a pool of blood seeps up from a dark stain. A flash of Wellington's mutilated face surfaces with the coarse, heavy feel of the tire iron clenched in my hand.

With a slow exhale, I blink away the disturbing imagery of the horrific scene I created in a haze of rage and vengeance. A detached moment in time that fractured my psyche is where Kallum and I were fashioned, twisted together. Stained deeper and darker than the soiled concrete.

I enter the unit and lower the roll door closer to the floor for privacy, but still allow enough natural light to filter into the small five-by-eight room. The manager gave me a decent deal, agreeing to let me rent it here in Hollow's Row week-to-week rather than pay for a full month, as it's uncertain how long I'll remain on the case.

That decision is yet to be made.

Unease churns in my stomach as I lift the hem of my skirt and drag the file box away from the corner. As recovered memories can be highly unreliable, I need something tangible to help me piece together the details.

I lower to my knees and insert the tiny key to unlock the lid. One fortifying breath, then I tear the top off like a bandage over a wound.

Within are the contents of the Harbinger killer case from the third crime scene. The scene I was frantically working before I discovered the cufflink with the college insignia and Wellington's initials that led me to Cambridge.

I shove aside files and a pair of joggers, my heart rate quickening as my gaze falls on what lay beneath. I touch the gray cotton fabric, needing confirmation of its existence, before I lift the sweatshirt from the confines of the box. Stretching the garment by the shoulders, I stare at the college name branded across the front in bold crimson letters.

A bone-deep tremor racks my body as a flash of memory assaults. The scream wrenched from my throttled airway. The cold, calculating look in his eyes as he crushed my windpipe. The sickening feel of my thumbs sinking into those callous eyes. The way the solid iron of the lug wrench reverberated off his skull when I struck his head.

The blood.

So much blood as it collected dark and shiny under the lamplights around his unmoving body.

"Breathe."

The stranger's deep baritone cracks into my state of shock.

"Come back to me."

Then the warmth of his suit jacket embraces me as he drapes it around my shoulders.

The memories crash against one another. Kallum's

actions throughout this case as he attempted to jog my memory fight for dominance with my very first recollection of him that night. Every interaction with him holds new insight and meaning. Like when he placed his jacket around me in the killing fields, and his frenzied demand as he commanded me to breathe during the ritual. Every time he slipped my hair tie off, or when he dragged my shirt collar down my shoulder in the interrogation room. His thumb swiping wine from my lip like the blood he once smeared across my mouth.

His fevered whispers and professions while he brought me to the brink, over and over, our passionate lovemaking an act of magick in its own right.

And in the end, all it took was one tiny totem— Alister's cufflink I discovered near the stream—to unlock my memory and send me reeling through time into a hellscape of my own design.

All the tangible proof is right here.

It has been the whole time, locked in a file box waiting to be unsealed, just like the latent memories were locked inside me.

With an aching sigh, I trace my finger over the collar. After Kallum gave me his sweatshirt, he burned my bloodstained clothes in his fireplace. I can still feel the heat, smell the smoke mingled with his woodsy cologne as he stood before me, his intense clashing gaze cast down at my bare shoulder.

I lightly press my fingers to that spot, the feel of his phantom touch heating my skin before I wince at the tender pain from where Devyn wounded me. Then I turn the sweatshirt inside-out to see the rusty stain—his blood —from the sigil.

Parts of that night are still unclear. By that point, shock and sleep deprivation were wreaking havoc on my mental state. I recall the intoxicating sensation that gathered inside me as Kallum traced the rough pad of his finger over my skin, the tantalizing friction burning beneath my flesh as his beautiful, captivating eyes seared through me. The way he reverently held my face, his breath brushing my lips and drawing me further into him. The dare to sever the last tether to my sanity before his lips crashed against mine.

Then everything that was past and hard and painful faded beneath the promise that kiss held.

It was sensual, and erotic, but it was also safe. I felt sheltered by his arms, where I could finally break.

A mysteriously sexy and intelligent man in an all-black suit fused himself to my soul in that moment. A man I had only just encountered made me believe in the illogical, like I was meant to find him, to belong to him. A man who witnessed me murder in cold blood and kissed me afterward, then harbored my dark secret like a shadow of the soul, waiting for me to come back to him.

Truth is, Kallum Locke is even more of a mystery to me now.

Whatever transpired after he marked a sigil on my body is still buried in my unconscious. I can only rationalize my mind wiped the traumatic event to protect its host from a full shutdown.

Kallum was willing to take all of it for me, even do the time, in order to protect me, to keep his word.

"I won't leave you in the dark."

Then I walked into the Briar Institute and asked for his help.

Apparently, the fates are not without an ironic sense of humor.

I futilely rifle through the box, knowing my search will come up empty. The only proof of Professor Percy Wellington's involvement in the Harbinger killings, that he was the infamous killer, was lost that same night during the attack.

The cufflink from the third Harbinger crime scene is gone.

"Dammit." Expelling a weighty breath, I abandon the flimsy hope of recovering it now. Realistically, its existence means nothing to the case, which at this point remains open and unsolved. As the perpetrator is dead, the serial killings will go cold.

No new murders, no more leads. No more case.

It's unlikely that even six months ago that piece of evidence would have resulted in Wellington's arrest and subsequent incarceration.

I knew this as I watched him try to escape—that even if his cufflink wasn't a tenuous connection that a pricy lawyer could explain away, I had already corrupted the chain of evidence.

I didn't set out that night with the intent to commit murder. Wellington was alive after I defended myself. At some point it altered. I felt the dark current sweep over me when I looked into his eyes and was met with a soulless fiend. I've never felt such conviction—and I was powerless.

He had to die.

Grief is a sickness. It's a corrosive acid that eats through us, burns away the very fiber of our existence.

I shouldn't have been working the Harbinger case.

I've studied killers. I've walked in their steps. To do what I do, to solve the most debased cases, I've learned to think like them, to mimic them. I've sunk down into the roiling pit of their tarred souls.

And in that moment, I took on the persona of a killer.

To some degree, we all have a shadow. We look at our dark side in the privacy of our mind, where we can raise the veil when the threat becomes too great.

I bring the sweatshirt to my nose and inhale the lingering scent of woodsy cologne and sandalwood, Kallum's scent mixed with a faint trace of smoke to rouse the chaotic emotions which stirred my soul that night.

Head canted, I curiously rub at a smudge of soot embedded in the fabric of the sleeve before I crumple the garment and stuff it down in the bottom of the box. Then I withdrawal the composition notebook.

Within the pages are my recorded thoughts and findings on the Medford crime scene, the Harbinger's third victim. I kept these journals for myself, my personal notes not logged into the CrimeTech database.

I told Kallum that I didn't regret what I did—and I still don't. I feel too removed from that moment, as if it was someone else who swung that weapon. But I do need to find a way to offer the families of Wellington's victims closure.

I stole that vindication from the victims' loved ones when I took the law into my own hands.

Slipping the notebook under my arm, I close the box and lock the lid.

As I stand and look around the small unit, I realize this is it—the end of the mystery. I have my answers, as Kallum promised I would by the end of the case.

Only the case isn't over.

As if to confirm my thoughts, my phone vibrates in my tote. I bring it out to read a message from Agent Hernandez. Special Agent Rana has requested my presence at the Hollow's Row Police Department. The locals have brought in Tabitha for questioning. The waitress from the diner, the one who served me the coffee laced with a hypnotic right before Devyn took me to an abandoned mine shaft.

I run my thumb over the cracked edge of the phone screen, my thoughts turning to the woman who literally tried to rend me apart and consume me during her ascension ritual. I had wanted to reach her, to help her, but she was too heavily under the influence of her own drug and delusion.

At least, this is what I've been trying to convince myself of ever since Kallum disrupted her ritual and carried me away, allowing Devyn to flee into the night.

The truth is much more sinister, and painful, and comes with a substantial dose of reality that I'll soon have to contend with. Despite the details I provided to Agent Rana during my debriefing, where I stated Devyn ultimately released me, I'm the one who let her go.

A choice I made knowing that Devyn is a potential threat. She heard enough of the damning details of what transpired the night I killed Wellington to piece together the facts. Only I couldn't let her suffer a fate that I myself evaded.

Lying on the cold floor of the cave, as I stared into her haunted eyes, I commiserated with the immense pain I saw there, and I couldn't let her be brought in like that. Not without knowing the full truth.

Why a brilliant and intelligent woman suddenly decides to try to deify herself and ascend into the *Übermensch*.

There are things she said to me during her ritual that shook me, that raise even more questions.

A part of me understands the lure, the addiction. I tasted the frenzy. I let myself become lost to it. The numbing balm is easy to be seduced by. If Devyn was provoked by her pain, then I've already walked in her footsteps.

And I can find her.

I touch my forearm, where the inked words of Voltaire have been defaced, the wound Devyn tore into me stitched in sloppy needlework with black thread by Kallum. Which is fitting, since it was Kallum who gave me the words to begin with.

When the verse came to me before I was assigned to the Hollow's Row case, I thought it was a remnant from an old college class. I'm good at giving the inexplicable a logical explanation. Kallum's words from that night imprinted on me, seared so deeply I branded them onto my body.

I see Kallum rolling up my sleeve in the hotel room, feel his heartbeat thundering under my palm as he traced his fingers over the tattooed words. On the bridge, he told me I inked my own sigil in script, that I recite my affirmation daily, my own way of keeping the past buried and forgotten.

Where do you think your subconscious picked up on that?

Despite the humidity, I shiver at the memory. He knew exactly where I got my affirmation, and why I inked it into my skin. He was just waiting for me to remember.

I drop my hand from the stitched injury. There are a number of scars desensitizing my flesh, layers of painful memories. Little by little, we are altered by life as it chips away at us. Most of the time, we fail to notice those subtle alterations. Then there are the catastrophic changes that alter us irrevocably.

The woman who I was before is a stranger to the woman I am now as I stand here, looking over a storage unit that holds the only thing I feel is of value to me enough to save.

The cases of the dead.

The evidence of how I became one of them.

With that, I haul another file box over and empty the contents of my tote, the bagged evidence of Alister's attempted assault on me. The skin cells I scraped from beneath my nails, the torn clothes I was wearing at the time. All of it goes into the bottom of the box before I seal the lid.

The evidence will need to be destroyed, as it's now evidence that could incriminate Kallum as a motive for Alister's murder.

I dip under the roll door and lower it to the concrete, securing the combo lock in place. Then I head toward the black SUV where Agent Hernandez leans on the door. Shades drawn over his eyes, he looks up from his phone.

"Get what you need?" he asks.

I hold up the notebook in answer. "Did Agent Rana reply to our request to interview the recovered locals?"

The derisive frown pulling at his mouth says how asinine my question is.

"Right," I say, walking around the vehicle. "That would be absurd, as I'm now a victim."

Agent Rana, the new lead on the task force, would have me removed not only from the case, but from the town if it was within her power.

She doesn't trust me.

My irrational behavior at the Alister crime scene might have helped influence that.

But seeing as I'm now a witness in regards to Devyn Childs, I've been remanded here. Technically, I should no longer be working the case as a consultant to the Hollow's Row Police Department. As a victim, it's considered unethical, but that hasn't stopped Hernandez and me from conducting our own side investigation.

Annoyed with my limited options of wardrobe today, I gather my black skirt and step up into the passenger seat of the SUV. While Hernandez navigates the vehicle through the narrow streets toward the precinct, I clutch my notebook and stare out the tinted window.

The setting sun slashes the sky in gashes of burnt orange, outlining clouds in a seam of blazing red, the color of violence. The tall trees are black silhouettes against the neon backdrop, a stark contrast to the drawn and morose elements of the town.

There's something wrong with this place. An emptiness, a hollowness that aches beneath the gothic architecture of its charming exterior, like a bated breath waiting to exhale.

I felt it the very first time I entered the killing fields, a brand of evil all of its own. It doesn't dwell in the trees, or the houses. It festers in the people.

This town has a sinister hold over all of us.

After Hernandez parks, I slip the journal into my bag and climb out of the SUV. As I situate the tote strap over my shoulder, my gaze hardens on the faded brick building ahead, and a kernel of anxiety digs beneath my defenses.

Hernandez takes up my side, his large presence a comfort. "It's just a creepy old building," he says, reading my hesitancy.

I nod once, my action uprooting my feet as I take a step forward with conviction. "I was just thinking that."

Memories can be as temporary as our existence.

Whatever lingering fear resides from Alister's assault is quickly obliterated as I summon the mental image of his severed head. From now on, that's how I'll remember him. The skin flayed from his skull. A symbol carved into the bone.

Selfishly, Kallum's act makes me feel not alone in mine.

As he's protected my secret, I have to protect his.

I'm the catalyst for Kallum's crime against Alister. Two mirrored moments in time, one woven over the seams of the other, like the harsh red outline of the lowering sun.

The night Kallum found me, I became his muse, his inspiration for the darkest acts of violence.

I'm the one who told him to sever the head.

I taught him how to stage the Harbinger crime scenes.

If we had never crossed paths, Kallum Locke would still be the bad-boy professor of academia, and not committed to a psychiatric institution.

He wouldn't be a killer.

We all have a dark counterpart. Even a muse of light and inspiration beckons the darkness when challenged. Where these forces are capable of gifting divine, creative genius, when pushed beyond the brink, they are just as capable of becoming a curse.

Throughout my career, throughout all the darkness I've encountered, each and every horrific, gruesome case, I never let it touch me. I was safely sheltered in a life of light and love. Then the moment my parents were taken from me in a hit-and-run, the darkness found a crack.

Violence leaves a stain, like soot after a fire. The tarry ash transfers to every surface, impossible to remove once it's touched you.

There's a terrible truth Kallum couldn't have known about that night, a truth that was impossible for me to admit even to myself, the actual reason I chased after a notorious serial killer.

No, I didn't set out that night with the intent to kill the Harbinger.

I had hoped he'd kill me.

3

PRIMORDIAL PAIN

HALEN

The atmosphere of the department is as sterile as the lingering scent of antiseptic drifting through the chilly air. As if the locals are trying to purge the rancid trace of betrayal from the system.

I follow Hernandez through the warren of cubicles, catching sight of many sullen expressions. One of their own has deceived them, and for members of law enforcement, this is a double slight. Devyn was a friend as well as a trusted member of their department.

A few curious looks are directed my way as we head into the interrogation section of the building. A local uniform guards the middle room, presumably where Tabitha is being held. As we enter into the monitoring room, Agent Rana and Detective Emmons are conversing in hushed tones with other task force agents.

A flush gathers beneath my skin at the sight of the brightly lit interrogation room through the two-way mirror.

Tabitha is seated at the table—the same table where Kallum and I shared a heated encounter. The memory evokes the possessive feel of Kallum's touch—his hands on my body, the demanding dig of his fingers in my flesh—and I'm entirely too aware of the achy need low in my belly.

The recorded footage of that intimate moment was deleted, along with my presence in the building when I broke into the evidence room and stole the carving knife. I was able to stealthily relocate the evidence from Hernandez's SUV to the safe in my hotel room.

Which I'll soon need to find a more secure location. As I've learned from my time in this town, nothing is safely hidden for long.

"Dr. St. James," Agent Rana addresses me, turning her full, probing attention my way. She nods briefly to Agent Hernandez in acknowledgment before meeting my gaze with scrutiny. "I appreciate you being here for the questioning."

She says this like Hernandez and I were not the ones to provide the tip on Tabitha in the first place. I fold my arms across my chest, mindful of the stitches on my forearm. "I'm glad to be of help," I say.

From my periphery, I see both detectives of the HRPD advance our way. Riddick is wearing civilian clothing, as is Emmons, though Emmons sports his ever-present, wide-brim police hat.

"Is there something we're waiting for?" I pose the question to the gathered officials.

It's Riddick who responds. "This is an interrogation tactic," he says, moving closer to my side. "Puts the suspect on edge, wondering what we're discussing, why we're taking so long."

I glance at the waitress through the glass. She's not showing any signs of distress. She's calm and collected and disinterested, like she's been every time I've encountered her at the diner where she works.

"To be frank, detective, Tabitha is the epitome of not on edge."

Agent Hernandez sends me an apprehensive look that states the locals are behind the times on tactics.

Instead of offering a response, Riddick regards my attire, his gaze lingering with too much interest on my skirt. "How are you doing, Halen?"

Anxious, I curl my fingers into my palm and take a step back to put distance between us. "To be honest, I'm a little under caffeinated," I say, forcing sarcasm.

He touches my shoulder, his expression conveying my attempt at deflection doesn't repel him. "I'm serious. What you've gone through... Difficult is an understatement. I want you to know that I'm here, that the whole department is here for you," he quickly adds. "Everyone's just in shock right now."

"Thank you. But I promise, I'm fine," I assure him, adjusting my bag strap so his hand falls away. "I'm actually more concerned for Devyn out there right now, potentially alone."

His features draw together curiously. "I would think that after what she did to you, concern would be the last thing you'd feel for her."

"Seeing justice served isn't part of my job," I say.

"Trying to understand what she's going through and why is."

A stab of hypocrisy penetrates my resolve. Six months ago, in a darkened university lecture hall, I wasn't interested in understanding Wellington or his reasons before I served him a dose of justice.

"Then why do you think Devyn has done this—" Riddick shakes his head, muttering a curse. He rubs the back of his neck with a hard exhale. "I can't even *say* what she's done, it's so far beyond comprehension."

I gauge his response, looking for any hint that he's closer to Devyn than simply a coworker or friend. "Is it because she's a woman?" I ask honestly. "If it were a man, would it be easier to accept?"

"No." He appears genuinely affronted. "Dev has been like family to me, to us all," he says, but leaves the past tense reference to Devyn unamended. "This just doesn't make sense."

Emmons bows his head to hide the brief wash of shame that flits across his strained features. "She still is family," he says tersely, and I can hear the raw ache in his voice.

This has to be particularly hard for him, possibly harder than any other person in this town. Emmons didn't just lose his brother during this case. As far as the detective knows, Devyn did more than betray him; she took Jake Emmons away from him for years, then forced the detective to identify his brother's decapitated remains amid one of her ritual scenes.

I offer him a useless, sympathetic smile, but don't try to downplay his anger or placate his emotions. I'm simply impressed he's here, and sober at that. He's still favoring his injured leg after taking a serious fall down the ravine.

"How are the others handling the news?" I ask Emmons.

"Once the shock wears off, they'll accept it." He touches the rim of his hat, his flat gaze as detached as his monotone voice. "Then they'll do what they have to do."

I feel as if his words are directed more inward, maybe trying to convince himself. I reflect on his statement, suffering a stab to my conscience. Shock does eventually wear off. And then, ultimately, we all accept what we have to do.

Agent Rana straightens her suit jacket as she steps in my direction. "I've provided you with a copy of the interrogation questions." She nods to the table that holds a stack of manila folders. "During the questioning, jot down any notes you have. Then I'll reevaluate later if needed."

I brush my overgrown bangs from my eyes, giving my hand an occupation to hide the tremor. I'm not intimidated, although being in such close quarters with this many law officials can make anyone nervous. My anxiety stems from indecision, the helplessness I feel where Devyn is concerned.

The FBI want Devyn for Agent Alister's murder.

During my debriefing, I noticed the case has become less about locating the remaining missing locals, and more of a manhunt for the person suspected of killing an FBI agent.

The woven thread that bound Alister's arms at the scene is a specific detail that points officials to Devyn as the accomplice.

I haven't yet figured out how to exonerate Devyn of the crime while also protecting Kallum. He wasn't a murderer until I brought him here. The weight of both their fates rests heavy on my shoulders.

"And if I have a question or recommendation during the questioning?" I say to Agent Rana.

Her dark, discerning gaze assesses me sharply. Her in her professional suit, me in my skirt and blouse. Regardless of my seemingly professional attire today, we're a paragon of opposites.

"Make a note," she reiterates sternly. "Do not interrupt the questioning."

An inky coil of irritation wraps my spine. The tolerance I usually harbor for my superiors is wearing thin, resulting in a stiff nod.

Trying to diffuse the unsettling feeling, I glance again at Tabitha. Her hands are folded neatly in her lap. She's sporting the same headband she appears to always wear. Like the hair tie Devyn gave me at the ravine, Tabitha's band boasts a similar knit pattern.

At the hollow pang in my chest, I turn away. "How are the recovered victims acclimating?" I ask Rana, steering the conversation onto the residents who fled the mine during Devyn's ritual.

During my debriefing, I was unable to recount for certain how many of the missing locals were there. I had assumed all thirty-three—but as I was drugged at the time, and under duress, I can't trust my memory. As of now, twenty-three of the missing locals have been recovered.

Rana's expressive eyes betray her distress, but she

quickly masks her features. "They're brainwashed and have no tongues. Makes communication difficult."

Her glib response feels forced, and in direct conflict with the worry I see creased in her expression. She's holding something back.

"I really would like the opportunity to try to interview—"

"That's not why I brought you in," she says, cutting me off. Her ability to avoid relinquishing information is unmatched. From the moment I met her at the crime scene, I've had a difficult time getting a read on her.

"Along with Professor Locke's insight into the esoteric angle—" her words cut short as the door opens "—your expertise in criminal behavior will provide a logical counter for the interview, which we can now start."

I feel him before he even enters the room, his intense energy a force that draws my gaze like a live wire seeking a connection.

Charles Crosby enters first, Kallum emerging right behind his lawyer, and my breath shallows. The pace of my heartbeat quickens to a frantic staccato pulse in my veins as an electric current heats my blood to a frenzy. The strong familiarity hits me in a whole new way as I try to reconcile my past and recent memories of him.

His dark presence slices through the tension in the room like the sharpest blade, his striking, lethal appearance just as honed. The stylish black suit and long overcoat taper to his toned build to emphasize every leanly defined muscle.

His hands are no longer bandaged, revealing the celestial tattoos and inked sigils. The memory of his

43

slashed palms grazing my skin sends a hollow throb between my thighs. I'm flint to his abrasive surface, and we're entirely too combustible.

On impact, his gaze crashes into mine to make that grounding connection, and suddenly we're the only two people in the room.

Time slows when Kallum looks at me, the rules which govern the universe no longer apply, and I can feel his gaze like a brushfire racing over my body, feel the unquenchable burn when his eyes settle on my lips like a brand.

Past and present collide, each memory layering one on top of the other to twist me, and I wonder how I was ever able to deny what's between us.

The crooked slant of his lips exposes that devilish smile, and I'm affected. Utterly. A light bruise dusts his jaw from his fight with Alister, which only serves to make his heady sex appeal more dangerous. Yet there's more behind his façade meant to charm and devastate, a shared, hidden knowledge between us that leaves me swirling in the molten blue and green of his captivating gaze.

Like that moment I first saw him at the Briar visitation table, and he looked right into me, disarming me and weakening my defenses.

I never stood a chance.

"Welcome back, Dr. St. James," Kallum says, failing to suppress a devious grin. Even his formal address sounds suggestive in his deep baritone. The way the syllables of my name curl around his tongue, the offending muscle might as well be forked. "You look recovered."

The innuendo to my recovered memories is delivered

with a conspiratorial wink before his clashing gaze touches on my skirt. Where I felt nothing but repelled by Riddick's obvious perusal, I'm a tangle of heat and yearning as Kallum drinks me in.

"I'm healing up fine. Thank you for noticing, Professor Locke." I intentionally glide my palms along my hips, earning a smoldering smile from him that pops the slight dimple in his cheek. I lock my arms around my midsection, afraid of my own body and the loss of control when he's this close.

I feel on display, as if everyone in this room can see the truth of us.

More concerning is the fact that I suddenly don't give a damn.

As I was in debriefing for most of last night, and Kallum spent majority of today conferring with his lawyer, we haven't been in contact since we parted at the crime scene.

His tongue deliberately chases the curled seam of his lips. There's so much deviant promise held in his heated eyes before he mercifully directs his gaze to the interrogation room. I know he's recalling what transpired there, and the following moments that led to Alister's attack on me.

Even after he delivered his retribution on the agent, I can sense the lingering ripple of anger as a muscle tics along his tight jaw.

He leans down close to my ear, and I shiver at his intimate proximity. "Did you wear that infernal skirt to fuck with me, little Halen?"

"Said like a true narcissist," I counter with a smirk.

"Not everything is done with you in mind, professor. As there isn't much time for laundry when working a case, these are the only clean clothes I have at the moment."

Something wild flashes in his eyes, a dare to make me as dirty as his thoughts.

I sense the curious press of Detective Riddick's gaze before he eases toward us. "I heard you've been cleared of any charges," Riddick says to Kallum, his eyes dropping to the evident bruises along Kallum's knuckles. "That's one hell of a lawyer you have there."

Kallum flashes a dark smile. "The best a psychopath's money can buy."

"There were never any charges pressed, Detective Riddick," I say, setting the record straight. "I believe the whole ordeal was a misunderstanding."

"Of course," Riddick says, his glare heavy on Kallum. "Although Agent Alister isn't around to give his side, but I'm sure it was just a simple misunderstanding between professionals."

Tension gathers as a beat of awkward silence settles around us. Hernandez tugs at the knot of his necktie before he slips off toward Rana, leaving the three of us standing, staring.

"This is taking too long," I say, trying to diffuse the tension. "We should already be out there searching for Devyn."

Riddick draws closer to my side. "You're not going back into the field." His tone is incredulous as his gaze pans over me, landing hard on the distinct bruises striping my neck, the ones left behind by Kallum's belt. "Not after what happened."

A hard mask descends over Kallum's face, and he tips his chin higher. "Be careful, detective. The last person who looked at her like that wound up flayed."

The air charges with the crackling intensity of Kallum's near admission. My heart plummets, leaving me suspended in disbelief.

"That sounds suspiciously like a threat," Riddick says.

Kallum's chuckle is caustic. "Excellent detecting skills, detective."

"Kallum," I say, my voice low in warning.

"No, I get it." Riddick turns a softer, somewhat forced smile on me. "The professor here is clearly marking his territory. In bad taste, I might add."

A measure of relief frees my constricted lungs, but only marginally. While Riddick's ego can brush off Kallum's remark, the fact is Kallum is skirting too dangerously close to getting himself detained. Again.

Before the situation escalates, Agent Rana addresses the team. "We need to recover a significant amount of time. Let's start."

Kallum and Riddick continue to stare at one another, each one waiting for the other to be the first to back down. I step in front of Kallum, my eyes saying what my voice can't.

He's garnering all the wrong attention.

Finally, Kallum takes a step backward, aiming a callous smirk at the detective before he pivots in the direction of the table. Rana begins issuing directives to the task force to further dissipate the male aggression.

In contrast to his primitive behavior, Kallum pulls out a chair for me in chivalrous offer. I set my tote on the floor and seat myself, and his finger traces my shoulder, unable to deny himself that single touch. I feel that touch ricochet against every cell in my body.

"*Stop* marking your territory," I say to him in a hushed tone.

He sits adjacent to me at the corner of the table, a smug smile lifting the corner of his mouth. "I apparently didn't mark it well enough the first time." He casts a scathing glare Riddick's way. "I won't make that mistake again."

I believe him.

Kallum has poor impulse control. He doesn't just like to rile people, he takes deviant pleasure in it. He doesn't fear Riddick or anyone else here, he thinks he's untouchable, and he's blatant about that fact.

And despite the crushing fear of what will happen to him if he can't restrain himself, the intense urge to drag him into the next interrogation room over grips me so fiercely, I have to press my hot palms to the cool surface of the table.

Something was unleashed within me the last time we were together, and it's wild and unhinged and tears at the cage of my chest. I felt it the moment Kallum released his belt from around my neck, and I slipped into some state between.

I've never been broken so immensely, and yet felt so complete, whole.

Sitting in this stark room with loud fluorescents, agitation worms beneath my skin, like an itch festering too deep. If I don't rake it free of my flesh soon, I'll come apart.

Kallum's gaze dips to the vee of my blouse, and I try to

ignore the heat flashing my skin as I force my attention ahead on the interrogation room.

What held him back before, what has kept him seemingly behaved on this case, appears to have disintegrated the moment I kissed him at the scene, and now he's unleashed.

To protect him, I have to find a way to contain him. Which feels like an impossible challenge when he's staring at me the way he is right now—like he wants to tear me apart.

I've never been a practicing psychologist, but I just need to get Kallum through this case without losing him completely to his unhinged urges.

Steeling my composure, I sit straighter as Agent Rana approaches and places a folder before me. "Your statement of events is here," she says, flipping to an inserted page. "Mark anything that Tabitha says which contradicts, and your own assessment of her behavior."

Rana places a folder in front of Kallum before she heads into the interrogation box with a markedly spurned Riddick, leaving Emmons standing at the back of the room with the other feds.

Agent Hernandez seats himself on the other side of Kallum, and they trade a look. Kallum parts the folder and angles it toward the agent, including him in the process.

As the questioning begins, Agent Rana has Tabitha state her name and occupation, her address, and other basic confirming details to get her comfortable answering questions.

With a frown, I glance back at Emmons. "Where is Tabitha's representation?"

"She refused a lawyer," he states simply.

"But you can provide her one regardless. She needs—" I stop at the hard draw of his features, understanding in an instant.

No one local wants to represent her.

I look at Crosby, and he shakes his head. "She can't afford me, Miss St. James."

"I wouldn't suggest it." Technically, I can't afford him, either. He opted to be my counsel only because it serves Kallum's best interests.

The lawyer hikes an eyebrow, amused. Apparently reading me pretty damn well.

As Agent Rana proceeds with the interview, each of her questions are met with either silence or a dismissive, "I don't know," from Tabitha.

Anxiety hitches to my already mounting nerves. I drum my pen against my thigh, curbing the impulse to pace the room. A slow simmer has been building within me, a threat to escalate into a dangerous fire.

And the way Kallum continues to stare at me is not helping to keep it under control.

Drawing in a measured breath, I try to write out a note on the page, but my thoughts are conflicted. I'm torn over whether I actually want Tabitha to cooperate or not.

There's no verifiable proof that this woman was the one who laced my coffee at the diner. As long as she remains quiet, the feds can't technically charge her with any crime.

Tabitha's demeanor has always seemed reserved. This could be her default coping mechanism, or her personality in general. Only as I study her body language, watching the way she periodically tugs at the headband, I realize this is a comfort object. Each time she situates the band, she's fortifying her defensive wall.

Someone has instructed her. Someone who understands the inner workings of law enforcement. Her tic is a learned behavior from a coach.

I think back to when Tabitha handed me the to-go cup at the booth. Right before I got the call from Crosby, as Tabitha retreated away from the table, she looked back at me—and I realize she knew exactly what was in that drink. For the briefest second, she felt guilt.

The first time we met Tabitha, Kallum pointed out her odd behavior at not questioning us about the remains at the crime scene. I brushed it off as her being untrusting, a part of a tight-knit community.

But Kallum never says anything randomly.

I lean toward him and whisper, "You could get her to talk." Kallum had a kind of rapport with her. He was able to obtain more information from her by simply winking at her than Agent Rana is getting now.

"I think the agent is doing fine." He covers his mouth with his hand, an action I've now studied enough to know is his tell. Kallum might not lie to me, but his body language discloses when he's holding back the truth.

Admittedly, the best-case scenario for us would be if Devyn was never found.

I mentally play out the ensuing months. Devyn disappears. The case goes cold. Kallum is relocated to a new facility to finish out his treatment, where he'd receive a shortened sentence after Crosby renegotiates his contract.

No trials. No prison time. For any of us. No tug-of-war

between my loyalty to Kallum versus my promise to help Devyn.

Ostensibly, it's the best outcome—the one where no one suffers.

Only I can't silence that tiny voice inside me.

I lean over the table toward the agent recording the session. "Tell Agent Rana to have Tabitha remove her headband."

The agent says, and somewhat annoyed, "Agent Rana can hear you."

Rana directs an incensed glare at the mirror before she says to Tabitha, "Miss Yarrow, can you please remove your hair piece."

From the fringe of my vision, I see Kallum's features darken. His bruised knuckles bleach as his hand fists atop the table.

Tabitha pulls her lip between her teeth as worry creases her forehead. She speaks to Detective Riddick. "Do I have to?"

"No one can force you," he says to her, "but it would work in your favor to cooperate."

Tabitha fidgets with the hem of her shirt. She's truly upset. She wasn't instructed on how to handle this situation.

My conviction winning out, I stand and exit the viewing room. The officer guarding the door rolls his shoulders and reinforces his stance, and a shot of anger injects my bloodstream.

Before I realize I've done so, I've stepped up to him. "Move."

He stands his place, but an unsure flinch in his features

reveals enough hesitancy for me to shoulder past him and push through the door.

I'm greeted with a rigid scowl from Agent Rana. "You're not allowed to be here—"

"Tabitha," I address her directly. "I know Devyn has told you not to help us. She really, really dislikes the feds." At this, a small smile twitches at her lips. "I know how worried you are for Devyn. Honestly, I'm worried for her, too. We both want to help her. She's out there alone, right? I know you don't want her to be alone. I promise, I'll make sure she gets help. That's what she needs, Tabitha."

After she considers my words for a moment, she reluctantly removes the headband.

And my heart crashes against my chest.

As I stare at the crown of Tabitha's head, Rana follows my line of sight.

It's Riddick who declares what we're all seeing. "Christ," he says, standing so he can lean over the table for better inspection. "What the hell are those?"

I swallow, my throat suddenly dry. Because I know.

I saw them on the victim at the hunting grounds. I saw them on the vanished locals as they danced around a circle of fire, and then on Devyn as she rocked me to the rhythmic drumbeat amid her ritual.

"They're implants," I say, tasting the bitter tension in the air.

Only where the victim's flayed scalp merely held the stainless-steel implants, Tabitha's harbor the finely shaped bone of antler nubs.

Realization washes over me with a cold prickling sensation. What Kallum said during our ritual comes back, about how antlers are adorned by an initiate of the mysteries, making them more godlike the closer they are to the sky.

The size is status. Maybe even a rank.

Devyn has a hierarchy, and it reaches outside of her inner circle of higher men.

I look to the mirror, as if I can find Kallum's eyes through the glass, but only my reflection stares back.

"Tabitha, I need you to explain what this is," Agent Rana says to her in a more subdued tone.

Bolstering her resolve, Tabitha says, "I want a lawyer."

Detective Riddick frowns with a severe draw to his dark eyebrows as he nods with finality. "All right, then. I'll see who I can find."

Agent Rana sends him an incensed look. "We're pressed for time, detective. We need answers now."

"She asked for a lawyer. I don't know how the feds do things, but we look after our own." He plants his hands on the surface of the table, then pushes to his full height.

Riddick brushes past me on his way out of the interrogation room, effectively ending the interview. Strained silence fills the room as Agent Rana nods to the officer, directing him to take Tabitha back to holding.

Once they've left the room, the agent fixes me in her stony stare as she stands and collects her folders. "I'd like to see you in my office, Dr. St. James." Then she looks at the two-way mirror. "All of you."

54

Outside Rana's office, tension thickens the atmosphere of the HRPD as what happened inside the interrogation room travels through the department.

I'm at least relieved the office Rana occupies isn't the same one Alister used, the one where he tried to assault me. I deliberately avoid looking in that direction as the violent scene attempts to play out through the blinds. Kallum purposely moves in beside me to block my line of sight, then reaches over and closes the blinds.

"I'm all right," I tell him.

His hand grazes mine reassuringly. "I know."

Agent Hernandez enters, and Detective Emmons files in behind him. Once we're assembled in Rana's office, she instructs Emmons to close the door.

She levels each of us with a serious look. "The Liptons are having a party tonight," she announces.

Surprise hikes my eyebrows. After the reveal which just took place during the interview, this isn't what I was expecting to hear. "A party," I say, questioning. "Right after a missing and traumatized member of their family has been returned to them."

The mention of the Liptons conjures the disturbing image of Vince Lipton through the wall of flames.

Rana seems to share my astonishment of this, at least. "Vince Lipton is still undergoing evaluation at the hospital," she says, as if this excuses the family's eccentric behavior. "Apparently, it's the Lipton's annual star gazing gathering, or something to that effect. During her interview, Mrs. Lipton stated, vehemently, that canceling the party would draw too much 'talk'." She makes air quotes for emphasis.

"Though inappropriate, she's not entirely wrong," I say, offering a partial shrug. "It's the psychology of small towns. They're built on status. The residents look to this family for support, for leadership to know how to handle their shared hardship. It makes sense Mrs. Lipton would feel it's her responsibility to provide a familiar sanctuary."

Rana doesn't shut down my analysis. Rather, she nods in earnest agreement, then looks at Detective Emmons. "Will all the residents be in attendance?"

He shifts his weight off his injured leg. "It's the second largest town event besides the holidays," he confirms.

"The Perseids," Kallum chimes in. "It's a yearly meteor shower, and one of the most brilliant to observe."

I direct my next words to Rana. "I'm not sure what the Lipton's social calendar has to do with the case."

"Mrs. Lipton has lawyered up and now refuses to cooperate with the task force," she says. "That limits our interrogation of Vince."

"I still don't understand what you need from me," I say more pointedly.

I've already stated to the lead agent where I feel my services will be best utilized. As a crime-scene profiler, I should be in the mine shafts, analyzing the habitat of Devyn and her followers. If there is evidence to be uncovered as to where she is now, it's likely in the place she's resided these past five years.

Rana maintains my gaze with firm resolve. "I need eyes on that family."

I tilt my head. "You're assigning us as babysitters."

"Essentially, yes." She crosses her arms in finality. "As much reservation as I have keeping you on this case, Dr.

St. James, the fact is you seem to always find a way to come into contact with the suspects."

I fold my arms across my chest in mirror stance with the agent. I'm not the babysitter. I'm the one being baby*sat*. With feds trailing me, watching me.

"Devyn isn't going to just stride right up to me," I point out.

"She did once before," she counters. "Look, I'm giving you a short leash with which to roam," she states, issuing a warning. "I'm excusing the behavior I witnessed at the scene yesterday as post-traumatic stress due to your recent encounters. I've officially recommended you undergo evaluation for professional counseling. I've also made a request for Professor Locke to be assigned a new doctor."

In other words, she's covering her own ass. Should any of my actions come back to bite her, she's making sure the paperwork states her reservations.

"A psychologist having her mental health called into question is beyond insulting," I say to her.

"Take it up with HR." Sarcasm laces her voice as she seats herself behind the desk. "Once Dr. Keller arrives, she'll officially take over as field psychiatrist."

A volatile current charges the air, and I can feel Kallum's ire simmering around me. "I'm here at Dr. St. James's request," he says, his tone dangerously low. "As she's the only one even remotely capable of working this case alongside me, I'm not being passed around like a puppet to perform tricks for the FBI."

Rana cocks an amused eyebrow. "Despite your impressive ego, Professor Locke, you're not the only philosophy expert out there. If you refuse to cooperate with the feds, then your services are no longer required and you can return to the Briar Institute."

I catch the smug curl of Kallum's lips before he adopts a somber expression.

When he doesn't push the subject, Rana plants her arms on the desk. "All right. Now that everyone's on the same page—" she returns her attention to me "—I need to know if Devyn Childs would flee the area."

I could deter the manhunt for Devyn right now. She didn't leave her hometown, but one suggestion to the contrary would divide efforts to locate her.

"I'll need to see the shafts of the mine to answer that question with any authority," I say instead.

Rana shakes her head. "There are teams of agents already covering every square inch of the tunnels."

"You mean, destroying any potential evidence that could be recovered by analyzing the scenes," I say, and Kallum cranes an eyebrow at my boldness.

Her sigh is heavy, filled with the kind of weight a leader bears. "Find me something useful tonight, and I'll see what I can do tomorrow, St. James."

For a moment, I witness her defenses weakening. I can see the strain she's under in the darkened skin beneath her eyes. "Bringing in Childs is top priority," she reiterates, her tone a touch softer. "A federal agent was murdered, heinously, gruesomely, in this town. Within forty-eight hours, my superiors will arrive and expect results."

The implied *or else* lingers in the dense air.

Agent Rana is on the figurative chopping block now. The higher ups need somewhere to place blame. Someone has to stand before the media and accept responsibility and explain the tragedy of this case to the public. If Rana doesn't secure a suspect, she'll become the one to bear that obligation.

Reading the room, Kallum says, "Someone always has to be the scapegoat."

"Unless I get some results, I won't be the only one," Rana says, her statement edged in clear warning.

Detective Emmons takes this as his cue to exit the office, leaving us in the brewing tension.

Hernandez waits until the door clicks closed before he says, "Is no one going to mention the fucking antler things on that girl's head? What the hell is going on in this town?"

Agent Rana glances at the door where the detective just left. "Something really wrong," she says wearily. "As sympathetic as I may feel toward the locals and their plight, we can't discount anyone here. Childs didn't do all this alone. She had help."

The weight of that implication bears down heavy in the small office. This is the angle Hernandez and I have been working since he recovered me in the mansion library.

"The locals won't talk to men in black suits," Rana adds, her gaze landing on Hernandez. "They don't trust the feds or outsiders. So…" She trails off, waving her hand. "Find a way to get them to talk before any more of them lawyer up."

Hernandez speaks up again. "Demanding to see their heads would connect the antler dots for who's involved real quick."

"I think the perpetrator is more hidden," I say. "They won't have such extreme body modifications. They have to

59

be the one people trust, who can go undetected." I shake my head, my thoughts delving deeper. "Tabitha likely doesn't know much. She served her purpose. While there are probably others like her around this town, I'm not sure what that means." I glance at Kallum, waiting for him to provide insight on the society angle.

He raises his chin with a hint of stubborn assertion. He's not just trying to be unhelpful, he's purposely being obstructive.

I exhale a lengthy breath. "But we'll look into it."

Rana nods slowly. "I'm working the inside perp angle with a special sub team. I suspect when we start to close in on this person, it could get volatile."

I hold her gaze, feeling the abysmal truth of her words, before she dismisses us.

Once we move into the hallway, Hernandez looks my way. "You got to remain on the case."

I drop my voice as we pass a group of officers. "And you know why that is, Gael."

He grunts his acknowledgment. "They're using you as bait."

"Precisely."

As the three of us exit through the doors of the HRPD building, the cool night air douses some of the fire still simmering beneath my skin, but only until I reach the back of the SUV and turn toward Kallum.

Noticing the sudden, unstable shift, Hernandez pointedly looks over his suit. "I'll change into civilian clothing first," he says before heading off in the direction of the hotel, leaving Kallum and me in the darkening parking lot.

Satisfied, Kallum gifts me a smoldering smile. "You're conveniently already dressed for the occasion." His gaze drops and lingers on my skirt, a sly smile twisting his mouth.

"You were cock-blocking the case." I grip my bag strap tighter, my body tense with the accusation.

He leans forward and plants both hands on the windshield to cage me against the vehicle. "When I'm doing anything with my cock, little Halen, you'll know."

I place my hand to his chest, keeping enough distance between us where I can breathe, can think. "Stop deflecting. I know what you're up to. Your behavior in Rana's office was obvious."

"Good." He tucks a strand of hair behind my ear, and his fingers sensually graze my jaw. He pushes aside my collar to expose the bruises along my neck. "Because I'm not trying to hide, and neither should you."

I curl my fingers into his dress shirt. The unbuttoned collar is parted open, offering an enticing view of the tendrils inked along the lower part of his neck. I let my gaze roam over his striking features as I try to unmask what's making him so vulnerable, and in turn, defensive.

"We haven't really talked." My fingertips brush against the mark I can feel beneath the fabric, the sigil I cut into his chest.

"We'll talk," he says, his jaw tight at the slight pain my touch brings. "We'll talk until our breath gives out and our bodies have to take over, but right now, all I care about is that you're safe. You're mine." He grasps my neck possessively. "And the sinful plans I have for this skirt."

A smile slips free, his charm never ceasing to sway me. "And the case," I say, adamant. "The case matters."

He wets his lips, a hard edge bracketing his features. "Your obsession with this case is delving to dangerous depths," he says, his deep tone no longer suggestive.

"But you know why I'm doing this, who I'm trying to protect." I position my palm over the sigil to convey my point to him, feeling the heat of the wound. "And you're making it difficult to do that."

Conviction lights the flinty shadows of his eyes. "That's because I'm the one who protects you, sweetness."

Hernandez appears in my periphery at a distance, and I expel an agitated breath.

Kallum places his hand over mine on his chest and leans in close. "To be continued," he whispers, sealing his promise with the soft scrape of his teeth along the shell of my ear.

As he pushes away, my palm blazes with the lingering impression of the sigil, my impossible desire scored just as deeply into me.

4

STELLARUM LAPSUS

KALLUM

Before one delves into the practice of chaos magick and sigils, one must first delegate their own personal banishing ritual.

Such a ritual empowers the chaoist to resist obsession should sigils start to become conscious.

A desire can only be obtained once the sigil is charged and forgotten. I've explained the basic concept of this to Halen once, but to truly comprehend the power of the subconscious, our will only realized once the sigil is lost, the magician must never think of their desire.

There are three main aspects needed to banish a sigil.

A magical weapon: an instrument used to reinforce the barrier of the mind.

A barrier: a symbol drawn with that weapon. Such as eight points of the chaos star, or three points in succession.

Then the ritual itself, the purposeful use of the object in expelling the obsessive thought from the mind.

I spin the silver ring around my thumb three times, my thoughts cast outward.

There's a danger in sigils becoming conscious, when our most coveted desires preoccupy our every thought. It's maddening, the constant craving, the endless yearning, as the intrusive *want* consumes, devouring us like a rampant brushfire.

As Halen walks ahead of me, I let my hungry gaze absorb every delectable inch of her. How her low ponytail sways back and forth with each determined step toward the gothic house. The way she wears flats instead of heels. The way she can't hide her sinful body beneath all those layers.

How could I ever banish her from my thoughts?

She is my only obsession.

And now that there's nothing preventing us from being together, the impatience to be rid of this case and this whole damn town is a taxing demand furiously pounding at my temples.

Weary of the ritual, I flex my fingers as Hernandez rings the doorbell of the Lipton home. The heavy thump of bass from within rattles the windowpanes, accelerating my heart rate.

When do we know the moment the danger is no longer a threat and insanity has consumed us?

Was I driven mad while I was locked inside a mental hospital for six months restlessly waiting? Or was it when Halen sat across from me at the visitation table, so close, but still so far away?

Was I already insane when I beat Alister into a literal bloody pulp and strung his corpse up before I flayed the flesh from his skull? To break the seal of her mind and harness the energy of a blood sacrifice, I delved to the darkest depths of the black arts.

Desperation for a woman can resort any man to his basest monster.

And if that base act is what ultimately brought her back to me, then I'd kill him a hundred times over. I'd flay his flesh while his heart still beat just for the way she looked at me at the scene. For how she's looking at me now.

I run my tongue over the ridge of my teeth and meet her eyes in challenge, dangerously close to doing something just as hazardous, like ramming Hernandez's head against the house so I can get little Halen alone.

Impatient, I say to the agent, "I think this party is open invitation."

Hernandez must sense my irritation, because he opens the door with no remark. A flood of music spills into the night to invite us in.

Halen arches an eyebrow in dare, exquisitely sultry as she turns and strides inside, her petite form engulfed in swirling lights. I touch the small of her back as we weave a path through gyrating youth, reminiscent of the night I brought her here to invoke the frenzy.

One of the revelers stops short in the middle of the throng to stare at us, his wide gaze stuck on the obvious FBI agent despite his dressed down appearance. He then points toward the back of the house before he escapes.

"I assume he's telling us where we'll find the adults," Halen says, voice cast over the house music.

Once we step onto the expansive veranda, we indeed find the main attraction of the Lipton home. The entire back yard overlooks the open marshland. Dusk is a swipe of muted pinks and purples across the dimming sky. Every gothic element of the house has been captured in deliberate embellishments. Draped over the many tables, black linen drips to the ground. Vines crawl along a giant arched trellis with swirled iron tracery that matches the revival home, and white lights glimmer from its canopy. Even the pavers that cover the sprawling yard are a dark slate with similar ornate design.

While the kids party inside, the outside is an opulent gala for the adults, boasting its own cellist to serenade.

"When we were here before, Devyn said the Liptons pretty much do what they want," Halen says, and I don't miss the pinch of regret between her soft brows. "Point made clear with their extravagant star-gazing party amid an active investigation."

While it's not a black-tie event, it appears most of the townies came dressed in their Sunday finest. Mrs. Lipton has gone all out in order to distract the locals from the bleak state of affairs.

As Halen eyes a bank of expensive telescopes, she says, "I also feel the Liptons just might be a tad eccentric and out of touch."

I press in close and lower my mouth to her ear. "If I don't touch you soon, I'm going to lose my fucking mind."

She angles her head back. "As opposed to the very sound mind you normally have?"

I smile at the venomous bite in her tone. She's still a bit irritated over my deliberate evasiveness at the precinct. I brush my lips over her ear. "I plan to show you just how crazy you make me."

A shiver quakes through her body, but before I can sink

my teeth into her, she pulls away, and only glances back to send me a wink that makes my whole body catch fire.

Devious little sprite.

I watch her approach who I assume is Mrs. Lipton. "How many feds are hanging around the house?" I direct the question to Hernandez.

He crosses his large arms. "Enough."

I nod once. His clipped responses and guarded gestures haven't escaped me. Ever since he interrupted my altercation with Alister in the holding cell, he's been defensive. The agent may have suspicions—but no proof.

And, considering his boss was a rapist piece of shit, he might even be a little conflicted over his loyalties.

I like Hernandez. I don't like many people. I don't want to have to hurt him.

"We both know it's unlikely for Devyn to show up here," I say to him, then step down from the deck. "But seeing as Halen keeps getting shot down on her requests, what do you say we take advantage of the gathered locals?"

It's an obvious tactic to earn his compliance, as his loyalties do in fact lie with Halen. But once someone has agreed to one suggestion, it's easier to get them to agree to another.

For good measure, I add, "We can see if any of them sport little antler implants."

The tension in his shoulders slackens some. "We can't just go around demanding to see their heads."

"Why can't we?"

His gaze narrows on me, then a faint smile graces his mouth. "I'll start on the left. You take the right."

As I work my side of the party, I actually do make an effort to collect information from the families, none of which is useful. But uncovering more of Devyn's minions is not my sole priority.

I eat up at least thirty minutes with trivial banter, keeping an eye on the lurking FBI agents around the perimeter of the party. By the time I make my way back toward Halen, she has Mrs. Lipton warmed up enough to talk with her phone out, discretely recording the conversation.

"Devyn was here quite a bit," the woman is saying to Halen, "overseeing our festivities, and as a guest, of course. Julian always respected her."

Halen bristles at the woman's use of the past tense. "How well did you know her and her brother, Colter? Her family?"

Mrs. Lipton adjusts the gaudy shawl wrapping her shoulders. "The father left when the twins were little. He didn't care for small-town life. The mother passed away when they were just out of high school, but I mean, Devyn and Colter had been on their own pretty much anyway. I helped where I could, of course, until Devyn decided to move away for school in the big city." She shrugs. "Following in her father's footsteps, unfortunately."

"The big city is…?" Halen presses.

The woman's penciled eyebrow arches. "New York City, of course."

"Of course. Did she stay in contact with her father?"

"I wouldn't know. When Devyn came back after Colter went missing, she was… Well, she wasn't the same." A frown deepens her makeup creases. "I suppose none of us were, really."

"Mrs. Lipton, did you ever notice a physical change in Devyn, or anyone else she was close to?"

The woman stares blankly. "Such as?"

"Such as extreme body modification, like horn implants on the head. Did your brother, Vince, ever show signs of this before he went missing?"

Her features harden. "Vince was starting to get into some peculiar interests and hobbies."

"And this didn't set off any alarms with you?" Halen asks.

Tightening her shawl more snugly, Mrs. Lipton turns rigid. "Why would it? Before you all arrived here, no one had any idea about rituals or any of that nonsense. Now if you don't mind, I need to attend to my guests, and I'm sure you have more pressing matters to handle. Anything else needs to be addressed through my lawyer. Please leave my party."

Halen stops the recording and tucks the phone into her tote bag. "Only old money can dismiss you like they're doing you a favor."

"As long as they say please." But I'm no longer concerned with founding families or their peculiar hobbies. My gaze captures and holds Halen, and with the slight part of her mouth, she senses she's been caught.

I seize her wrist and pull her against me, linking her arms around my neck as I lure her into a slow dance to the deep and melancholic notes of the cello.

"Smooth, professor." She glances around anxiously. "But we're the only ones dancing."

"Does it bother you?"

Staring up at me, she tilts her head. "No."

I tighten my arms around her, drawing her closer. Halen stopped worrying about what others thought of her a while ago. When you've experience true suffering, you no longer perceive the world's trivial concerns as relevant.

"We can do whatever we want," I say as I nudge her bag aside and cup the curve of her lower back. She gauges me carefully, my little seer reading more into my statement.

"Kallum..." I hear the disapproval in the way she trails off from my name. "Your joke to Riddick was extremely impulsive and reckless."

I lick my lips, loving the hint of clove she's giving off. "It wasn't a joke." I possessively dig my fingers into the sexy flare of her hips and drop my voice. "I never should've let Alister get that close to you."

Had I done away with Alister from the start, then Halen never would've been alone where Devyn could get to her.

I read the torn uncertainty in her, and a wisp of anger threads my insides. I rarely suffer regret, it's wasted energy, but I absolutely regret not eliminating the priestess also when I had the chance.

Halen thinks she's protecting me, but if she keeps on this course, she'll undo everything I've done to protect her.

"You need to implement some impulse control," she says. "I can help you with some exercises."

"Oh, I have all kinds in mind." I sway her and grip the back of her skirt in my fist. "But while I'm looking forward to those sessions with you, Dr. St. James, right this second, this skirt demands my undivided attention."

A tinkling pixie laugh escapes past her lips to ensnare me. She glances around. "God, I'm going to hell."

I lower close to her ear. "Luckily the devil has the hots for you."

She releases another light laugh. The moment she yields in my arms, that constant ache in the center of my chest eases. The sky has darkened, transforming the marsh into a scenic backdrop as stars begin to appear.

Too soon, the burden of the past dims her features, and I mourn the loss of her laugh.

While the guests turn their attention to the sky in anticipation to view the Perseids, my only view is Halen. "The myth of wishing on shooting stars supposedly originated from Ptolemy," I say to distract her.

Her gaze hung on mine, she says, "It really is a sign of antisocial personality to divert topics in such a way."

A smile tips my mouth. "It connects, I promise," I say with a wink. At her placating sigh, I continue, "Ptolemy claimed when the gods became bored, they'd look down on their creation. The stars were scattered when they did so, and we were closer to them as a result. So if your heart desired a thing, that was the moment to wish for it, while the stars were falling from the heavens."

She stares up at me, her fingers caressing my neck. "Three thousand years later, and we're still in awe of the stars."

I pull her searing scent into my lungs with a deep inhale. "Science may have killed the romance in them, but it can't kill our desire to be distracted with ethereal beauty and wonder."

"I understand wanting to use a distraction to avoid reality." A hard swallow dips along her throat. "But when the enchantment is over, there are still gruesome crime scenes and harsh realities to face."

I can feel her slipping away, and I tether my arms stronger around her. "The enchantment never has to be over," I say as I dip her, holding her angled beneath me until a beautiful smile touches her lips. Soon as I draw her upright, it vanishes.

She drops her gaze, and I hook a finger beneath her chin to lift her face. "I'm not going to let you punish yourself."

Her mouth parts, as if she's going to debate, but the rise of the cello dissuades her efforts. "We'll discuss this later."

"Perfect, because I have far more evocative tales to distract your thoughts. I won't stop until you're a puddle in my arms, little Halen."

A smile fights to break across her face. "You're relentless."

She has no idea. I clasp her neck, a devilish smile slanting my mouth. "After a life of study, I'm prepared to offer you the single most poetically beautiful piece of philosophy I've uncovered."

She laughs, this one more powerful, and I'm spellbound.

Halen's laugh holds power.

It holds power over me.

Peter Carroll asserted that laughter is the highest

emotion. As it encompasses all others, from ecstasy to grief, it's the passion that fuels the soul. And the musical cadence of Halen's laugh does so many fucking things to me.

"All right," she says on a breathy exhale. "Enchant me, Professor Locke."

It's a dare I vigorously accept. "Aristotle—"

"But of course," she says with a deliberate eye roll.

I refrain from nipping her bottom lip and say, "According to that ancient dead guy, unexplained phenomena like lightning and shooting stars was the result of two events. The first hot like fire, the second vaporous and wet. This was the Aristotelian vapor theory, and it was the dominating theory for, oh, two thousand years while natural philosophers pondered how the earth emanated flammable vapors that could ignite the atmosphere."

She shakes her head lightly. "And yet, my panties are nowhere near wet or vaporous," she teases, but I feel the truth in her body. We're barely swaying, rocking only slightly to the melody, and yet there's a heated current lashing between us to be sealed together.

I lick my lips and move in closer, chasing her breath. "The theory was, when the sun's heat broke water into steam, it was the earth exhaling. In essence, the core of our planet heated until the violent force of it built and built into an eruption, a climax. Which Aristotle called an earthly exhalation."

Dark hunger flares behind her eyes, tempting my demon within.

"Ignorance makes for such poetry, such beauty," I say, tipping her face higher with my thumb. "The passionate exhalations of the earth. The result of which we experience as a beautiful light show in the sky. There's nothing that poetic or lovely in our conquered logic, sweet Halen."

The fiery embers in the depths of her eyes are as hot as the raging stars. "Consider me an enchanted puddle, professor."

A sudden crack of applause announces the event. Halen tilts her head back as the first visible shower of meteors streak the night, her features awestruck. "I have to admit, it is beautiful." As the sky flickers with flashes of light, her eyes glimmer. "I don't think I've ever experienced anything this lovely."

"Neither have I," I confess, but I'm not looking at anything but her.

I'm held captive amid a sea of falling stars by her beauty alone. The power of it could rival the universe.

Her gaze connects with mine, and no more words are necessary. She removes her arms from around my neck and takes my hand in hers, threading our fingers together.

"Since I'm already going to hell, I might as well have my way with the devil," she says, leading me away from the party.

My whole body fucking ignites.

I'd follow my dark muse anywhere, right down into hell itself.

But since the Lipton's have a terrace with the perfect view, I tug Halen in that direction.

As we reach the path, she pulls me to a halt. "Kallum, wait," she says as her gaze trails up to the house tower, and her hand slips from mine. "I don't like heights."

"I promise, I won't let you fall."

She expends an uneven breath. "It's not the falling part that scares me."

The raging need to uncover what does scare her burns through me.

"Trust me." I extend my hand.

A tense moment of hesitation gathers between us, and like she did all those months ago, she takes my hand, allowing me to breathe.

Guided by wrought-iron rails, we ascend the narrow stairwell and step onto the stone landing, where the pitched roof overhangs three feet of the quaint balcony. A stained-glass window wraps the tower above, and a French door leads into the dark recess of the house.

The height affords an expansive view of the marshland, where the night sky seems endless as it sits atop the dark woods in the distance.

A pure and beautiful experience before we become as hot and violent as the stars themselves.

Halen keeps her distance from the railing. "This is a bad idea."

I grab the strap of her tote, using it to tow her closer before I remove the bag, letting it drop to the terrace. My hand captures her neck, palm welded to the sexy slope as I tip her chin up. "I agree. It was a very bad idea to wear that fucking skirt, sweetness."

She arches a delicate eyebrow. "Are you going to shred this one?" But all flirtatious banter is replaced with raw, carnal want. "Shit. Kallum, don't shred this one—"

Then my mouth is on hers, swallowing the tiny moan that escapes her parted lips, determined to rectify the hours I've spent away from her. Hell, the fucking months of torture spent without her. Gripping the thin material in my fist, I drag the skirt up her legs and push my hand between her thighs, earning another sweet moan.

I swirl my fingers over the soaked material, a guttural curse wrenched free as I confirm how aroused her fear makes her. I have her in my arms and pressed to the stone wall, my need to taste her unleashed. Her moans turn breathy under my fierce demand as I trap her wrists against the stone, my body pinned to hers as I greedily devour her sounds.

She turns her head to drag in a breath. "Kallum—"

"I should have never stopped kissing you," I say, the confession dredged from the vile depths of me. "I should have taken you to bed and made love to you until you could no longer comprehend the meaning of shame." I draw in air past my constricted lungs. "I should have never left you that night."

Eyes wide and cast upward, her gaze solders to mine. Freeing a wrist, she places her hand on my chest. With her index finger, she gingerly traces the crescent she carved into my flesh to inflame it further. "I don't know why I ran away," she admits.

Moving her hand to my face, she kisses me slowly, tenderly, answering my suspicion. While Halen has recovered most of her memory, there's still a vital piece missing.

A selfish part of me wants to accept the gift of her selective memory, but that's not how this works. As time passes, she's going to suffer her guilt more acutely.

When she attempts to pull away, I kiss her harder, brutally stealing her breath to make it my own, as if I can siphon her grief. Everything between us has been topical, a calm but fragile surface with delicate banter and traces of passion to mask the dark and torrid vortex beneath.

Only when she's breathless and gasping against my mouth do I break off. "So I'm going to keep kissing you," I swear to her. "I'm going to keep touching you, and making love to you, and fucking you, until I exorcize the shame you're suffering from every cell of your body, even if I have to exhaust you in the process."

I'd eat every bit of it for her if only she'd let me.

She latches on to my shirt, clenching the material in her slender hands. "None of it was your fault." Her swallow is painful. "I wasn't able to solve their case, and that pain... I don't know. If I could've found the person responsible, then I wouldn't have been so obsessed with the Harbinger. I needed someone to punish." She shakes her head, hiding her eyes. "I'm the one who lost touch with reality long before that night."

Her parents. The tragic accident that left her with no family, and no one to punish for that crime. The very first tipped domino.

"But I can't go back there," she says, and I'm unsure if she's referring to the physical place or the hell inside her mind. "Just...touch me. Keep touching me until I shatter. God, make me feel anything else."

A primal growl tears free, and I have her insufferable skirt hiked up her thighs before I push a hand beneath the hem to feel her, wet and ready for me, the thin fabric of her panties dangerously close to being shred right along with my restraint.

"I'll give you anything you ask of me. Just don't

disappear." I breathe the words across her lips before I recapture her mouth.

While sparks of light rain down like falling celestials from the darkest court of heaven, I feast on my own fallen angel, devouring her sin with each greedy, lust-filled kiss.

Fuck, I'll be the one to commit every deadly sin to keep her mine.

Our tongues tangle and lash with each heated exchange of breath. Our touches become desperate, fighting to be closer. She has my overcoat pushed off my shoulders and the buttons of my Oxford pried open so she can flatten her palm over the crescent, ratcheting my heart rate to the climbing beat of a drum.

And fuck, she's soaking her panties as I rub her, coaxing me to intrusively push at the barrier, the soft give of her pussy driving me right out of my damn mind. I tug the elastic away from her body and slip my hand under the fabric, my fingers seeking the perfect center of her.

She gasps over my mouth as I pinch her clit between the slat of my fingers. Her blunt nails track across my skin before she pushes against my chest for leverage as she provocatively works her hips to shred my sanity. She rides my hand so fucking sexy, grinding her clit against the heel of my palm as I plunge two fingers inside her cunt.

Jaw clenched, I brace one hand on the wall above her head and fuck her pussy with my fingers, my cock straining against the closure of my pants at the seductive feel of her arousal. Her scent torturously invades my system as her inner walls tighten around my fingers, warning how close she is to breaking, and I can't take my eyes off the erotic way she's rolling her hips.

"Fuck, so fucking sexy," I grit out between gnashed teeth. "Do you want to come on my fingers or my cock?" I demand, my voice gravel.

Her heated gaze snares mine. "I want your cock."

"*Christ...*" Untamed need unfurls in my veins, and I swear she's already incinerated the last of my control until she tugs at the clasp of my slacks, and I come undone.

With pained effort, I take a deliberate step back, chin tipped up as I tear the belt buckle open and lower the zipper, issuing a silent command. Beautifully disheveled, Halen pushes off the wall, her hand finding my pants before she takes me out. Her soft palm fisting my cock is such sweet torture, I bite off a growl.

As I capture her mouth, tasting her exquisite mix of sin and virtue, the buzz of her phone sounds out in an infuriating disruption.

Breaking away, she breathes a curse as she kneels and digs out the device from her bag. I glimpse the Briar Institute on the screen, and a hit of fury spikes my bloodstream.

Fucking bastard.

Rationally speaking, we can never identify the precise moment insanity overtakes our mind, as we're already gripped by madness. But by then, we are also too possessed by our desire to suffer any remorse for what we've had to do to obtain it.

5

SHADOWS

KALLUM

A s Halen's phone vibrates with an annoying buzz, she stares at the screen, her thumb hovering between Decline and Accept.

Composure all but stripped, I confiscate the device and send the call to voicemail.

"Dr. Torres has been trying to contact me," she says. "I should find out what he wants."

And I should have had Torres stab his jugular instead of his hand.

I drop the phone on her bag, tempted to crush it beneath my boot. Instead, I let my hands fall to the wall on either side of her, brazenly settling my cock against her belly. "Maybe the good doctor wants to retain your services. You do seem to have a thing for psychos."

Her glare is disapproving, but beneath that obvious reaction, a hint of doubt crests.

With a forced breath, Halen places her palms to my

chest and steps around me, digging the loss of her deeper as she cautiously eases toward the railing but stops a safe distance away. "We're too exposed up here. There's not enough shadow to hide us."

Despite her avoidance, I sense her torn emotions. My dark muse is in there, yet as always, she just needs to be pushed past the edge.

"I don't need the shadows to make you come." I press up against her and wrap my arm around her waist, forcing her toward the railing.

"Kallum—"

Her fear spikes my adrenals, dosing me with a pure fucking hit to render me drugged. I grab her hands and anchor her palms to the cool iron, trapping her between my body and the bars.

"Keep your eyes right there," I command her, "on the constellation Perseus."

Her breathing erratic, she pushes into me, her backside delivering satisfying friction. "We're right in view—"

"To whom? The bored agents who lost interest in us after the first ten minutes. To those dull fucks below us? We're just a couple watching the sky." My grip tightens over her hands to hold her in place, my body caged around hers. "They can't hear the filthy things I'm whispering to you, or feel how your body responds to them."

"Kallum, stop." Her panic is tangible as she looks down.

Towering over her, I collar her throat from behind and force her head back as I drop my lips against her ear, lowering my tone to a lethal decibel. "There are no safe words between us. You want this to stop, you know how to make it stop."

Her swallow pulses enticingly against my palm, her heart taking flight.

"Slow your breathing," I instruct as I loosen my hold. Gently, I stroke her throat, taming the wild creature in my grasp. "That's it. Good girl. You know with one command, you can enrapture me or end me. You felt it in the room as you watched me come undone and lose my goddamn mind at the sight of you riding your fingers, coming so pretty for me as your eyes held me captive, and I was *dying* as I came so fucking hard for you, Halen. That's the power you possess over me."

She doesn't have to own it. We both know she can annihilate me right this instant, and I'd praise her while she delivered her lovely damnation.

Her body relaxes into mine, her breathing deep and slow as I tenderly trace her neck before I remove her hairband, loving the way the soft layers fall over her shoulder. "Fuck, at that moment, I would have traded what's left of my black soul for just a taste of your sweet, sweet pussy." My cock throbs at the prospect. I spear my fingers into her hair and pull her head back. "Tell me how wet you are."

A reflexive tremble grips her muscles. "Soaking my thighs," she says, shamelessly torturing me.

A guttural sound works free from deep within my chest, and I fasten my eyes closed as I release her and press my lips to the top of her head. The air has no temperature. There are no scents. The sounds of the party have faded away. Even the meteoroids in space have ceased their course.

She's all that I sense.

"You consume my fucking cells, Halen. I'm always touching you, always inside you. I know you feel me." I slide my fingers through hers on the railing. "Admit it."

"Yes," she breathes, her voice scarcely carrying over the cello. "I always feel you."

Like a fiend, approval inflates my ego. "It's our own unique chemistry. Just like quantum particles whose fates are intertwined, we were created together during the same event. We're entangled, our properties forever linked wherever we are. Opposites that continuously communicate across time and space."

She shakes her head in silent rebuttal, yet I know she understands every word, *believes* every word. It's her logic that wants to deny our connection, because it's inexplicable.

So what I'm about to do to her will blow her damn mind.

My voice drops to a low rumble. "Don't remove your hands from this rail."

She clings to the safety of the bar, her body tense, as I slip one hand away. I graze my palm up her arm, over the stitches, coasting higher until I'm positioned between her shoulder blades where I unhook the bra closure.

She gifts me an involuntary flinch. "Doing your bad-boy moniker justice," she teases, but I can hear the breathy uncertainty in her voice.

"Oh, I'm absolutely about to do it justice, sweetness." I seal my words in a threat as I grind the length of my unrestrained erection along her ass. "You want me to shatter you, then I'll shatter you from the inside out."

I push the bra straps down her shoulders, allowing the garment to slip to her abdomen, her breasts free to experience the satiny sensation of her top. Like a masochist, to torture myself further, I unfasten the button right below the low neckline, granting myself a sexy, teasing view of her breasts. The temptation to capture her peaked nipples between my fingers is a hot demand in my groin, but I return my hand to hers.

"While touch is addictive, the mind is what makes the sensation real." My claim is backed by the cool caress of night, the haunting notes of the cello. "An orgasm is more cognitive than physical, but my little Halen knows this," I whisper in her ear. "When the mind and body are in tune, an energy orgasm can clang the fuck out of that tuning fork, and there are no two people on this planet more aligned than us."

Recovering her memory is only one facet of her awakening.

Halen doesn't just have to face her fear, she has to look into the eyes of her monster and surrender. Emergence of our darkest aspect is not a sickness. It's not psychopathy.

It's providence.

To deny this part of ourself is *contra naturam*—a sin against our very nature.

And Halen's denial will damn us both.

"Don't take your eyes off the sky," I command, the ache in my voice guttural and raw. "Watch those flickers of light and know their beauty could never compare to yours, Halen. Not for me. There is nothing in this world or the next that will ever rival you. I knew that the very first time I saw you, with the setting sun your backdrop to illuminate you like a goddess. You owned the elements. You owned me."

Her breathing shallows even as her pulse screams in her veins, beating wildly as I press my lips to the throbbing point in her neck.

"You're so fucking beautiful in every light," I say, my voice thick with arousal, "yet even more striking in your shadows, where you think you're safely hidden. You should know by now that you can't hide from me. Everything you say and do twists me, makes me a feral heathen. You're so fucking perfect the way you shamelessly ride my hand, your needy clit seeking friction, your pussy gripping my fingers and begging for my cock. So fucking sexy when you give yourself over to the frenzy, you make me a madman who wants to watch you come on my fingers and fuck you at the same time."

The backs of her thighs rest along mine, and I jam my foot between her feet to unlock her knees and splay her legs wide.

Unprepared, she tips forward past the handrail. "Jesus, Kallum." A muttered curse falls free as her gaze snaps to the ground far below. As she pushes back against my chest, I seal my hands tighter over hers on the rail, my bruised knuckles pulsing in painful time to the quickening of her heart.

"I swear, I won't let you fall." I nuzzle her hair, deliriously drunk on her fear. "But I won't stop until I discover what scares you, sweetness."

Her resulting shiver ricochets through me, and I band

my body tight around hers. Every soft curve of her figure aligns with my unyielding form to tear at my control.

"Every night, I taste you on my tongue," I whisper over her ear, "becoming a ravenous beast as I'm torn awake, desperate for a chance to bury my face between your thighs and lap your cunt." My cock jumps as she arches her back and rocks into me, her impulse overriding her anxiety. "And I know you feel me. I know the mark on your thigh is fire in the middle of the night when you stir awake to the hollow ache between your thighs. Because I feel you. I feel your fingers, shaky, as they explore over your trembling belly to touch yourself."

I greedily meet the slight roll of her hips with my own, catching the flames of her fire as she burns hotter, eliciting an erotic moan that slides beneath my flesh at the tantalizing friction.

She's trying not to move, to keep from drawing attention, yet her body demands the abrasive caress of her panties over her clit, her thighs quivering with need to clench closed and offset the ache.

"Do you know how many times I've imagined you wrapped around me, what you'd feel like as I buried myself deep inside you?" I say with a dark groan. "God, you have no idea how I've tried to satisfy my need for you, thinking the next moment we were alone, I wouldn't be able to stop myself from taking you. All the times I had to restrain myself from pinning you down and tearing your panties off, thrusting my cock inside you at least one fucking time just to get a taste of relief."

My molars grind at the sound of her gasping whimper, my jaw locked as hard as my body to prevent me from ripping the barrier of her skirt away so I can take her right against this railing.

"And then the misery, the sheer fucking torment of you when I know you're doing the same damn thing. When I sense you push your fingers inside, cloaked in the dark, seeking that achy need. Trying so hard to satisfy the desire. I feel you when it's not enough and you grind into your bed"—I thrust against her ass in graphic demonstration—"burying your throaty moans against the pillow, your hips thrusting so lewd and sexy as you chase that elusive orgasm, your thighs spread wide to feel as salacious as you do when you look into my eyes and see that raw, carnal heat, and are tempted to let go and fall."

Her body held captive in my embrace, every subtle roll of her hips drives me out of my mind. My lips graze the thinly raised welts along her neck, choking my throat in a thick vise of lust. I breathe over the sensitive joint of her shoulder, the painful desire to sink my teeth into her skin a throbbing pain at the head of my cock.

"But you only drive that maddening ache deeper," I say, my voice coarse, my sinew corded like ropes of fire around my bones. "You can never satisfy the need. Just like now, how we're right here, so close, but unable to satiate our desire. The craving threatens to make us mad, tear us apart, until we're clawing at each other and fucking like debased, wild and wicked things."

"God, Kallum. Please..."

I groan at my name pleaded on her trembling breath. Her begging nearly unravels me, and I shove her closer to the rail, sparking that flame of fear higher. "Please what, Halen? Fuck you and make you scream out in front of every person here?" I demand, breath hot in her ear. "Will that satisfy the craving?"

She hesitates, her overstimulated nerves a web of need tormenting us both. "No," she admits. "It's not enough."

I drive her farther, her toes positioned right at the edge of the terrace. My own fear is tested as I dread the moment she slips from my arms. The tighter I band my hold around her, the more that fear thrashes at the last of my sanity.

Her instinct is to run. To hide. To deny us.

Yet the feverish flush of her skin bares her innermost desire to me, those dark little yearnings she refuses to confront.

"Your appetite is just as wicked as mine, and I'm the only one who knows what you need, sweetness. The dirty things you want to hear." I lick over the marks I placed on her neck, letting my teeth take a greedy nip of her skin. "You want to tell me to stop, but that's only so I'll push you past that refuge. I wonder if you even know what truly scares you."

She locks her forearms, the heels of her hands braced against the railing, her belly pressed to the iron as the dizzying sensation grips her.

"The fear is a fucking aphrodisiac as we edge closer." I rut against her, pushing her another inch over the railing. "Don't close your eyes, Halen. Watch those fucking meteors fall, feel every fiery pulse rush your veins, how your heart pounds in fright. Let me taste that saccharine fear, baby, the one that really terrifies you."

Lust gathers her muscles tight, her body tensed as she grinds against me in need. I bring my foot next to hers and force her legs together, dying as her broken moan rakes over my skin. Her head falls back against my chest as a shiver of relief races through her body.

"Fuck, you're not actually scared of being caught. Your fear of heights won't stop us either." My voice is gravel as my erection stabs her ass. "You're not even scared of what I'm going to do to you when I get you alone. You're frightened of what you're going to *let* me do to you, *beg* me to do to you. And how much you're going to love every filthy, deviant second."

A breathy moan escapes as she arches her back, her nipples desperately seeking friction from her blouse, and my heart crashes against my chest wall at the erotic sight.

The stirring notes of the cello float to the terrace to rouse, and her body is possessed as she yields to the desire. It takes all my willpower to harness a fraction of self-control, to stop myself from fisting my hand in her hair and bending her over the rail and fucking her like her needy little cunt is begging to be fucked.

"Dammit, tell me what terrifies you, Halen," I demand.

Her whimper sets my blood aflame, the sensual roll of her hips pure torture as she salaciously rubs along my cock. My unfastened buckle snags on her skirt, and the feel of her frantically reaching for her release is fucking hell as I deny her.

I run my tongue over the smooth surface of my teeth, my lungs seared with her arousing fragrance. "Tell me," I say with a low growl.

"Us." The word escapes her on a rushed breath. "I fear us. The terrible things we're capable of…the loss of control."

But the way she's squeezing her thighs together reveals

the dark current of truth beneath her confession, just how much those terrible things excite her, how badly she craves that loss of control.

I can feel her so close, so damn close to that edge. "God, Kallum," she breathes my name. "The ache…it hurts. Make it hurt so much worse."

"Jesus, fuck." I grit back my need to gnash her skin and deliver the pain she craves from me—the sharp delivery of which can be the sweetest relief.

"Bewitching little siren, be careful what you ask for," I whisper roughly into her ear.

The explicit way in which she's arching her back in pursuit of contact levels me. I drag my arms over hers, shifting her blouse to offer her nipples the stimulation she's seeking, and when she tries to stifle a soft cry, I'm ash amid her fire.

I wedge my hand in the confined space between our bodies and gather her skirt at the waist. I tug the back of her panties just enough to slide the soaked material over her sensitive clit, and she greedily takes the friction.

"If you work those sexy hips any harder, I'm going to come all over this fucking skirt, Halen." A growl claws free of my constricted chest. Every tender wound on my body blazes as she defiantly undulates against me.

With marked effort, I uncurl my fingers from her clothes. "If I taste your pain right now, I won't be able to stop."

Her reactive shiver tempts me to the bounds of my control, and as I force my hands over hers, she turns her palms up and threads her fingers through mine. "I trust you."

Hell will swallow me whole.

I lower my mouth to her neck and breathe her into my aching lungs, tangled around her as she infuses my whole being with her delectable scent, her desire for that hit of pain strangling me.

"Breathe, sweetness," I coax her. "Clench that sweet pussy around the throbbing ache. Hold the fire deep inside. Feel my hands touching every beautiful inch of your body. And stop fucking moving, or I swear I'm going to be forced to fuck you in the most obscene way in front of this whole gala."

Her body locks tight, the dare to move and end the torture is a charged current strung too viciously tight between us. If she even shivers, I won't hesitate to shove her infuriating skirt up and bury my cock inside her until she's screaming my name.

"I need your touch," she whispers, flaying the last of my restraint.

Unable to deny her, I splay my hand low on her belly, feeling her pelvic muscles contract. "That's it, angel. Feed those dark and needy things right here out in the open. You can't hide from me, ever. I know the sordid thoughts that surface from the fringe, and how you want me to take you there."

Her body trembles against mine in concession, and I slide my hand down to her inner thigh to touch the sigil I carved there, stimulating one of her erogenous zones. I've mapped her body. Nipples, ears, thighs—all places Halen's body responds to, but nothing surmounts mental stimuli when it comes to making my muse lose her mind.

Her throaty moan is pained as she tries to trap my hand between her legs.

"You don't know if you want the pain to go on or stop, it's such sweet agony. That's how you make me feel, Halen. Every second with you is lovely agony, and the pain feels so goddamn good—that satisfying, edging bliss that's right there, balancing between torture and ecstasy."

The back of her head rolls along my chest, her body shuddering with desperate need for release. I'm so fucking hard that with one well-timed thrust sewn to her sexy movements, I'll come apart.

The relief would be sublime, but fleeting.

I want to exist in her frenzy.

Despite her whimper of protest, I return my hand to hers on the rail and shamelessly rock against her perfect ass, becoming a madman as I abstain from giving in to her need. The violent, unrelenting urge to sink my cock inside her soaked pussy thrashes inside my chest like a caged animal.

"God, that's it," I urge her, my voice a coarse whisper. "You can feel me. I'm always inside you. Clench that sweet, needy cunt tighter and take me deeper. You can feel me as I thrust harder, becoming unhinged as I hit that deep, empty ache."

Her breathing intensifies, and I swear to whatever divine entity hung the stars, I could get off on the erotic sound of her breath alone. The throaty cadence sends an arousing jolt to my groin, and I lock my jaw against the feral need to spread her ass and spill deep inside her.

"I'm losing my goddamn mind, Halen." I groan over

her ear, rocking harder into her. "I need to feel you come for me, sweetness."

Her body responds to my demand as she pulls her core tight, her yearning to quench the insatiable hunger provoking the demon within to take her far past the edge.

We are not a dead philosopher's soul mates. We are not born from divine thoughts. We were forged in the darkest recess by primal fire and base elements, where not even the gods dare to cross.

We could spend eternity locked in each other's embrace, with me whispering my passion into her ear, feeding off her arousal, bringing her to orgasm again and again, and I could be sustained by her heightened emotions alone.

And I'd still crave more.

"I know why you seek the shadows, little Halen," I say, my voice guttural. "I know what thoughts stir you awake at night, the panic that invades your mind when the silence gets too loud."

I taste the full hit of her fear as she pushes back into me, her desire to run a hot lash down my spine. I bracket my body harder around hers and inhale her intoxicating scent of honeysuckle.

"I'll be there in the dark with you when you wake," I whisper, "when you're trembling, terrified at how turned on you are by the thought of taking a life, the taste of revenge so satisfying and arousing it nearly makes you come in your sleep. I'll be there for you to take it out on, to rake your nails over my flesh and draw blood and punish me as I fuck you senseless, until you're unable to think about anything at all. You can lose yourself in the rage, and I promise, when you're spent, I'll make tender love to you."

God *damn*, she's so close, her entire body trembles with her pending climax.

"That's my wicked girl," I say with a deep groan. "All those dark, deviant thoughts you hide away…I sense them, Halen. I see them in the storm of your beautiful eyes, feel them when you pierce your nails into my skin. And I taste them like the sweetest sin in your kiss, the blood stained on your lips."

"Oh, fucking god…Kallum…" She's unintelligible as she fastens her eyes closed, her body flushing hot and rioting with the agonizing desire to come as her orgasm fights to grab hold.

I dig my fingers into the backs of her hands, refusing her escape, a monster as I feed off every painful current tearing through her body.

"I'm the only one, Halen. Say it."

She arches her back, her chest rising to chase each breath. "You're the only one."

"I've felt your pain, so beautifully broken. I've seen you at your darkest, and you never looked more exquisite. You're a vision bathed in moonlight and blood." I catch her earlobe between my teeth to earn a soft moan. "I'll be the one to worship you until the end of time, when those forgotten gods scatter the last of the dying stars from the sky."

My body is one white-hot strike away from igniting. To regain leverage, I look past the terrace. The marsh is a band of black in the distance, the dark all-consuming. The meteors race and burn up in shimmering trails across the night sky as the cosmos die right along with us.

Breaths ragged, she reclines her head against my chest as she straddles the divide between pain and pleasure. "I need the pain, Kallum. Please."

A growl rips free. "And I need you thoroughly wrecked."

Restraint annihilated, I thrust my cock against her, so close to hitting that wet heat as I draw a torn moan from her mouth, hellbent on keeping my word.

Everything that is violent and lovely about my muse is reflected in the chaos of her suffering. She wants me to hurt her, to punish her—to let her experience physical pain in place of the one that haunts the darkest corner of her soul.

I drag the collar of her blouse down her shoulder to expose her silky skin, and the sight of her injured flesh drives a fire-hot brand into my sternum.

I'm all fury and wrath as I run my thumb over the gash along the joint of her neck from where the priestess destroyed my teeth imprint. The very place I marked a sigil on my muse has been defaced, and I've never wanted to burn the world to ash the way I want to right now.

Suppressing a furious roar, I give in to the base monster and sink my teeth into the delicate arch of her shoulder.

I breathe her in as I bite down, feasting on her flesh like a ravenous devil, my craving for her renewed as the sigil she scored in my skin flames against the seductive friction her fight offers.

Closing my hand around hers on the rail, my gaze falls

to the ring circling my thumb, the weapon which has failed me time and again to banish my muse from my thoughts.

The danger in sigils becoming conscious lies in the madness. Consumed by our desire, psychosis is inevitable.

And I am a fucking maniac for her, my sanity lost when I failed to purge her from my mind. To feed my obsession, I welcomed utter ruination.

No one can ruin me more utterly than Halen St. James.

6

PLEASURE PRINCIPLE

HALEN

I've only ever experienced this sensation on the fading edges of sleep, in some lucid dream where I wake right as an orgasm takes hold. Some tantric, elusive pleasure that teases and edges in an infuriating climb, the pressure in my core a painful ache, desperate for release.

I stop breathing.

I stop moving.

As Kallum bites into the soft curve of my shoulder, every muscle locks in agony that the pleasure will never break. I release a small cry before I catch my lip between my teeth to stifle the sound. Moisture gathers in the creases of my shuttered eyes, and finally, the heartache that's been building into an unbearable pressure surrenders with the piercing of his teeth.

Kallum affectionately kisses the bite, his lips trailing

across the tender throb. "Open your eyes," he breathes over the enflamed skin of my shoulder, his breath heated, arousing. "Breathe."

My eyes open, my lungs steal crucial air, as the roll of his body along mine plunges me over the edge. The hard feel of his chest is maddening as he grinds into me, forcing my back to arch and my blouse to graze my nipples with satisfying friction.

Meteors shower the night as my climax grips me. The beautiful, shimmering lights fade and blink out as fast as they blaze across the sky. Just like pleasure, the height of which is such sweet, fleeting bliss, and then we're burning out.

"*Come*, sweetness. Come so fucking hard for me," Kallum commands, unleashing a growl that travels right to my center.

Like clinging to the dying wisp of an erotic dream, I grip tight to the eroding edges, where the cruel tease of that elusive pleasure teeters on the fringe.

Painful and torturous and maddening.

As I pull a satisfying breath into my starved lungs, my entire body tightens around the negative space. My inner walls clench, and my hips lewdly thrust to drive the aching throb deeper.

"*Oh, god.*" My muscles burn and contract. What started off as a slow build peaks all at once and shatters through me. A strained moan tears free as liquid fire pours through my veins, leaving me trembling, every cell fluttering with aftershocks.

"Goddamn." Kallum's voice is guttural and abrasive against my ear, the sound of his rapid, heavy breaths an erotic chord strummed across my body in pleasure's wake. "You are so fucking sexy, you kill me. It's fucking torture not touching you."

It's his strong arms that keep my limp body from crumpling to the terrace. I linger in his firm embrace, his warm and lean muscles hard along my soft curves, his distinct masculine scent a comfort. The furious beat of his heart ricochets through his cells to mine.

I slip my hands from his on the rail and turn in his arms, hit with the fierce desire burning in his striking gaze. The threat there undeniable as the embers of lust are fanned into flames. Kallum feeds off my pleasure, but he is the epitome of insatiable.

He's so devastatingly beautiful in this moment it aches.

And if he doesn't touch me, I'll go out of my mind.

Mad with pleasure.

The pleasure principle is the psychic force that motivates us to seek gratification of our instinctive impulses—hunger, thirst, sex—as the id demands replete gratification.

It never stops *wanting*.

Kallum's desire to eliminate my pain is still a selfish one, only rivaled by his need to be the one to derive pleasure from it.

By that design, the delirium I feel at having him at my mercy is intoxicating. It's like wielding the power that fuels the sun, and it's darkly addictive.

As the party commences below us, possible leads and answers all gathered in one place, the need for those answers is overruled by my desire for Kallum to touch me, be inside me, blissfully caving to his ravenous demand for hedonistic pleasure.

It's the pained expression on his face that tears at my weakening resolve. I cling to his shoulders, my mouth inches from his, so close to tasting the blood stained on his lips, as I push my body against him to feel his fight—how badly he wants to take me this second.

"It's not enough," I say.

Sweat dampens his hair as his gaze ignites, and I swallow his agony as it's expelled in a coarse groan. I lower my hand and circle my fingers around his thick erection. "I need you inside me."

The words have barely left my mouth before he has me lifted in his arms, his fingers digging into the backs of my thighs in bruising demand as he hauls me to the other side of the terrace.

I'm swept into Kallum's turbulence, the impact of being hit by a tidal wave. Any fear of toeing the edge is a fading memory as I face the unbridled demon in his eyes.

It's not the hit at the bottom that is terrifying.

It's the loss of control during the fall.

With Kallum, the fall may never stop.

I'm pressed to the glass door, my back braced between his body and the hard surface, as he frees one hand to work the doorknob. When it doesn't turn, he issues a heated curse. His gaze solders to mine and, with a fervent groan, he bears down and twists the handle. The shattering *clink* of the broken mechanism heightens my arousal.

I arch an eyebrow. "You have a bad habit of breaking doors."

"Fuck it." His voice is coarse like gravel as he

wrenches the door open. "I'll buy them a whole new creepy house after we're done tearing down these walls."

The muffled beat of music filters from the lower level as the room instantly insulates us in the dark. I shiver at the blast of cool air over my sweat-slicked skin. "Where are you taking me?"

"The shadows." My back finds another unyielding surface as Kallum plants me against a wall, his body caged around mine. "The filthy things I'm about to do to you are only for me, sweet Halen."

His hips pin me to the wall, allowing him to shove my skirt up my thigh before he tears the seam of my panties, roughly forcing the ruined material out of the way. Then he captures my mouth in another sensually brutal kiss.

I hear the distinct rustle of his belt buckle, then his pants are shoved down, all while my legs stay locked around his waist. He wraps his hand around the base of his cock, and just the lecherous act of him grabbing himself and notching the tip to my entrance works a desperate sound from my mouth.

"Nothing about this will be gentle." He's barely voiced the warning before he thrusts forward. The hard warmth of his cock fills me fully, hitting that deep ache low in my womb and earning a hitched cry as I dig my heels into the slab of muscle in his lower back.

His rising growl is broken by his teeth sinking into my neck.

My hands move of their own accord, tearing at the buttons of his shirt until I have it wrenched open. I roam the sculpted contours of his chest, trace the inked skull of the stag, touch the hollow eyes that stare right into my depths.

I dig my nails into his shoulders as he immediately drives into me again. Deeper, harder. Rougher. Shredding right through my clenched inner walls and sanity.

"God—fuck, you're so fucking wet. Let me die buried in this sweet pussy." His hot breath fans over my shoulder as he kisses and marks me, teeth scraping possessively.

My body responds instantly to his praise, my arousal slick between us, a conduit to summon his darkest cravings.

His arm anchored around my lower back, he rails into me with relentless need, every thrust more forceful and devastating than the last. He has my blouse tugged open to touch and lick my breasts, his movements frantic, control annihilated.

My moans come uninhibited, drowned out by his furious growls and the music, torn from my chest in ragged, desperate sounds. When Kallum finds my mouth again to seal a kiss, he digs his fingers into my hair, tilting my face up to him as he ruts into me like a feral beast. He releases my hair only to fasten his hand around my throat, the healed over cuts on his palm coarse friction as he braces me to the wall in the perfect angle to deliver his brutal thrusts.

He fucks me ruthlessly. He fucks me with his whole body. Harsh breaths fall between us as he keeps a severe, wild pace, like he's punishing me for making him want me so badly.

He fucks me like he's scared to stop.

My body doesn't just take the cruel treatment, lust fires

through me with vicious yearning as his hips bruise the inside of my thighs, his chest crushes mine.

My shoulder blades take the brunt of his brutality, bones pounded against the unforgiving wall. His palm cuffed around my throat prevents a full breath, the pressure building into a crushing ache. My heartbeat pounds against my eardrums, and flaring sparks of light burst against my eyelids like the shower of meteors in the sky.

"Fucking hell...I need all of you." His avow falls over my swollen lips, and I'm not sure if he's even aware he's uttered the words, he's so gone. His eyes blaze with hunger and something dark and primal.

Kallum is frenzy.

The pained expression on his face clenches my heart as he rails into me, his need to be closer, my need to be felt, the constant, agonizing demand for *more* that ruins us. I cling to his shoulders, swallowing his guttural moans as I crave oxygen.

He dips his head and sucks hard at the bite to draw fresh blood, and the abused skin flares with a satisfying throb. He's frantically devouring me, teeth raking over my skin before he bites into the soft flesh of my breast. As his teeth sink deep, the pain locks my muscles and I contract around him.

His growl forces my hands beneath his shirt, nails seeking greedy purchase in his skin as I claw into his back. My sleeve snags one of the stitches in my forearm, and the resulting pain scratches an itch so deep, I arch off the wall, my hips rolling in time to meet his merciless thrusts.

Only vile creatures could love so violently.

Lost in our relentless desire as we rend each other apart, we are these wild, wicked things.

The web of his hand becomes a vise, depriving me of air. Fear is tactile and smothering, encasing us in the darkness—yet it's not the dark we fear; it's what's in the dark, the things too fragile to voice, the terror of what could be lost.

The fear of what we could do to each other.

Once a monster tastes blood, they crave it all the more.

Violent and depraved, Kallum didn't just kill a man—he flayed his skin from his skull, stripping him of his identity for daring to cause me pain. I took a life, snuffed that living spark out of existence with my own hands.

Kallum chokes me in deviant craving, yet he also seeks to take control of his fear, edging closer to that dark act which promises a release from his obsession.

Knowing the hurt and damage we're capable of, and wanting it—every sick, painful part of us—we're not given a choice.

There is no escape for either of us.

Fire thrashes my overused muscles until I'm languid and dissolving under his ruthless thrusts. I feel his muscles spasm beneath my palms, his body racked with shivers against mine.

"Ah, goddammit...*fuck.*" Mindless obscenities spill from his mouth in fervent assertions like a helpless plea, and my body answers each one, responding to the needy pain, the consuming, aching demand.

I cup his face and kiss him, my lips hard on his, biting into his lower lip as I fall over the edge, my back arched against the rough wall, my hips rocking into his furious thrusts, lewd, uninhibited.

He frees my throat, and air tunnels into my deprived lungs, the intense sensation alone orgasmic.

"Kallum...oh, god. Fuck me harder." Every broken word is torn from me as he obeys, hips slamming against my thighs. Every time I cry his name, he drives harder, deeper, like his name falling from my lips further strips him of control.

He knows what I'm begging for, what I need, and he delivers that pain.

"You were made for me, sweetness. And I was made to destroy this perfect pussy."

The fire rises until we come together in a violent crash.

I shiver at the erotic feel of his ejaculate coating my thighs as he continues to rock into me, teasing out every last bit of pleasure before he stills. His breaths labored and falling over my neck, I cling to him as the wave recedes, leaving me shaken.

Slowly finding my gaze, Kallum first tracks my features with his eyes, then his thumb gently swipes over my lips, his ring cool against my fevered skin, before he kisses me until I'm again struggling for air, the taste of metallic blood heady on his tongue.

Kallum meant every word of his promise to me. He would expend every energy source to never stop touching me, to never stop fucking me—he would let us wither in his desire to satiate.

And I'm not sure if I'm strong enough to stop the destruction.

When finally he releases me from the kiss, his forehead

touches mine. "You have to leave," he says, issuing his heated request against my tender lips. He pulls away, and there's just enough faint light for me to see the broken expression creasing his face. "Leave this town, Halen."

The appeal is reminiscent of the moment in his townhouse where he asked me to stay with him. Had I not left, had I stayed...then how different would our lives have been these past six months?

"Okay," I say, nodding my answer.

His relief is a smoldering smile breaking across his beautiful face before his mouth descends on mine, kissing me until I'm spent.

I owe this to him, to choose him—to choose *us* this time.

I suddenly dread this monstrous fear that he's plagued with, worried it will destroy him. I don't know how else to save Kallum from his own destructive path.

When he's unable to keep me held aloft any longer, he lowers me to the floor, forcing me to unlock my legs from his hips. My muscles are weak and burn as I find sure footing in the dark.

Seeking my panties to clean up, I hold the hem of my skirt and search the floor. Kallum seals his hand around my wrist.

"I want my cum dripping down your legs," he says, his voice thick with lingering lust. He then yanks my skirt down before he retrieves my torn panties and shoves them in his pocket.

"You're a troglodyte," I say as I fasten my bra into place. I grab my tote from the terrace, unable to deny the thrill buzzing my veins. He makes me just as savage. It's not healthy, I know this—yet I've also seen the devastation a supposed healthy relationship leaves behind.

The arresting smile that stretches his abused lips steals what's left of my breath as he shamelessly tucks himself away. "But this troglodyte did leave you with a whole skirt."

I curb my smile. With trembling arms from my exerted muscles, I dig through my bag and unearth my phone. Two notifications display when I light the screen. The missed call from Dr. Torres and a text from Agent Hernandez inquiring where we are.

As Kallum slips into his long overcoat, my gaze lands on the steady red light of the GPS monitor secured to his ankle, recalling the last time we were inside a dark room within the Lipton house. I shiver at the memory, feeling untethered.

He drives a hand through his disheveled hair, then motions for me to walk ahead toward the terrace.

"You didn't fuck my fear of heights out of me."

"Yet," he says, challenge darkening his tone as he sends me a wink. "All right. We'll take the easy way."

Sometimes, the descent down is harder and scarier than the climb up.

As he takes my hand in his and leads me into the depths of the house, we abandon all the torn open fear in the maddening echo of that dark room.

The hallways are lit by the dim glow of sconces as we navigate our way to the other side of the house. I'm thankful for the near dark that conceals my bruised skin and tousled appearance, even as I try to comb my fingers through my tangled hair.

A sense of something unfinished pulls at the back of my mind, leaving a hollow pang in my chest. So I tighten my hold on Kallum's hand, shoving all thoughts of Devyn and the case aside as we arrive in the large kitchen area.

There's a spread of serving platters with appetizers on the marble counters. Kallum grabs a bottle of red wine and uncorks the pourer before he takes a swig.

He offers me the bottle. "I stay my claim that the Liptons have decent taste in wine."

I point toward a serving tray of bottled waters. "I'll hydrate, thanks," I say, my words trailing off as I look back at the bottle in his hand.

I didn't notice it the first time we were here, but the wine looks homemade. Accepting the bottle, I turn it around and read the handmade label. "What type of wine was found at Landry's mansion?"

Kallum braces the heels of his palms on the edge of the counter and leans back. "I'm not sure," he says, but I know he's following the logic.

I set the bottle aside and send a reply text to Hernandez to meet us inside. "I wonder where the Liptons keep their wine collection." At his heavy silence, I look up. "It's at least a lead for Hernandez to follow."

Kallum pushes off the counter. "No, you're right. You didn't say you were leaving tonight."

I catch the flash of anger before he masks his expression. "As long as we're still here, this is our job."

He turns abruptly and captures my neck, shocking my breath in my lungs. "I'm in this town for you, sweetness. I'm not here to solve cases, catch killers, or save lost priestesses."

"You've mentioned as much before," I say, a tremor of derision leaking into my voice. "The feds want Devyn locked away, to punish her unjustly for a murder she didn't commit. They're looking at her for Alister, a scene you orchestrated."

"She tried to frame me first," he rebounds, his voice pitched below the thumping music. He inches his hand higher and swipes his thumb across my jawline. "There's a merciful way to solve this conundrum, but you've made it clear I can't kill the priestess."

I try to pull away, but he backs me against the counter, placing his mouth next to my ear as he tightens his hold. "But if I find her, I promise you, Halen, if she so much as breathes a threat in your direction, I'll be forced to break that promise."

I angle my head to find his eyes, and as his gaze locks with mine, his tongue drags across the inside seam of his lips. "Deep down in the dark little oubliette of your mind, you know the truth," he whispers. "You can't say it, but that's why you have me, to be the villain and do what's necessary."

I swallow the forming ache in my throat as silence fuels the tension between us, the press of Kallum's desire at battle with my will. He believes I hold the power, he's told me this repeatedly, but for the first time, he's furious over it.

And suddenly, I'm staring into the intense eyes of the same cunning devil I met at Briar, the one who issues ultimatums.

I pull in a steadying breath. "You know I won't let that happen."

"We'll see, sweetness," he whispers against my ear and pushes his hand between my thighs, intimately touching the sigil and sending a current of renewed heat to make me inhale a sharp breath, effectively earning the response he wants from my body.

Before either of us are given the chance to say more, Hernandez appears in the arched doorway. Touching the back of his neck, he clears his throat, further disrupting the heated moment.

Kallum's gaze flits over my face searchingly, his jaw clenched until a muscle flexes. "Halen thinks there's a secret wine cellar with mysteries hidden somewhere in this house," he says to the agent.

"Then she'd be right." Hernandez removes his earpiece, letting it drape around his neck where he covers the feed with his hand. "The team found something in the basement."

My gaze collides with Kallum's, and his resulting, despondent smile is devastating on his beautiful face.

I question whether I'll be able to walk away if I see what's in that basement, and Kallum knows this. I'm seconds from doing just that, walking away completely, when he says, "Fuck it. There's no satisfaction in an open ending, is there?"

He turns and brushes past Hernandez, the music suddenly too loud, the bass hitting my chest to mask the rampant pounding of my heart as I watch him leave.

The pleasure principle demands replete gratification, and in surrendering to it, we're denied something vital in return.

Pain.

The id avoids pain at all costs, and is only opposed by the reality principle, that crucial balance needed to weigh our actions, what acts as a control to our impulses.

I follow behind Kallum, feeling as if I'm still suspended in the free-fall. Yet knowing there are some laws that can't be broken. It's only a matter of time before gravity takes hold.

7

CAGED

HALEN

Agents in black suits and earpieces filter through the basement, crowding the space with overpowering scents of cologne and coffee. I suppose it's a more favorable blend than the urine and feces that lingers beneath the dank air.

Dull fluorescent lights flicker on the ceiling, washing the cinderblock walls in gray light. Like any other basement, the Lipton's is stacked with clutter. Old vacation supplies. Camping gear. Skis and life vests.

Ritualistic artifacts and jars of human organs.

Kallum and I trail behind Hernandez, following the obstacle course of caution tape and task force members as they bag and tag evidence. Maneuvering around a row of stacked boxes, I glove my hands, way too aware of my lack of underwear in this questionable environment.

According to Hernandez, a rookie agent thought it would be clever to get the son—the intoxicated teenage son—to open the basement door. As the feds can't legally enter a locked room of a home to conduct a search, Agent Rana was able to secure a search warrant through a judge on the west coast, stating the urgency of the case.

The deeper we journey into the basement, the more pungent the odor. "Where is that smell coming from?"

Hernandez beams his flashlight on the wall across from us. "I suspect the stench has something to do with the makeshift toilet over there."

I light my phone flashlight to pan the area, landing on a cot tucked into the opposite corner. Black material has been draped across to conceal a small living space.

"Not a bad arrangement where Vince Lipton could hole up," Hernandez remarks. "If you don't mind the disturbing murder house feel."

"How do we know it was him?" I ask, and snap a few pictures before I drop my phone in the tote at my hip.

"Mrs. Lipton confessed as much before her lawyer shut down the questioning," Agent Rana says as she approaches. Her hair is pinned out of her face, the circles beneath her eyes more pronounced in the garish lighting. "Apparently, she was harboring her brother down here on and off over the years."

"This is why you wanted eyes on the Liptons," I say to the agent.

"I've had suspicions about how involved certain members of the community are. It's the psychology of small towns, right?" She arches an eyebrow. "People look up to this family, so how many others have been doing the same as Mrs. Lipton?"

A new degree of respect develops for the lead agent,

even as her perceptive gaze bounces between me and Kallum. "It's nice you both could finally join us," she says. "Come on. I'll take you to where the action is."

Rana directs us toward the far wall where a line of agents and forensic analysts are being funneled. Careful not to disturb any evidence, Hernandez hunkers near an ancient water heater. A section of plywood has been slid away to expose a crawlspace along the floor.

"This connects to a shaft of the mine," Hernandez explains. "The tunnel is old, probably here since the house was first built. Presumably how Vince was able to come and go without detection."

"I didn't think houses this close to the marsh could even have basements," I say.

Kallum moves closer to my side. "Old money likes to circumvent the rules."

"That's an understatement." Hernandez sweeps aside the material to reveal a section where cinderblocks have been dismantled to create an opening large enough to walk through.

The air changes as we step into the dark space. It's thinner, colder. Vile. I wrap my arms around my waist, my blouse insufficient to shelter me from the soiled feel.

A single naked bulb hangs from the low ceiling, a cord feeding it power from an unknown source. The gathered task force members work in tense silence, the dark illuminated with a strobe effect of camera flashes to offer glimpses of a gruesome sight.

Like sinking into an oil slick, a tar-like substance adheres to my skin. Nothing about this space feels similar to the previous ritual sites. There's a sense of malevolence down here that knocks angrily against my bones. It seeps down deep in my lungs until I'm forced to turn my head, seeking a breath not tainted with the stench.

Kallum touches me, just a simple placement of his hand to my forearm, but I lean into the solid feel of him. "This doesn't seem like Devyn," I whisper.

Despite the harsh words we exchanged upstairs, he hasn't abandoned the case or left my side. "No, the priestess doesn't deal in *Goëtia*." His gaze lands on a wood plaque featuring an intricate pentacle that's being photographed by a tech. "But then, the artifacts down here feel more like decorations from a collection than a practice."

"You sound skeptical, and strangely impressed," I say, drawn to where his hand rests on my wrist. His thumb absently rubs over the delicate arch, the sigils and bruises along his knuckles faint under the dim light.

"Impressed that this person is still sane enough to stay hidden." He looks down at me, and a hard crease forms between his brows. Without explanation, he strips off his overcoat and takes my tote strap from my shoulder. Then he proceeds to drape the jacket around me, his hand coming to rest on the nape of my neck. "Whatever you ask of me, I'll always give it to you. Just make sure it's what you want. Some asks come with a high price, and you can't take them back."

I stay locked in the intensity of his eyes, lost in the wary caution I glimpse there, the way the gloom blends his irises into a steel gray.

Offering a nod, I draw his jacket tighter, unable to voice my response as his penetrating gaze bores into me, triggering a hot flare of pain along my shoulder from where his teeth tore into my flesh.

Whatever answers are uncovered, I have to walk away. Kallum has already paid a high price for me. I can't allow him to continue to pay that price. It's time I find closure for those who deserve it—for him, for Wellington's victims. Even for myself.

"*Goëtia* is a form of black magick," I say, shifting the topic to the disturbing scenery of the caverned room. "I came across it while researching Crowley."

"Now I am impressed." The corner of his mouth tips up, and I hear the approval in his voice. He drops the canvas strap over his head to carry my bag, and despite the grisliness surrounding us, this makes me smile.

Crime-scene tape has been strung to section off the different quadrants of the isolated room. In one area, metal buckets are stacked haphazard, a dark substance staining the sides. In the next section over, crude shelves have been carved into the clay walls, where Mason jars are lined like a mad scientist's lab.

As I look up, the sight of chains dangling from a crossing support beam ices my body. A tech mists one of the chains with luminol, and the rusty links give off a white-blue glow to confirm traces of blood. The distinct glow touches the void of darkness all around. It's deceptively beautiful, like a bioluminescent cave deep underground, as the sinister truth of this room is uncovered.

This is a torture chamber.

A buzz courses through my veins. I've always felt this rush at scenes, and I could lie to myself and claim I was

119

altered after all the loss—but this chamber unveils my own sinister truth, setting my inky parts aglow with a luminescent light.

I gravitate toward the macabre cases because stepping into an offender's persona curbs the dark urges. If I feed the monster in the dark, then I'm not tempted to stray from the path. Kallum said as much upstairs as he teased the dark tendrils out of me, offering pleasure in the wake of my fear.

I shift my focus to Kallum. "The task force found evidence of surgical implements and medical supplies in the mine tunnels. It was clean, hygienic. Nothing like this place." I turn to inspect one of the murky jars. "You know what this chamber was used for."

Kallum steps in front of me, the scent of sandalwood a welcome invasion to my abused senses. A forensic tech ducks under the yellow ribbon of tape, and without looking her way, he says, "Can you determine how old the blood is?"

She pauses and looks at me, since I'm the one to meet her eyes. "Could be just hours to days old. Won't know conclusively without tests, but it's my best guess."

"Thank you," I tell her, and she nods once before resuming her work. I return my attention to Kallum, who hasn't taken his penetrating gaze off me. "Did you have a theory to go with that random question?"

Charged tension arcs between us as he takes his time rolling up his sleeves. "You'll put the timeline together," he says. "But my guess is, this is the ravine. Where failed attempts go to die."

Instead of deer carcasses dumped in a ravine after

failing to summon the divine madness, this person dumped people, the victims. I suddenly realize Rana will never recover the rest of the missing locals alive, because parts of them are right here.

A chill attaches to my bones, and I again look at the chains hanging from the rafter.

A sickness roils my stomach as I piece together a terrible and cruel scene. I profiled that the offender would resort to a primeval alchemy incorporating human sacrifice, after which I became the offering in Devyn's ritual—one where she attempted to cannibalize me.

While she was unsuccessful, she has many other higher humans at her disposal. Despite the evidence, I don't want to believe she's devolved so far that she's now torturing these people...that she's lost all connection to her humanity.

"Where are the bodies?" The question escapes me.

Kallum immediately senses my distress, knowing where my thoughts are heading. "If it was me, I'd go with fire. It's a primitive means of disposal, but it's still the most thorough. Organ harvesting was likely done beforehand on the unwilling subject." He eyes one of the Mason jars that appears to hold a spleen.

I nod slowly, even though his assessment may only be for my benefit, to offer me some measure of relief.

"Unwilling," I echo his word choice. Scanning the bowels of the dark cavern, I decide that word is key.

Unlike Devyn's higher humans, willingly following her, dancing seductively around her fire, giving themselves over to the frenzy in pursuit to their priestess's cause, the ones brought here were victims. The

121

proof of their unwillingness lies in the densest part of the darkness.

A custom-made cage has been erected central in the room. Large enough to hold a human captive, it incorporates an aviary design with mesh and wire bars. Metal cuffs are welded to the top grid.

I saver the warmth of Kallum's overcoat for a moment longer before I slip it off my shoulders and hand it over to him. Then I brace myself to face what the analysts are documenting right behind us.

Runes and markings garnish the backside of the cinderblock wall. The rusty color is indicative of blood.

I want to turn to Kallum, to seek that easy camaraderie I found with him while working this case. I know no matter what happens, he won't deny me that. If I asked him to stay, to see this case to the end, he would.

That has to be enough.

Agent Rana appears in my periphery, bringing along Hernandez and another black suit. "This is Dr. Markus, the Bureau's expert historian. He's been sent in to help assist us." She introduces the man to her right, apparently keeping her word to replace Kallum should he fail to stay in line.

"You're up, Professor Locke." Rana hands him a pair of gloves. "I need your highly qualified expertise on that." She tics her head toward the wall of bloody symbols.

Kallum looks over at me, a silent question delivered with the leisure arch of his eyebrow.

To remove Devyn as the FBI's most wanted for Alister's murder, we need a new prime suspect. Before I step away from this case, I need to make that happen.

Nodding once, I give him permission to do what's necessary.

Undisturbed by the blood, Kallum drapes his jacket over my bag and wanders close to the wall. He studies the symbols briefly before he says, "They're a derivative of alchemical glyphs." He points to the top symbol, depicted with a cross inside a circle. "*Prima materia* always comes first. It's first matter, chaos, the formless base of all material. What the ancients referred to as aether." He then points to the hierarchy of glyphs that cascade below. "Salt, mercury, sulfur, etcetera. Basic elements, but with variations to incorporate demonic sigils. Not an uncommon practice. Every alchemist had their own style."

Rana folds her arms across her FBI jacket and trades a look with Dr. Markus, circumspect. "This sounds way off base for our perpetrator, Professor Locke."

With a derisive curve to his lips, Kallum removes his gloves and stuffs them into his pocket. "If my expertise is in question, you're welcome to have Dr. Markus take a crack."

A wave of anxiety crests within me, and I accept the challenge. "Alchemy isn't just transforming material into gold," I say, providing Rana some context. "It's the study into the mystical existence of all matter. The death and rebirth of everything."

Kallum's mouth slants into a smoldering grin as his eyes alight on me. "Everything is alchemy," he says, then motions toward the jars of blood and wine. "Distillation and fermentation are attempts to accelerate the natural order and bring a state of being to perfection. Works on people the same as wine."

As he says this, I think of Devyn, of her desire to reach a higher plane of existence, of her quest to defy the natural order to achieve this very state of perfection.

"That aligns with Child's motive," Dr. Markus comments in echo of my thoughts. He adjusts his thick glasses. "Reaching the state of divine enlightenment."

"Thank you for pointing out the obvious, Dr. Markus, expert historian," Kallum says, sarcasm heavy in his tone.

The man clears his throat, undeterred. "This method is an extreme deviation, however. Childs is straying drastically from her philosophical map."

As I meet Kallum's gaze, a charged battle of wills snaps between us. I ball my hand at my side and dig my nails into my palm, using the bite of pain to offset the emotions at war.

"All right. Here's your lecture, agents." Kallum swipes his hand over his mouth before he folds his arms across his chest. "Hermes is the basis for alchemical practice. As such, there are two opposing forms of magick that derived from texts within the Hermetica. Theurgy and *Goëtia*. The first is divine and calls on the service of deific spirits, such as angels and gods. The second is dark or black magick, which is dependent on alliances with demons."

Kallum is a striking figure as he paces in front of the cinderblock wall. I watch him now just as I watched him in the killing fields that first night of the case as he lectured me, rapt, enthralled by him.

"Since its conception, Theurgy has been the chosen practice," Kallum continues. "Its goal is to become united with higher counterparts in attainment of divine consciousness."

Hernandez shakes his head as he speaks up. "If this is the best practice, then why resort to black magick?"

Kallum's smile is devious. "A trade," he states evenly. "If you want something bad enough, will sacrifice anything or any*one* for it, then the dark arts is, in a sense, a shortcut. Basically, you're making a deal with the devil."

I'm held captive by those beautifully clashing green-and-blue eyes, the ones I stared into as I made my very own deal with a devil.

If I sold my soul the day I signed Kallum on as a consultant, then this is my trade.

Not only does Kallum's evaluation help profile a second suspect, it's an answer to the question of who will take the fall for Alister's murder.

The suspect who tortures his victims, the one who practices the darkest of alchemy.

Someone always has to be the scapegoat.

Kallum looks at the chains. "Childs is a purist, incorporating shamanism in her rituals and alchemy from the three metamorphoses in Nietzsche's allegory." He delivers his next words directly to Agent Rana. "Childs isn't the culprit of this torture room."

As Kallum's gaze settles on mine, understanding passes between us. He's done what I've asked, and the price is high.

With gloved hands, Dr. Markus inspects a broken clay tablet. "Professor Locke, while I don't disagree with your assessment, I would like to point out an oversight."

A nervous flutter pulses in my neck as he lines up the pieces of clay along the dirt floor.

Dr. Markus points to a symbol scored into the clay, an

ouroboros depicted by a snake consuming its tail. "While styles vary, since when does a practitioner utilize two different period techniques? You can see here fragments of the *Chrysopoeia*, dating centuries before medieval alchemy."

Tension brackets Kallum's features. "Since human sacrifice tends to make a practitioner a little insane and unstructured, Dr. Markus."

An ache forms in my chest at the turmoil I sense in Kallum. He's a purist, too. It has to pain him to have his expertise called into question by a historian and not rise to the challenge.

I wait for a rebuttal from Dr. Markus, and a tense breath eases past my lips when he nods with acceptance and bags the evidence.

A small measure of relief frees the tightness in my chest, allowing me the opportunity to break down the scene. I mentally remove all the task force members and distractions. Kallum said the artifacts seemed more like decorations, and I agree.

This room feels staged, and not by a professional who works crime scenes—like someone like Devyn. The wall of glyphs was splashed on the cinderblock like an afterthought, maybe to divert from what's in this room, or rather, from what's missing. It all feels rushed, like the suspect was in a hurry to remove the real evidence.

Moving close to the bagged tablet, I tilt my head and study the design of a double *ouroboros*, depicted here with two rings, representing two snakes swallowing one another.

Out of habit, I go to reach into my bag for my

notebook of research, realizing one, Kallum has my bag and two, my notebook has been missing since the day we worked the ravine.

What I do recall of the symbol indicated it's a sign of volatility, suggesting opposites join together and exist in an eternal, recurring manner.

Shit. An ill feeling coats my stomach as I tie the scene right back to Devyn and her methodology.

A theme in Nietzsche's *Thus Spoke Zarathustra* centered on the eternal recurrence: *Everything goes, everything comes back; eternally rolls the wheel of being.*

"Do you have any insight into this suspect, Dr. St. James?" Agent Rana turns my way, her question breaking into my thoughts.

"I do, yes." A chill clings to my limbs, and I wrap my arms around my waist. "As I said before, this offender has to be someone people trust, someone they respect. This scene only confirms that. The suspect would make them feel safe and protected, at least long enough to lure them here. According to Professor Locke, dealing in this type of alchemy would stress one's mental state." I fidget with the cuff of my blouse. "They'd start to show signs of deterioration. Becoming agitated, suffering at their job. Yet they believe they're above laws and can evade consequences. Someone who's already in a position of power—"

My analysis is cut short as Detective Riddick enters the room. I quickly avert my gaze to the flickering light above, and a wave of dizziness seizes my head as the light sways, casting dancing shadows across the walls.

"Like someone in law enforcement," Rana says, her voice dropped low.

Suddenly, the den of the chamber feels alive with activity. Camera flashes, the rustle of evidence bags. The murmur of voices echoing through the hollow cavern. The flutter of wings.

I touch my temple and blink hard, trying to chase back the pending headache. "Right, exactly," I say, but I've lost the thread of our conversation.

The fluttering grows louder, and I again look up at the bulb, noticing a moth flitting around the light. I squint at the insect, struck by the franticness of its movements as it beats its tiny, winged body against the lamp.

"Dr. St. James, are you all right?" Hernandez's deep voice breaks through the muffled sounds.

"I'm fine." I swipe my hair off my damp forehead. "What about the herd symbol found at the grove?" I ask as I try to recenter myself.

Rana regards me curiously, but says, "Dr. Markus was just stating that the herd could point to a secret occult society, saying it stands to reason that as this is Mrs. Lipton's basement, she's the most likely suspect."

"It's simple heuristics," Dr. Markus states. "You said this suspect is a prone leader, the person this town looks to for direction. She fits your profile, no?"

Riddick chuckles as he approaches the group. "No offense, but I've known Mrs. Lipton for years. She's eccentric and overbearing, but the leader of some cult? That's absurd."

Kallum steps in his direction, and a nervous flutter bats my chest, my heart thrashing as hard as the moth's wings.

"Not cult. Occult," Kallum stresses. "There's a critical difference, detective."

Riddick squares his shoulders. "Christ, am I about to be tortured with a longwinded lecture on the subject?"

A muscle tics in Kallum's jaw, his smile tight as he twists the ring around his thumb. "Well, you have come to the right place for torture."

Dr. Markus interrupts, seemingly oblivious to the aggression. "It's quite simple to distinguish the connection," he says, flipping through pages on his tablet. "Hermetic magick was practiced by many secret occult groups. For instance, the Hermetic Order of the Golden Dawn. This society was heavily involved with alchemy, and kept very hidden."

"Until their secrecy was broken by Aleister Crowley," I supply.

Kallum sends me a subtle wink. "After Crowley revealed detailed accounts of the Order's teachings, other orders started incorporating their practices, deemed renegade members."

Riddick interjects, "If these secret groups were so secret, how would the suspect even know them?" He doesn't try to mask the incensed skepticism in his expression as he narrows his gaze on Kallum.

Rana's eyebrows draw together as she studies the detective's apparent animosity toward the expert consultant.

Kallum doesn't waver. "Perhaps this person is a descendant of one of those renegade members. Families pass down all kinds of creepy histories. Or they're just lazy and impatient and copied right out of one of the books in the mansion library." He matches Riddick's defiant stance. "But I assure you, they're no proficient."

The accusation in Kallum's words is unmistakable, his remark delivered as a direct insult to the alchemist suspect.

The shrill flapping comes louder, the unnerving sound raising the hairs along my body, and anxiety prickles my chest as I watch the wild flutter of the moth's gray wings, the way the insect savagely rams its frail body into the bulb.

Shadows bounce along the ground, the rocking motion assaulting my head with another wave of dizziness. The moth probably hitched a ride on someone's clothes. Now it's stuck, attracted to the one source of light, unable to find its way out.

Out of habit, I seek the comfort of the verse inked in my forearm. Only my fingers are met with the course stitches rather than my scar, and my anxiety mounts.

Through the ringing in my ears, I hear Hernandez mention motive, then a flurry of voices rise around me and pulse in time with the pounding at my temples.

I'm having an anxiety attack.

Hernandez breaks through the haze as he says, "He wants something pretty fucking bad, whatever the motive."

"Obsession," I blurt.

A number of gazes fall on me. "What was that, Dr. St. James?" Rana asks.

I watch the moth spiral down into the cage, where it flaps, helpless, unable to take flight.

"This room is full of dark obsession," I say, my throat dry. "From a person who would go to any length, even hurt the ones he's trying to protect in order to obtain that obsession."

The bulb stops swaying, and I blink to clear my vision. When I look over, I'm met with the intensity of Kallum's gaze. What's not being said between us as polluting as the stagnant air of this chamber.

"I'll take that into consideration," Rana says absently, her attention aimed on a point past my shoulder. She then offers a curt "thank you" to the team before heading in that direction.

I yank off a glove before touching my forehead, the floor feeling unstable. A tingling cold sensation touches my lips as black borders my vision.

I feel the press of Kallum's hands on my body as I'm held upright.

"You're bleeding." The deep baritone of his voice grounds me.

Shock has me covertly checking my legs before he brings my forearm up, a bloom of bright red staining the material with fresh blood.

"Shit," I say, feeling how inflamed the skin is. "Okay. I'll tend to it later."

"We'll tend to it now," Kallum says, adamant.

"Jesus." Riddick inserts himself into our space. He takes my wrist in hand, his touch firm but gentle. "Who the hell sutured your arm, Frankenstein?"

"I did, actually," I say, releasing a forced laugh. "My skills are lacking."

"I have a medical kit in my truck." Riddick's thumb glides over my irritated skin. "Why don't you let me mend you up right?"

Kallum's nostrils flare, his fury simmering beneath the stifling air. I lock onto the dark flare of his eyes and issue a warning with mine.

As I lower my sleeve, I try to remove Riddick's grasp on my arm. "I appreciate the offer, but I really don't like needles. It'll be fine. My equilibrium is just off down here."

Kallum secures my wrist, forcing Riddick to release me. "What she needs is water. I'll get you a bottle."

"I don't want anything from this house." My eyes fall on the jars of blood. "I just… I exerted a lot of energy before." At my coy smile, the tension I sense coiled within him eases a fraction, but only just.

Riddick doesn't take the hint. "You need proper treatment, Halen."

"She doesn't need it from you." Kallum's fingers thread through mine possessively.

Nodding his head slowly, Riddick smiles. "She damn sure needs more than water and philosophical bullshit from pretentious professors."

Kallum wets his lips, a dark smirk overtaking his features. "How long have you been practicing that line, detective?"

"God, *enough*," I say, failing to bite back the burst of anger. "Give me your jacket," I demand of Kallum.

With smug countenance, Kallum effortlessly removes it from my bag and holds the garment open. I slide my arms into the sleeves, effectively covering the blood on my blouse.

"Professor Locke," Agent Rana calls, garnering both our attention, and I'm thankful for her interruption.

She heads our way with a middle-aged woman in a sophisticated pantsuit in tow. "This is Dr. Keller." She makes the brief introduction. "As she's arrived on-scene, we can complete the transfer paperwork at the department later, but Professor Locke is now under her monitoring."

Kallum still hasn't removed his gaze from me, and my skin heats under his intense study. The hard press of his clashing gaze states his concern for me, and the only way to move this forward is to make some reassurance.

I face Agent Rana and my replacement. "It's nice to meet you, Dr. Keller. I'll head back to the hotel and clear my belongings from the joint room. I'm sure Iris can find me accommodations for the night."

Agent Rana tilts her head, a suspicious pull to her mouth as she looks over Kallum's jacket. "That's helpful, Dr. St. James. Thank you."

I nod, then meet Kallum's shrewd gaze, the one I'm not fooling. "Good luck, Professor Locke." I take my tote bag from him, then turn toward Rana. "I'll reconvene with the task force tomorrow."

Riddick enters my line of sight. "I'm heading back that way. I can drop you off."

"She has a ride." Kallum directs a stern look at Hernandez, giving him a silent command.

"I'm all right to walk," I snap, a hot surge of anger twisting my insides.

Even though there was never any charges levied against Kallum for the altercation with Alister, rumors can be just as damning. If Kallum can't resist his violent nature and hurts Riddick or worse…

Violent offenders are locked up in places far worse than Briar.

Rana's discerning gaze sharpens on me. "You're not walking. Agent Hernandez will drive you back to the inn. I can place another agent with the professor and Dr. Keller. In fact, I'll walk you out."

I can feel Kallum's scrutiny on me as I follow behind Rana. I can *feel* his battle at letting me walk out of this room.

As I pass the cage, I stop and stare down at the moth. Still alive, it flops on the ground. I drop my glove over its body and scoop the insect into my palm.

As we reenter the basement, I see Mrs. Lipton seated on the cot. The woman looks out of place here in this dingy environment, her shawl pulled tight around her shoulders, her crusted diamond earrings sparkling under the fluorescents.

Her lawyer speaks to her in a hushed tone as she stares off vacantly, tears tracking her makeup, the search happening all around her.

"They can probe all they want," she says, her voice pitched over the ruckus. "My brother's dead. I said goodbye to him five years ago. I have nothing left to say."

Her lawyer touches her shoulder. "Regina, please. Say nothing else."

Soon as we reach the basement stairwell, I take a full breath, relieved to be out of the confining room, yet I'm hung on Mrs. Lipton's words as a memory is triggered.

Devyn had said something similar to me outside the precinct when I accused her of murdering Jake Emmons: *Jake was already dead. I haven't taken a single life.*

Hernandez shakes his head. "I can't decide if she's ignorant about a whole torture chamber being under her house, or if she's hoping hosting a party right on top of it makes her look innocent."

Agent Rana pauses. "Maybe she wanted us to find it." At Hernandez's confused expression, she adds, "Discovering the chamber might be a relief for her."

I raise an eyebrow, impressed at the agent's insight. "Agent Rana, you need to search the victims' medical records."

She regards me suspiciously, but something else is banked there in her gaze. "I've already had the unit combing through them."

"Not the local records," I say to clarify. "You need records that haven't been through town channels. They need to be requested directly from any noted specialists."

Understanding lights her gaze, and she nods. "The updated lab results on the remains should be in tomorrow. We outsourced everything, every piece of viable evidence is in the process of being retested. I'd like for us to go over it."

I hold her dark gaze, sensing a tenuous camaraderie. "Sure," I say, knowing I won't be here tomorrow to go over any of it with her.

As long as I remain here, Kallum will remain here. And the only way I can ensure he won't fall prey to his violent nature is to remove any temptation.

I'm responsible for the monster I created.

"But feel free to also email me anything you want eyes on right away," I add, hoping she'll follow up.

Her forehead creases, but she says nothing else as her

phone rings and pulls her in another direction. The lead agent is in the process of securing search warrants for all the victims' homes.

Rana is not like Alister. Despite the bureaucracy of her agency, she appears openminded. She doesn't just want to resolve the case, she wants answers, the truth.

By the time I reach the night air, my head has cleared. Maybe it was a touch of claustrophobia, or the shifting light toying with my equilibrium—but I can't stop seeing the moth flitting around the bulb, like a dark silhouette against the setting sun.

I climb into the passenger seat of the SUV, the frail moth still cupped in my palm.

"Back to chauffeuring duties," Hernandez says, but there's no trace of malice in his tone.

I look his way. "We need to make one detour first."

With a resigned breath, he keys the ignition. "No rest for the wicked."

A despondent smile pulls at my mouth. "*Nemo malus felix*," I say under my breath.

"What's that?"

"Latin." I glance down at my closed hand. "It means, peace visits not the guilty mind." Those debilitating thoughts which plague the guilty, we're offered no peace to rest. "First from the book is Isiah, then later, Ozzy Osbourne."

He chuckles. "Christ, he's rubbing off on you."

Literally, he's all over me.

I shiver despite the warmth of Kallum's jacket, and Hernandez shuts off the A/C.

On the terrace, Kallum said he first saw me in the

setting sun, yet it was night when we collided on our path. With Kallum, it's all poetry in the words, beauty in the language, the startling intelligence that seduces the mind.

And that's all it could've been, an arbitrary verse delivered to seduce.

I let my hand fall open. The moth lies on the bed of latex, its wing crushed from the light. Or it's possible it's my doing, trying to hold on too tightly.

I can't entirely fault Mrs. Lipton for her actions. When it comes to the people we care about, when we see them suffering, we'll do almost anything to spare them pain.

Because selfishly, we want to spare our own.

Trying to hold Kallum back from his own violent, self-destructive nature is like trying to stop a star from going supernova. It's paralytic, the fear that I can't protect him.

I put Kallum in that cage of violence. I told him to sever the head. His psychopathy should have never come into contact with that level of violence.

I lower the window and open my hand, allowing the moth to float away.

If the moth survives, I can't stop it from returning to its source of pain, just like I can't stop myself from being drawn to Kallum. It's the light we're drawn to.

The light is so lovely it's blinding.

Some cages, we design for ourselves.

8

ALCHEMY OF MONSTERS

KALLUM

The marshland surrounding Hollow's Row is haunted.

But it's not ghosts or ghouls that roam the tall grass, or monsters that cling to the eerie swamp trees.

This wetland is haunted by pain.

It's a ghostly whisper of agony breathed through the barren, twisted branches as it curls up spines and raises hair from flesh. It's a mourning specter dancing to the rhythmic drumming that imbues the muggy air. And it's the blood-red moon hanging above the bleeding wound of this land.

With every stroke an artistic slash of heartache delivered with purpose to paint the crime scene.

The dark energy buzzing through the sodden field grips the task force members as the science begins; the deconstruction of art and melancholic beauty to analyze and strip that which cannot be defined.

Pain.

It haunts us all.

As a scholar, I rarely praise literary works, but I'd be as banal as Wellington if I completely disregarded the works of a few select novelists in their alchemical pursuit. Such as William Godwin who—though his philosophical contribution was largely as a political theorist—explored Hermetic themes of immortality and life extension.

There is little wonder, then, that Godwin was the father of the renowned Mary Shelley. The intertextual links between father and daughter's works are undeniable once you uncover them.

The desire to escape death.

Monsters and their makers.

In Godwin's gothic tale of *St. Leon*, our main character is determined to obtain the philosopher's stone and the elixir *vitae*—the alchemists' elixir of life. But along his journey to acquire such coveted gifts, he finds himself becoming weak and isolated.

The moral of the story is a theme as old as alchemy itself: When we achieve superiority over humanity, we in turn become exiled from it, as obtaining everything we desire is a descent into a solitary abyss.

In the end, stripped of the very thing which gives him the hope, the very will to live, his immortality becomes a death sentence.

Oh, the fucking irony.

Love is nothing if not punishing.

Above the crown of spotlights, where the black and twisted branches of the marsh trees claw toward ominous clouds, cosmic debris flickers across the early morning sky. It's an arrangement of eerie and lovely that sets the perfect backdrop for Devyn's newest display.

Her very own work of art, a lonely cry into the abyss.

Her pain lashes out in all its fury, her pursuit for her coveted stone raising the question of whether she's the maker or the fiend.

Goddammit. Once Halen sees this, there will be no convincing her to leave Hollow's Row.

Devil's hour is when wicked deeds are done, and I can attest to this, all my darkest, most nefarious deeds whispered to me in the pitch of night. As I stare at the scene, the flurry of activity trying its damnedest to wake the dead, my mind delves to my own solitary abyss.

No one wants to be alone.

The ungodly hour calls for a devil, and I plan to deliver.

Jaw clenched tight, I roll the pad of my finger over my thumb ring, nose wrinkled at the boggy scent in the air. I spy Dr. Keller amid the reeds and wonder how difficult it would be to make this nuisance disappear. The pounding on my door started just before three a.m., the urgency of a new crime scene demanding the expert on call to the FBI.

I stand behind the bobbing yellow caution tape, breathing in the flavors of marsh water and decay, deciding which way to direct them.

Unlike the previous ritual offerings, where select organs and body parts were put on display, Devyn has taken a more creative approach in her staging of the body. The corpse of a woman has been adorned in fresh deer skin, blood of the animal coating her flesh. Alchemical symbols mark her skin. Bone-white antlers protrude from the crown of her head, circled by a ring of ivy.

The severed, deformed ears and black thread stitched across the sunken eye sockets establishes the victim as one of Devyn's higher men.

The woman has been posed on her side, in a position as if she's falling, her hands stretched up into the air and held aloft by woven string. Of course, Devyn's signature. The arms have been entwined in a web of gauzy yarn, like a spider caught its prey amid the woman's last breath as she tumbled down.

It leaves an echo of emotion. I circle my finger over the sigil Halen scored into my chest. It's become a compulsion to feel the hint of pain that touch brings. I now understand why Halen sought the comfort of her pendant.

The reeds rustle in the still dark as Dr. Keller moves into my periphery and swats at a bug, interrupting my introspection. "What time was your last round of meds?" she asks me, wiping her palm off on her slacks. "I need to update my chart, then schedule to dispense."

I keep my gaze fixed to the execution of Devyn's misery. "I don't take meds."

"How is that possible, Professor Locke?" Her tone is incredulous. "Your file states you've been receiving two milligrams of risperidone and lithium since your induction to Briar."

A wry smile lifts the corner of my mouth. Halen didn't bother with these inane questions and procedures. She knew it was futile to push drugs on me. Hell, she knew right away I wasn't on them, and that I'd find a way to dispose of them.

Instead of giving Dr. Keller a canned response to further waste both our time, I shift my focus to the tree line where an immediate pull grabs me on a cellular level. I can always sense her, her atoms dancing with mine. She's crawled inside me, and I'll never scratch her out.

Halen emerges from the high reeds with Agent Hernandez at her side. She's changed into jeans for the occasion, and I shamelessly wonder if she bathed, or if I still coat her thighs.

As soon as Halen sees the body amid the maze of webs, she halts. Bag dropped to the wet earth, she stays frozen in that pose, lost in her thoughts. Crime-scene techs and agents swarm around her, yet she's the still marsh reed amid the winds of chaos.

She did the same thing when she first glimpsed the Harbinger display in the quad. I watched her then, waiting for the spark of recognition that never came. I watched her for three days before I finally approached her, when I couldn't bear to stay away from her for one second longer.

Seems I'm remiss to learn my fucking lesson as I start in her direction now. The unrelenting need to be near her supersedes my self-preservation, always.

As I approach, her gaze stays trained on the scene. "Madness is welcomed over suffering and death," Halen says, her voice as soft as the early morning breeze. She then turns an inquisitive gaze on me. "You said something to that effect before, whether Nietzsche actually achieved self-deification, or if madness was his escape."

I share a look with Hernandez, my drawn features conveying our need for privacy. Carting her tool case, he tics his chin toward the illuminated crime scene. "I'll go

143

find out who discovered the body," he says, then steps away in search of Agent Rana.

Stepping closer to her, I say, "No, you likely said this." Halen has a bad habit of denying her brilliance, what she attempts to hide from everyone. "I'm a student of philosophy, which means I ponder and question, but offer no absolutes."

She touches her forehead. "It's too early for existential...anything, Kallum."

A potent mix of turmoil and anxiety swirls within her, and my suspicion flares. Something has changed since she left the Lipton house.

Her eyes finally meet mine, and I see the glassy sheen of unshed tears banked there. After a tentative beat, she says, "I was planning to leave in just a few hours..."

Apprehension cords my spine at what she leaves unsaid. "Until this," I supply, and nod toward the body adorned in animal skin and bone.

She swallows hard. Then she again looks at the grisly exhibit. "This isn't a part of her ascension ritual," she says, blatantly avoiding the sore topic. "It's not a part of her delusion at all. This is her suffering."

"I agree with your assessment."

Her gaze darts to me. "Don't patronize me."

I lick my lips, tasting her fury in the open air. It's tantalizing, and the depraved craving to feel her rake her nails over my skin simmers beneath my flesh.

"You're angry because you think Devyn is devolving," I say, calling her out and provoking her further. Whatever happened between then and now, she needs a figurative punching bag. I can take her hits. "Which means the window to help her is closing."

She arches a fine eyebrow. "Don't psychoanalyze me, either, Kallum."

"You could have never helped her," I say outright.

She shakes her head, gaze slit. "God, such narcissism. This is exactly what you want."

With a dark smile, I clasp her wrist and draw her into the shadows of the spindly trees. "Yes, we've covered that. I'm a selfish, greedy, covetous devil over you."

She attempts to twist free of my hold. "Let me go."

"Not happening, because I gave you my word," I say to her, my voice rough. "That means I will go to whatever dark place you're slipping into and drag you out. Over my goddamn shoulder if you make me."

She stops fighting, and I reluctantly release her arm. "And you'd derive all the sick pleasure from that," she accuses.

An amused sound hums past my lips, and I advance on her, sliding my palm along the slope of her neck as I back her against one of the trees. Because we're made of combustible elements, I crave her vitriol as much as her passion. She can lash out at me and I'll swallow every harsh word, drink it right from her sultry, venomous lips.

I lower my mouth near hers, claiming her breath as my own. "My smell is all over you. *I'm* all over you, my violent little muse." She latches on to my hand, trying to free herself with a weak fight. "Fuck, the way you want to hurt me right now…want me to hurt you…" I lick the flavor of her on my lips. "I'll make the pain taste so sweet,

Halen, you'll beg me to never stop giving you such sick pleasure."

Her rioting pulse kicks against my palm in challenge, but the stoked embers in her hazel eyes reveal that fire that wants to burn us both to cinder. A broken whimper escapes to rouse my cock, but she bites it back.

"That's a shame," I say, jaw clenched around my disappointment. "I don't mind if you take it out on me. But if you do, use your claws."

Her mouth hardens. "This is how it's going to be with us," she says, livid, her tone questioning. "Fighting, fucking…hurting each other."

"Sweetness, you can fuck me and fight me at the same time. Whatever you need." I glide my thumb over the thrashing pulse in her neck, drinking in every expressive emotion. "I'll even fight you for us if I have to. Hell, I'll be the one to fight *for* us. But you can't lie to me, you need the fight. The hurt wouldn't feel so good otherwise."

"You're a deviant," she snaps. "A fucking sexual sadist who gets off on punishing me for having feelings for you. I know you, Kallum. Anger excitation is nothing unique. No matter how charming and intelligent you are, you're still just a textbook deviant trying to fulfill his psychosexual needs."

I tighten my fingers around her throat, loving the way her skin pinks, her eyes flare, the tantalizing frisson vibrating through her body.

"*Hmm.* Psychoanalyzing me gets my little profiler so fucking hot," I say, catching her bottom lip between my teeth before I release her. "But don't sell yourself short, Halen, it's where you live, too."

Her narrowed eyes threaten to flay me, but the reflexive tremble of her body exposes that buried need.

"What do you fear?" she demands, lowering her voice to control the tremor. Our first night on the case, she asked this of me, and I refused to give her any answer. "Come on, Kallum. You've probed all my fears to get your rocks off. I want to know what terrifies the notorious bad boy."

The earthiness of pending rain mingles with her alluring scent to test my control.

"In twelve hours, I'm boarding a plane to the Graystone Institute," I say, dropping my heated words in the charged air between us. "That's the time you have to find whatever answers you need to part with this case."

She runs her fingers over her neck, the delicate space between her brows creases. "Crosby got you the transfer." Her insistent gaze touches mine, demanding the truth.

A confirmation would alleviate some of the guilt she's drowning in at my incarceration, but she's not wrong in her analysis; I really do enjoy seeing her squirm.

The squelching sound of footsteps disturbs the gathering tension as a shadow falls across the moonlit reeds.

"Dr. Keller, you have impeccable timing," I say as the woman moves into view. She is more of a nuisance than Stoll ever was.

Keller glances between me and Halen. "Agent Rana is asking for you and Miss St. James."

I pull farther away from Halen. "Doctor," I correct her as I move out of the shadows. "It's Dr. St. James." To Halen, I say, "Twelve hours."

Agitation strings my sinew tight as I advance toward

the scene and dip beneath the caution tape to meet Agent Rana and Hernandez inside the perimeter. "So who found the body?" I demand, surprising Rana with my direct question.

"Officer Michaels." Rana nods to one of the local uniforms. "The vic has been ID'd already as Bethany Elsen."

As Halen appears at the fringe of the scene, Hernandez hands over her gear across the band of tape. "I recognize the victim from the mine. She was the Thyrsus holder."

Rana seems to understand that role amid the priestess's Dionysian ritual, requiring no further details. A stark contrast from Alister. "ME's estimated TOD is between two-to-six hours, but there's no clear cause of death. Elsen was discovered an hour ago. We can't patrol every inch of the killing fields and search the mine tunnels at all times." Her tone is bordering on exasperated. "But I'm more interested in why this site is so cryptic and deviates from the others."

"I'm not sure it's cryptic," Halen says, motioning to the woven patterns in the web as she unzips her bag, her movements hurried to disguise the lingering tremble in her hands. "The yarn work is similar, still encompassing an esoteric connection. While the artistry is ritualistic, this is not a rite or ritual in and of itself."

"Childs obviously spent a good deal of time here." Rana props her hands on her waist. "If it's not connected to her objective, why risk exposure?"

"You're only looking at Childs for this," Halen points out, dropping her camera around her neck. "The Harbinger killer likes to leave nonsensical riddles with the victims."

I swipe a hand over my mouth. Though she may want to, Halen can't exonerate Devyn of every crime, especially when there's a flaw in her logic. If she wants closure on the Harbinger killings, then she can't revive the killer from the dead in Hollow's Row.

Choices choices.

Agent Rana tilts her head. "How likely is it that the Harbinger is actually here? It's more plausible that Childs was using a link to you, one of your past cases, for her own purpose. It's Occam's Razor, St. James."

I study Halen's profile, noting her open stance. Despite her own agenda, she appreciates Rana's logical outlook.

"I was told by Agent Alister to incorporate the Harbinger in my profile as it was your theory, Agent Rana."

"Well, he's obviously no longer in charge." Rana crosses her arms.

Halen raises an eyebrow. "Yes, ma'am." She moves around the exhibit, using her camera lens to zoom in and study the details of Devyn's design. The rapid-fire shutter click fills the dense air as Halen photographs the scene.

"The weaving is ceremonial, the act itself sacred," she says, walking around the woman suspended between the marsh trees. "Where the other scenes were crafted as ritual offerings, this one is more intricate. I think the perpetrator is attributing this specific skillset to Athena, making it divine." She lowers the camera, her gaze cast upward on the slender antler tines. "She's taken the time and care to honor this victim."

Halen's use of generic verbiage in place of a name is telling, trying to distance herself from the woman she's profiling, but she can't disguise her anguish, the connection she still feels to Devyn.

At Rana's confused expression, Halen says, "Athena the goddess. She was a weaver."

Rana's tough exterior softens a fraction as she studies Halen. "I remember my mythology classes," she says. "That doesn't answer why Childs deviated in method. Why display this victim rather than dismember her for a sacrifice?"

Halen slides on a pair of latex gloves and leans in to examine the symbols traced in blood, focusing on the circle within a triangle, the philosopher's stone. "Because she cared for this woman. Because she couldn't bring herself to offer her to Dionysus. They were friends." Emotion cracks her voice, and she looks away. "I think once the medical examiner conducts an autopsy, they'll conclude the victim died of natural causes." Halen snaps her gloves off, the sharp sound concluding her examination.

Rana holds up a hand. "That's a huge leap, Dr. St. James. Care to share a theory?"

Still chasing away her unsettled emotions, Halen reinforces her stance. "Based on the deviation, it doesn't fit the other ritual scenes. The perpetrator could also be devolving."

The way Agent Rana scrutinizes Halen spears my chest with apprehension, and I move in closer. "Your perp has lost most of her higher men, her sacrifices," I say, diverting the lead agent. "Symbolically, she may believe this exhibit will garner her more favoritism from the god."

"I've never once heard you utter an indecisive word,

Professor Locke." Rana pins me with a skeptical look before returning her attention to Halen. "The *perp* is Devyn Childs. She murdered an FBI agent and decapitated him. Yes, clearly, she's devolving. I'd like to stop her from devolving further."

I watch the tension gather in Halen's shoulders as she purposely avoids looking my way at the accusation. While I did as she asked, pointing the proverbial finger at the alchemist suspect for the murder, Rana still has her sights set on Devyn. Respected or not, Alister was FBI. One of them.

Rana shifts her gaze to me expectantly. "So, professor, I want more conclusive insight from you where the word *may* doesn't enter your extensive vocabulary, or I'll send for Dr. Markus, and your evaluation will reflect that."

I rub the back of my neck, sick of the humidity. Sick of this town. Sick of performing. "It's a replica of *The Bacchae*," I say decidedly. "An ancient Greek tragedy set in Thebes. The scene depicted here is iconic, ornamented on vases and murals from the era. Do you also recall the play from your mythology classes?"

The agent doesn't flinch. "Refresh my memory."

My smile is cutting. "Fearful of the raving ones, the *maenads* empowered by divine madness, men chased the women up a mountain side. It was barbaric, branded as the pursuit ritual. Their fear of these women was so tremendous, they chased them over the cliffs of the mountain."

My gaze drifts to Halen, registering the sadness in her expression, the residual ache of loss I always sense within her. The desire to taste that ache deep inside her thrums through me with vicious need, and I give the agent my closing statement so she can be rid of this scene.

"Overall, I agree with Dr. St. James," I say, sinking my hands in my pockets to curb my desire to touch her. "This is a shrine. Childs views her followers as the mad women regardless of gender. Their groupthink mentality is so strong and loyal, their devotion to their priestess earns them a commemorative death." I tic my chin toward the exhibit.

"Childs hasn't deviated from Nietzschean philosophy," I continue. "Nietzsche used Greek tragedies to express how life is cruel and unfair, how illogical our suffering can be." But I'm looking into Halen's eyes as I say this, my words meant solely for her. "As Childs has clearly replicated here."

Halen doesn't break my gaze, a certain understanding passing between us. "Nietzsche also felt that to make sense of our suffering, we have to have 'a recognition that whatever exists is of a piece, and that individuation is the root of all evil'."

A faint, hopeful smile graces my mouth at her direct quote from *The Birth of Tragedy*.

"In other words, Dionysus offers deliverance from our pain, where we don't have to suffer alone." Halen looks at the exhibit. "Devyn's shrine denotes her pain, but in this way she also reconciles it, mitigating her loss by making herself one with this woman through the god."

The crime scene all but falls away. Halen's saccharine melancholy infuses the air and reaches right into my sternum to strangle the muscle that beats only for her. I'm tempted to set this whole field on fire and make love to her as it burns to ash around us.

Rana cranes an eyebrow. "You two do work well together," she says, her innuendo not so subtle. She's not oblivious, but at least she's also not tactless, giving the moment sufficient time to taper before she addresses me. "Thank you for your thorough analysis, Professor Locke. I expect a detailed report on *The Bacchae* before the end of the day."

Yet another reason to set fire to this town and be rid of this whole charade before the day's up. I don't do fucking homework.

Finally, I break away from Halen and give Agent Rana a compliant nod, satisfied when she turns her full attention to Hernandez and another task force member.

The activity of the scene bleeds into the sudden stillness incasing us, the chirr of the crickets too far off, the rustle of disturbed deer buried beneath the whine of cameras and ringing devices.

Nothing feels sacred anymore.

With a final zip of her bag, Halen hefts her gear. "Since I have nothing further to offer, I'm heading back to the hotel." She directs her statement to Rana.

After a measured beat, Rana excuses her. "Keep your phone on in case there's a new development."

Halen nods her agreement before turning toward Hernandez past the crime-scene tape. "Would you mind bringing my gear back to the hotel later? I don't feel like lugging it all to my rental car, and I need to get some sleep."

At his accommodating nod, she walks off the scene.

I feel the weight of his stare on my back. "Are you going to let me in on what happened with her earlier?" The demand in my tone makes it not really a request.

Hernandez moves into my field of vision, his features stern. "Maybe she's figuring you out."

Despite the smile that slants my mouth, the implication digs beneath my skin. A flash of the Briar Institute on Halen's phone rears before I tamp it down.

"You know, Gael. It's pretty easy to get locked up in holding cells with madmen around here."

His nostrils flare. "Is that a confession?"

"A truly smart fed would take it as a warning."

Facing him, I reach out and take Halen's gear from his grasp. He says nothing more as I back away, keeping my gaze hard on him as the threat lingers amid the reeds.

Right on cue, like an irritating gnat, Dr. Keller crops up in my periphery. "Professor, you're not permitted to leave the scene."

A growl rumbles from my chest, and it's enough to catch Halen's notice. She looks back with a severe glare to deliver her own warning.

I hold up a hand innocently. "I'm just helping to carry gear."

Halen seals her eyes closed briefly before she slogs through the reeds toward the woman. "Dr. Keller, I need a moment alone with your patient."

"It would appear the both of you spend too much time alone," she says derisively.

Halen cocks her head, a dangerous twist angling her pretty smile. "Is that a professional assessment?"

A thrill sparks my blood at the threat edged in her tone, so close to touching that wild fury.

Dr. Keller flicks her humidity-frizzed hair from her shoulder. "Just an astute observation."

The standoff between them stretches until Halen says, "Until your services are required as more than a babysitter on this case, you will respect all requests from every member of this task force despite your limited observations."

Goddamn. My blood is molten watching Halen mark her territory like an apex predator.

When Keller ultimately relents, walking a distance away, Halen levels me with a knowing stare. "Do not do anything to her," she says.

"I don't think I'm the one Dr. Keller should be worried about. Damn, baby. Those claws are sharp." I reach down and shamelessly adjust myself. At her unmoved expression, I say, "I have no intention of making the doctor piss herself." Though the memory of Stoll doing so brings a crooked smile to my face. "Besides, I can't anyway if I'm no longer here."

"You lied back there," Halen says, accusation heavy in her voice.

"No more than you did," I challenge.

Her dark layers of hair escape the band at the base of her neck. She holds my gaze a moment longer before she admits, "I was just trying to make Devyn appear—"

"Compassionate," I say. "Remorseful. Like she's incapable of murdering a member of law enforcement in cold blood."

She brushes the shock of white from her eye. "And you were lying to protect me."

"Always."

A charged current pulses the air between us, and I chance a step closer.

"If you want Devyn vindicated, someone has to take the fall." I roll my shoulders as I anchor the strap of her case higher.

"There always has to be a scapegoat," she says, slinging my words back at me.

Always.

"Rana's right, the Harbinger has no logical reason to be here. The alchemist suspect is the best target. Nudge Rana toward him with your profile, and I'll back it up in my... report." I bite the word off with a hint of derision, making Halen's captivating smile surface. Just as suddenly, however, that smile turns crestfallen.

My thoughts focused, I rest my tongue in the corner of my mouth and close another step toward her. "The person who spent time in the Lipton basement conjuring the dark arts, that person probably isn't trying to manifest rainbows and unicorns, Halen. You don't even have to suffer any guilt—"

"That's not it." She shakes her head lightly. "It's all pointless anyway."

"Tell me what happened," I demand.

She drops her camera case and crosses her arms, pensively rubbing her thumb over her forearm where I stitched her wound. "Devyn's sick," she says.

I lift my chin, waiting for her to offer more as I watch her lower to her bag and remove a hardback.

She rises to her feet with a medical journal. "I saw this in the stacks that day at the mansion library," she says, showing me the cover. "I couldn't make any connection to it at the time. I just knew it felt out of place amid all the other esoteric books."

"You're getting real comfortable with removing evidence," I say.

She releases a breathy laugh. "It's the least questionable thing I've done."

The large print on the front cover has two words that stand out: Huntington's Disease.

And suddenly, as I stare into Halen's watery gaze, I understand the hopeless vortex I feel churning inside her.

She cannot save Devyn.

And she knows this now with finality.

"Devyn's sick," she says again, her voice catching. "She's dying." She lifts her shoulders in a resigned shrug, a despondent laugh slipping free. "Nothing I do here to try to help her much matters anymore. It's a lost cause. The only thing I can do is let her escape into her madness."

Her statement from earlier makes sense now. "Madness is welcomed over suffering and death."

"Her escape." She sniffs hard, lifting her head higher. "So...lie to them. Hell, lie to me, Kallum. It doesn't matter. The case is closed. Over."

I'm frustratingly at a loss for how to console her.

"Don't pretend as if this news doesn't delight your wicked heart," she says, the venom resurfacing. "There's no reason for you to threaten her life anymore. She's no longer any threat to me."

"What causes you pain causes me pain." I want to lead

157

her farther into the dark marsh, where I can touch her and distract her from that pain.

I understand why she was hesitant to tell me, to say the words aloud, so she wouldn't have to face the resulting guilt at the relief she feels. In the dark chasm of Halen's mind, she's relieved. She doesn't have to choose. She doesn't have to decide who to protect.

She's such a delicious tangle of emotions.

"So why did you even come to the crime scene?" I ask her. "If it's pointless."

She shrugs, her gaze fusing to mine through the dark. "To be with you."

Every cell in my body strains to be connected to hers, but I can feel all their eyes on us, watching, judging. Hernandez, with his suspicions. Dr. Keller, with her annoying, asinine obligation. And Agent Rana, who knows Halen is hiding something.

"No snowflake in an avalanche ever feels responsible." My mouth twists into a lopsided smile as I offer her what comfort I can. "Voltaire."

Gaze cast outward, she wraps her arms around her waist tighter. "Voltaire didn't flay a man," she counters. "Or crush his face with a lug wrench."

"That we know of."

Her laugh tumbles out, and she's unrepentant for a few brief, blissful seconds before she fights it down with a broken sound. "I think we're responsible for more than a few snowflakes." She looks up at the night sky. "I don't think she's a murderer, Kallum," she says softly, her emotions drained. "I just wanted to prove that before I leave."

"It's too risky." I drive a hand through my hair. "All risk poses a threat of ruin."

Her anger flashes hot. "What the hell am I supposed to glean out of that?"

"I won't risk you. I won't lose you to your own ruin, no matter how damn hard you try, Halen St. James."

I stopped exactly that from happening once, and I'm prepared to do what's necessary to prevent it again. Even if I have to charge sigils, spill blood, banish her thoughts— risk her forgetting us all over again. Fuck it, that *is* the risk I'm willing to take.

"For once, Kallum, please... Just tell me what you're trying to say."

I eat the distance between us, forcing her head to tip back as I tower over her. "You went willingly with Devyn. While I was locked up, unable to protect you. You went with her and put your life at risk."

"I get it. You're upset—"

"No, I'm not upset. I'm goddamn furious." There's a pit in my stomach trying to gnaw me from the inside out at my admission. "You already tried to save her once, and you nearly died. Now here you are, with your answers and no hope, and you're still trying, like you have a fucking death wish."

The truth burns through us like a destructive wildfire. Unable to douse the roaring flames once the tinder has caught fire.

She won't deny it, because she can't.

The ache in the center of my chest flares until I'm strangled by the force of it, constricting my throat with fear's razor-sharp talons.

"You asked me what I fear," I say, my gaze holding hers. As she reads my expression, I lower my defenses, allowing her to see the brutal truth of what her death would do to me. "If you want to destroy me, don't take your next breath."

A hard swallow drags along her slender throat. "Kallum, I came back," she says, her eyes searching mine, a promise held there. "I came back for you."

A deep groan barrels free of my chest. "Fuck them. I'm handing in my fucking notice anyway."

She came back for me.

Instead of running, she came here to be with me—to fight, and fuck, and hurt—to get what my dark little muse needs that she can't get from anyone else.

My whole body ignites as I drop the gear and grab the nape of Halen's neck. I pull her to me, my mouth descending on hers as I crush her body against mine.

Her hand roams my chest, her fingers finding the crescent sigil through my shirt, delivering that sweet hint of pain that screams *mine*.

Alchemy's stones and elixirs, the endless quest for eternal life. But what is eternity if spent without the fire of your twin flame?

Fear of loss is such a brutal bitch. But hope... Hope is a cruel and sadistic monster, one of our own desperate design. Yet even the most monstrous of us cling to the frail wisp of it.

9

ICEBERG

HALEN

In one of my psychology classes, we were presented a structural model which displayed the two-dimensional rendering of an iceberg in comparison to the psyche. This was Freud's iceberg theory, and it essentially broke the mind down into three layers.

The tip of the iceberg is where our conscious exists. The layer right beneath the frigid water is the preconscious. And the rest of the berg below is the unconscious. It is in this vast region below the water where the psychological forces of the psyche reside, there in the dark, endless void.

The deeper the unconscious, the darker the abyss.

I would stare at that iceberg, unnerved, the image evoking a sense of dread and hollowness that left me shaken and suffering some form of Thalassophobia. Possibly the reason why I've never used Freud's model as a reference. That, and his approaches have since been widely rejected.

And I'm only thinking of it now, as I hit Send and fire off the finalized profile to Agent Rana, because of the connections I can no longer deny, the ones stirred by Devyn's shrine.

Everything connects.

Kallum said this in the killing fields our first day on the case.

While it's not so mysterious that Freud would reference Nietzsche's Duality Dichotomy to explain the id —he often used philosophy and the Greek mythos to lend to his psychology endeavors—it can be insightful.

Such as how Nietzsche stated the Dionysian represents raw energy from which everything originates. The ancients referred to this state as a void. Kallum cited this as *prima materia*, the chaos of the universe.

To Freud, this raw energy embodied our most extreme emotions, from terror to ecstasy. In its purest state, the Dionysian is powerful yet equally destructive without a way to control and focus it. Not unlike the id when deprived of a counterbalance, which would enslave us to our desires.

When comparing the ego to the id, the Apollonian is a necessary contrast. It creates a way to incorporate the Dionysian. As Dionysus represents existential reality, Apollo gives us the means to live this intense, passionate reality without being consumed by it.

Otherwise, regardless of its evocative beauty and alluring creative genius while in the impassioned throes of the Dionysian, we are not actually free, as we're still doomed to the self-destructive forces of our base desires.

While there is beauty in the chaos, like the fiery dance of the cosmos, there is also pain and tragedy in its unruly violence.

Freud stated that it is the excess, the id, that makes us violent.

It doesn't take an expert in philosophy or having a doctorate in psychology to see the parallels.

These two forces must work in tandem to survive and exist in harmony. No matter how badly my logical disposition wants to argue, once all doubt is removed, the result is a life worth living, even if it's chaotic and dark and painful.

Kallum consumes my excess, and I balance his extreme nature.

I close my laptop and move to the foot of the hotel room bed, where my suitcase is mostly packed. I drop the tear-shaped diamond in the palm of my hand, feeling the coolness of the rock as I pool the white-gold chain around the pendant.

Some distant part of me wants to keep this token of my past life, yet there's now a stronger part that desires to release it and the pain its tied to. Like tossing an anchor away from a vessel, I set the necklace on the nightstand, freeing it one finger at a time as a buoyant relief untethers the weight within me.

If Devyn was here, I'd give her the pendant. A piece tied to my grief bestowed to her with the hope that it could somehow set her free also. That's the part of me she needed, that she connected with. This memento should stay with her.

After a few hours of sleep, I'm mentally recovered enough to accept the outcome.

There's no help for Devyn.

Even if I somehow exonerated her of Alister's murder, she would still be charged with desecrating remains, and a whole host of other offenses. She'd serve a lesser sentence for these charges, but even then, she'd die in prison or an institution before she earned the chance at freedom.

I don't know when Devyn's symptoms first showed, but I know she had to be young. On average, someone with the juvenile form of the disease may live up to a decade after symptoms appear. With the little research I've done on her disease, I think Devyn could have potentially months to a year left.

I'd been trying to walk in her steps with each ritual scene, trying to uncover the reason—the *why*—that sparked her obsession with ascending into a philosophical existence.

The moment of clarity came when Mrs. Lipton confirmed a single theory, that her brother was terminal. The rest of the pieces connected in quick succession when I uncovered the medical journal at the mansion.

That was Devyn's cave, her solitude of meditation for years. The journal could only belong to her.

Sometimes, two and two equals four. It's just that simple.

Once the updated lab results come in and are matched to the proper medical histories of the missing locals, it will prove all thirty-three of Devyn's higher men are—or were —terminal.

But Agent Rana already knows this. It's why she's been so guarded, keeping the recovered victims quarantined in the hospital. They're all severely ill, and likely getting worse. I just hope my suggestion to obtain their records does help to get them treatment.

While there's still the mystery as to why the residents kept this information about their loved ones hidden during the investigation into their disappearance five years ago, Dr. Markus's theory on highly secretive societies is the most logical theory. People sworn to secrecy, clinging to the hope of their loved ones' recovery.

I could delve further into the town's groupthink dynamic but...

It's no longer my case to solve.

Along with the profile that includes a list of suspects, I also sent her my notice.

I have to move on from Hollow's Row.

Kallum is still concerned Devyn will reveal my secret, but that was never truly my fear. Even if she announced it to the entire world, it would be perceived as the ramblings of a clinically disturbed woman with no physical evidence to back her claim. No official would take the allegation seriously. She was obsessed with me during this case, she tried to cannibalize me. It would be easy enough to generate a profile showing how she twisted the crimes to justify her desire to use me in her ritual.

I do not want to be forced to do that.

With a long exhale, I look at the closed door of my hotel room. Even from across the hall, I can feel Kallum.

Where we go from here is what I have to answer. Once he's transferred to a new hospital, I have no doubt Crosby will argue in his favor for a reduced sentence.

Whatever happens next, we'll be together.

And I want to be with Kallum. The man who can take my pain and consume it like a wildfire, who can kiss me harder as he devours the ache. The man who looks at the blood and carnage in the unhinged depths of my psyche and doesn't shy away in horror, but rather craves the dark depravity, who can even find the beauty in it. A man who laps at my tears of fury when I'm drowning in the torrent, and who will never let another person cause me harm, because this world will always bring pain. It's never-ending.

I have almost given up once already, given into the weight of it all, and he will refuse to lose me. He will always find me, and force me to keep fighting.

The truth is, I did die the night I confronted the Harbinger.

And this is the woman who was resurrected in her place—the one designed for a man like Kallum Locke.

I reach for a clean shirt and begin folding it. Iris was kind enough to lend me the use of her hotel washing machines. As I lay the garment in the suitcase, my phone screen lights up with a video call.

I stare down at the unknown number. Brow furrowed, I accept the call.

Dr. Torres appears on the screen. *Shit.*

"Hello, Dr. Torres. I'm sure contacting me is against the sound medical advice of your doctor."

"Have you figured it out yet?"

His face shows marked signs of sleep deprivation, and his thinning gray hair is unkempt. He drives his fingers through the sweaty strands, and I note the bandage wrapping his hand. Dr. Torres is not well.

"I promise I don't know what this is about," I say, turning toward the window to gauge the coming storm. With the media invasion and road blocks, bad weather will congest the roads that much more. "But I'm positive you're not supposed to have access to a cellphone."

He huffs a manic laugh. "You refused to answer my calls from the facility," he says, as if this is a reasonable explanation. "Besides, this is my hospital. I can use what devices I see fit to." Even so, his gaze darts around the white room warily.

"And the reason for your call?" I prompt him to hurry him along.

"I was certain, with how intelligent you are, that you'd have put it all together by now, Dr. St. James."

He's baiting me. Otherwise he would have already told me what he wants me to know. From what I've heard from the psych department at Briar, Dr. Torres is suffering a form of persecutory delusion. Which, I have no doubt Kallum helped exasperate, but he didn't create the psychosis.

"I'm ending the call now, Dr. Torres. Please make sure to take your scheduled medications and do the work to get well. I wish you the best."

"Professor Locke was communicating with your suspect."

The dark, chilly waters funnel over my head as a sinking feeling tows me under the iceberg.

I draw the shades closed across the window. "While he was remanded at Briar," I say, needing to hear him say it audibly, clearly.

"Yes, Halen."

"You want me to believe that Kallum was in contact with the Hollow's Row suspect before I came to the institution." I speak the words slowly, deliberately, so I can hear each one for myself in some lucid format.

"Yes," he bites out, his teeth ground in frustration. "His manipulation of that person is, in fact, the very reason for your visit."

My chest pangs with a residual ache, the floor beneath my feet shifts. "Dr. Torres, I don't see how that's possible."

His chuckle is derisive. "You don't think a talented mind like Kallum's, who deftly manipulated a court hearing to obtain a judgement of not guilty by reason of insanity, could maneuver you onto a case?" His smile falls. "You know the truth."

The anchor tethered to my ankles tightens, the weight submerging me farther down the obscure void.

I sit on the corner of the bed, stare at Torres's blood-shot eyes through the screen. His gaze isn't on me, he's watching my reflected image as I'm watching his. "You have a sick obsession with Kallum," I say, keeping my voice steady.

"I'd argue you do as well, Dr. St. James."

"I refuse to hear anything more on this matter until some proof is produced." Despite every cell in my body screaming, I owe Kallum my trust.

"Fine," Torres snaps sharply. "I can see the demon has

his talons sank deep. I have plenty of evidence for the criminologist who needs proof. But once you see it, I want your word you'll help me get out of here."

A small measure of relief loosens the tight cavities of my heart. So this is Torres's motive. Playing into his delusion will only further his psychosis. I shouldn't have answered the call.

"Sure, Dr. Torres," I say. "Once you provide this evidence, I'll gladly help secure your release."

As I go to end the call, he says, "I am sorry, Halen. I was an opportunist, and single-mindedly focused on my case study. For not being truthful with you and allowing the manipulation to go this far, I am sorry."

My thumb hovers over the red button. I school my features even as a tiny fissure of doubt cracks my resolve. "It's all right," I assure him, trying to placate the doctor. "You were a pawn."

"I'm afraid when it comes to the great Professor Locke, we are all pawns," he says. "Even you, Dr. St. James."

Three beeps signal the call disconnecting, and still I stare at the screen after it's gone dark. I'm reaching for the anchor tether, desperate for a breath as my lungs ache from the pressure.

A knock sounds at the room door to mercifully pull me out of my spiraling thoughts. I pocket my phone, the device feeling heavy, and open the door to find Hernandez on the other side.

A deep groove carves the skin between his thick eyebrows. "What is it?" I ask.

"The ME report came back on the vic from the recent

scene," he says, like he's pausing for dramatic effect. I widen my eyes to urge him on. "While it was confirmed she had a rare disease, that's not how she died."

"Gael, just say it."

"Hemlock poisoning."

The last bit of solid ground erodes beneath my feet. I'm falling through a crag at the bottom of the ocean basin, a vortex sucking me down past any rays of light.

"All right," I say, trying to sort my thoughts. "Let me get ready and grab my bag." I toss a glance around his shoulder at Kallum's room door.

"Do you want me to grab them?" he questions, referring to Kallum and Dr. Keller.

Doubt is poison injected into my bloodstream. I can only shake my head in answer, my voice lost.

I close the door and glance at the safe, where I stashed the carving knife. One second to deliberate, then I unlock it and shove the bagged knife into my tote. I pack everything else that remains into my suitcase. I hesitate a moment as I look at the nightstand before I stuff the necklace into my pocket.

Then I meet Hernandez in the hallway with all my belongings.

I won't be returning.

FORCES COLLIDE

HALEN

The medical examiner's office is located in the minor building adjacent to the police department. In smaller towns, they're even sometimes nested within the same building. This is a convenience for more than just town officials; it's convenient for any person who wants to tamper with evidence and reports.

The chilly air is laced with the stringent scent of antiseptic as Hernandez and I wait at a stainless-steel table in the main office for Rebecca Forester, the chief ME of the county. She was brought in the first day of the investigation to assist the office when dismembered eyes were discovered on eerie marsh trees.

She arrives with a couple folders and a tablet nestled in her thin arms. "I just gave this information to Agent Rana," she says, as if we're disrupting her process. Which, admittedly, after the abuse of this office and scrutiny it's been under due to the evidence tampering, I understand her distrust.

Regardless, she hands me the tablet. I scan the document, confirming the finding of hemlock poisoning to Bethany Elsen. A puncture wound was discovered at the base of her spine, the same location as Leroy Landry—the beast of a man who attacked me and Kallum at the ritual crime scene.

I set the tablet on the table, disbelief clawing at my conscience. "We need to see the body," I say.

Her slight features purse. "My findings are sound."

"No one is questioning your autopsy," I say. "I need to know if there were any markings on the body I overlooked." I accept full responsibility of my negligence. I was distracted at the scene, moving too quickly through it, wanting to shut down my own pain.

Hernandez's phone rings to break the tension, and he accepts the video call. A partial view of Agent Rana's face appears on the screen. "Good, you already have St. James with you." Apparently, she hasn't yet checked her email to receive my notice. "I've been trying to keep this quiet from the media, but the medical reports have leaked that the local victims were all terminally ill."

Hernandez adjusts the phone. "How was this kept so quiet from us?"

She flashes a look my way. "The medical histories were buried. Nearly half of the victims weren't initially town residents, having moved here beforehand from other states."

I see Devyn before me in the cave, her eyes flashing wild when she said: *I've liberated them.*

She wanted to liberate them from the suffering of their illnesses, their pending physical deaths. She could have been communicating with these people for years before they moved here to disappear.

"What I want to know is how you put this together, St. James?" Rana asks me.

Snapped back into my thoughts, I touch my forehead. "There was a medical journal at the mansion library." I sneak a glance at Hernandez. *Was* being the operative word. "It was conjecture."

"Good conjecture," she says. "The father's death certificate was recovered to confirm he was the gene carrier for their disease. He was checked into a hospice facility at the time of his death."

My limited research indicated that juvenile onset of the disease is almost always inherited from the father. I suspected that Devyn's father likely passed away from complications not long after he left town. Possibly, so his children and wife wouldn't have to watch him deteriorate.

"You profiled that if the gift of the Overman was rejected by society, then the perpetrator would devolve and take their own life or the victims' lives."

I immediately see the connection the agent is making to the torture chamber and internally curse. On my second revision of the profile, I concluded the hemlock would come into play as a means of elimination. Which, by all appearances, looks to be what happened to Bethany.

"That wasn't a definitive conclusion at the time," I say, attempting to deter her. "Considering the recent developments, the alchemist suspect fits that profile more reasonably than Childs. Closing up loose ends, eliminating any potential leaks that could expose and implicate them."

"If that's so, then Childs would logically be in danger, as she's also a loose end," Rana says, and the hairs along my body lift away. "But it's more plausible they're working together. Childs staged the scene yesterday. No matter who injected the hemlock, she's an accomplice."

Unless Devyn was trying to tell me something with the scene. I know it's not rational and even biased, but I want to believe Devyn's desire was to help these people, to offer an escape, even if a delusional one.

"I'm sending Keller and Locke your away to team up," Rana says. "I want the crime scene analyzed in daylight before the storm can hamper any potential evidence."

At the mention of Kallum, my heart rate quickens. "Agent Rana, did you receive my—?"

"I got your notice, and I don't accept it. Professor Locke is scheduled to depart this evening, and I can't lose the both of you on this case."

"Agent Rana—"

"I know why you want to leave," she cuts me off. "I understand you feel a connection with Childs—Devyn," she amends. "And though I typically subscribe to the sound advice to never commiserate with the suspect…use it, Halen. Use your connection with Devyn to find her."

Chest constricted, I can only nod, not fully appreciating what I'm agreeing to before she ends the call. All I can think about is what she said.

Devyn could be in danger.

Hernandez pockets his phone in the inseam of his jacket. "So you're not leaving now."

I expel a tense breath and look him in the eyes. As he was the one to help load my luggage in my rental, I couldn't keep it from him. "I still am. I'll check out the scene once more before you drop me off. But like I said before, if anything pops up that you need assistance—"

"I'll reach out to you," he says with a wan smile. "For what it's worth, I think you're making the right call. I have a bad feeling about this offender. Like Rana said, as we close in on them, it could get volatile."

While we wait on the second half of our team to arrive, I conduct a more thorough examination of the victim's body, looking for anything that I could have overlooked during my cursory evaluation.

Using the ME's photos on the tablet to compare to the autopsied body, I study the figures drawn in animal blood on her skin. I recall most of the markings from Devyn's circle in the cave as part of her ascension ritual. The only symbol that stands out is the philosopher's stone. It's the only symbol that appeared in the ravine, Devyn's sacred space.

An image of the symbol carved into Alister's skull flits across my vision, and I squeeze my eyes shut to force it away. Kallum has woven himself just as intricately into this case, and if I start pulling at the thread, I'll be the one to unravel.

What are you trying to tell me, Devyn?

I glance up from the body. "Was Colter Childs ever identified among the remains?" I ask Dr. Forrester.

She presses her lips together and digs out her phone. After I provide my email, she sends the full report to my device.

"Thank you, but can you just tell me if his remains were recovered—"

"The initial report on the vic's remains was doctored," she says, impatient. "Eleven of the victims were determined to be deceased prior to organ removal. Colter Childs was one of them."

I again look at the body, unable to refer to her as a victim even in my thoughts. If Devyn gave this woman so much care and love upon her death, then what did she do with her brother's remains? Where is his body?

I nod my thanks to Dr. Forrester, and she covers the body before sliding it into the locker.

The chill of the room settles deep into my bones as I imagine Devyn sitting in her ravine, her emotions a chaotic storm after losing her twin brother to the illness they shared. Her belief system being challenged, her optimistic delusion crumbling.

That was her moment of no return, the heartache and rage I felt there in that chasm. That's where she engraved the philosopher's stone into the clay wall as she slipped right over the edge.

But she didn't jump off that cliff all by herself.

She had a push.

I expel the thought as soon as it surfaces. My hand curls into a tight fist as I try to breathe through the tight ache.

Agitated, I push through the swing door and crash into a solid wall of chest. I reflexively step back and am met with the fierce green and blue of Kallum's eyes.

He uses his foot to catch the door before it swings in, an arresting smile easily crossing his face as his other hand cups my arm to hold me in place. "Just the sexy little criminologist I was looking for."

A reactive flame licks my skin at the way his gaze brushes over me. "I'm wrapping up my final inspection of the scene before I leave." Swiping my bangs out of my vision, I add, "Devyn could be in trouble."

He cocks his head, the intensity of his gaze searching me. "That's a given," he says glibly.

"I mean danger." I sink my teeth into the cushion of my lip as I try to block the doubt creeping in. "But even so, what if her actions were influenced?"

His features draw together in confusion.

"What if someone—" I edge closer to the hallway "—manipulated her to go to extreme measures? Are the consequences solely hers, then?"

He reaches up and grabs hold of the doorframe, effectively blocking my escape. "Like the alchemist," he says, reasoning with infuriating logic.

"Yeah. I told Rana this person could be tying up loose ends, trying to remain hidden. She suspects that could put Devyn in danger. She's too much on the feds' radar. Killing her before she's caught and can reveal anything incriminating..." I trail off, letting the implication linger in the chilly air between us. "A morally corrupt person could justify doing so, as she's already terminal to begin with."

"*Hmm.*" He makes a sound of thoughtful deliberation. "I doubt having the FBI and media invade his town was ever part of his plan. It's all gotten very unruly."

I study Kallum's eyes—the eyes that swallow me, that I fell into from the first moment he put me in his sights.

177

"Kallum, if there's something you want to tell me, please. Do it now."

He lowers a hand and clasps my cheek as his heated gaze bores into mine. "It is not enough to conquer, one must learn to seduce."

Unease tightens my chest. His cryptic quotes have never felt so damning.

He pushes in too close, his next words dropped hot against my lips. "If you don't want vague answers, don't ask vague questions, Halen."

As footsteps approach from farther down the hallway, Kallum let's his hand fall away. He takes a step into the corridor, allowing me the chance to fill my aching lungs.

"Noted," I say.

He releases the door, sending me a wink before it swings closed.

I catch the corner and flatten my palm against the cool surface, dousing some of the heat beneath my skin. "Goddamn him."

Kallum's words burrow under my skin as I follow Hernandez outside the building where, once we're all assembled, it's decided that Dr. Keller and Kallum will ride with us to the newest scene.

I should be driving my rental out of this town, not cruising down a desolate stretch of road toward the killing fields. Kallum didn't point that fact out, but his intentional silence was loud.

The internal ticking inside me feels more like a countdown to an implosion than the finality of this case. To divert my anxious thoughts, I pull up my email and scan the reports from Dr. Forrester.

The Bureau's official lab results state six of the remains' tissue samples revealed burst cells, denoting the bodies had been preserved via a freezing method. After a reexamination of Jake Emmons, it was confirmed he was alive at the time of his death.

He was murdered.

Devyn told me Jake was already dead, and I made the assumption it was an illness that took his life, not her. I made an assumption, because I didn't want it to be Devyn who took his life.

A new email pings the top of my inbox, and my stomach pitches as I read the bold words in the subject line.

PROOF

I've been here before, staring at an email that could expose a dangerous truth, warring with my feelings on whether or not knowing that truth would change my feelings for Kallum.

Eventually, the enchantment does end.

With a tremor in my hand, I open the email. I skip over Dr. Torres's ramblings and tap the attachment, my breath held as I wait for an image to load.

A picture of a hospital room materializes. Posters of Nietzsche and Greek philosophers are displayed on the walls. The next image shows a collection of pictures—all of me. One was taken from the first crime scene the very first day I arrived.

Kallum has never denied his obsessive behavior. It would be hypocritical of me to pretend to be disturbed, as I wasn't necessarily innocent in my fixation with him.

There's a room in my apartment with a wall dedicated to Professor Locke.

My relief is tangible. If this is the extent of Dr. Torres's claim…

The last attachment loads, and my heart riots against the wall of my chest.

Correspondence transcripts from Briar. I flip down the email log, my heartbeat so loud it muffles all sound around me. My pulse accelerates as my eyes land on one single line contained within an email.

He who sees with his eyes is blind.

I see Kallum standing across the Briar visitation table, his calculating gaze assessing me, his smirk derisive, as he said that very line to me—the line that convinced me I needed him on this case.

As I scan the other two emails, my breath catches on the typed signature.

The Alchemist.

"Son of a bitch," I whisper beneath my breath.

A thought occurs, and I open my contacts and scroll down, looking for the Briar Institute. The number has been Blocked. I think back to the moment Kallum took my bag in the chamber, giving him the opportunity to access my phone.

The sting of furious tears blurs my vision as I darken my phone screen. I shove the device in my bag, and my nails bite into my palm. I can feel the intense weight of his eyes on me. I've felt his eyes on me since we left.

Whether or not forensics can prove it, I know those emails were to Devyn. I have no doubt that Kallum has some measure in place where this won't come back on him. He's already conveniently given another suspect the moniker.

There always has to be a scapegoat.

What's insulting is his assumption that I would never figure it out.

Kallum has to know these emails wouldn't remain hidden. Every one of Devyn's accounts are being combed through, analyzed. When she's arrested, every single piece of evidence that can be brought forward to make a case against her will be crossed in court.

Not if she's dead.

I wipe a hand down my face, a cold sweat blanketing my skin. I grab hold of the door handle, the thought hitting me so powerfully to escape the vehicle I have to forcefully pry my fingers away.

I barely register Hernandez's voice as panic crashes through me.

I touch my forearm, desperate to gain a sense of control. Only the coarse feel of stitches drive my anxiety higher. It feels wrong...*everything* feels wrong.

Kallum has woven himself into me more intricately than this case—every sin, every dark truth, every wicked, salacious feeling—we're bound together by this sick and twisted world we've designed.

As I struggle to pull in a breath around the ache smothering my lungs, I turn to look at Kallum in the backseat, and I'm struck by the disarming beauty of his eyes all over again, falling right over the edge.

The fall is endless.

Those same striking eyes that once pulled me from the

depths when I was so lost are now a treacherous void dragging me under.

There are no beautiful surfaces without a terrible depth.

Kallum is that terrible depth.

And I've been sinking into him since our first encounter.

I hold Kallum's knowing gaze until the second I'm forced to shift my focus to the back windshield, to where the vehicle behind us is gaining speed.

It happens suddenly. The sound of crushing metal, the shattering glass. The screams. The soundtrack to my nightmare.

11

DOOMED

KALLUM

Homer wrote: *Everything is more beautiful because we are doomed.*

We never know if the next moment may be our last. In a matter of a blink, all that we've loved, every breath we've taken, every memory created can be snatched away by something as ordinary as a tree.

As sound bleeds into the muted chaos, a hazy white gas clouds the interior of the SUV. Past the deployed airbags and cracked windshield, the crushed hood makes the crash a reality.

I blink hard through the wave of dizziness, only giving myself a second to recover before I yank off my seatbelt and lunge toward Halen in the passenger seat.

She's disoriented but conscious. I roll her face toward me, and her unfocused eyes close and open slowly as I unstrap her from the belt.

"Halen." Her name feels muffled in my ears, the

ringing grows louder as I search her body for injuries. "Come back to me, sweetness." When she gives me no response, I groan and push past a frantic Dr. Keller and kick the door open.

The vehicle is right-side up but perched on a steep embankment, creaking as though it's ready to give up its weak grip on the ground. If not for the thick willow, the SUV would be at the bottom of the ridge. The tree wasn't the culprit for this much damage, however. The blame goes to the testosterone-injected truck that slammed into the backend at full fucking speed.

I wrench the passenger-side door open and pull Halen into my arms, catching sight of Hernandez on the cusp of my periphery. "Get out. *Now*," I say to him as he rubs a trail of blood from a cut on his forehead.

The urgency lies not in any fear of engine combustion, but in that same truck currently reversing behind us, gearing up to deliver another hit to send the SUV careening down the embankment.

As the agent attempts to free himself, his struggle becomes futile when the latch jams. He glances back once to gauge the truck's distance as the engine revs, then the truck lurches forward.

I look at Dr. Keller. "Run. *Go*."

Her shrill scream proceeds her sloppy scramble from the vehicle. She stumbles and quickly rights herself, not stopping even when she's made it safely across the street as she bolts into the dense thicket.

I curl Halen tighter to me, then spare a glance at Hernandez.

"Get out of here," he says, his wide gaze on Halen cradled against my chest.

With the fraction of a second I have to weigh my options, I predict Halen's grief at the loss of the agent. Muttering a curse, I reach across the front seat and grab hold of the belt, releasing a furious grunt as both Hernandez and I fight to muscle the latch free.

Giving the belt one final yank, I break the buckle. Our eyes connect briefly before Hernandez escapes his seat.

I wrap my arm around Halen. Now more cognizant, she reaches for her bag. "Wait—"

"Leave it."

The storm in her hazel eyes traps me, imploring. "It has the evidence."

"Fuck." I sacrifice my hold on her just long enough to snag the strap and then have her rocked against me, falling backward out of the SUV seconds before the truck smashes into the backend.

The screech of metal on metal rends the air upon collision. The SUV is dislodged from the trunk of the tree and sent barreling down the embankment.

As the truck flies past, Hernandez pivots and draws his service weapon, taking aim at the tires. He fires off two shots before the truck kicks into Reverse.

I have Halen's arms locked around my neck as we slide down the side of the steep incline. I glance up in time to witness the rear of the truck clip Hernandez before he's able to escape its path.

The truck brakes, kicking up a cloud of debris.

Lowering Halen to the rocky earth, I unlink her arms from my neck and drop her bag. "Get the knife."

Her beautiful face sheened with sweat, she captures my hand. A raw abrasion reddens her cheek from where the airbag took aim. And while I'm struck by how lovely she is in her damaged state, those silvery eyes spear me with cold fury.

She holds me bound no longer than a heartbeat, but I read each turbulent emotion raging within her.

This moment was unavoidable.

I reach out and sweep the white streak behind her ear. "If you need to loathe me, I can accept that. But loathe me with a vengeance while you take that fucking knife out."

The slam of truck doors severs our connection, and I suffer the loss of her touch as I turn to see two men exiting the hulking vehicle.

Clothed in black sweatshirts, they advance with their hoods drawn up, their faces masked by large, unnerving stag skulls. The white horns are filed into sharp points to resemble spikes projecting from their heads.

I'd be impressed with their resourceful endeavor to intimidate if not for their supreme stupidity in endangering the reason for my fucking existence.

Hernandez is sprawled on the ground, his gun lost at some point during the impact. Where his pant leg is torn at the thigh, deep-red blood escapes the injury. One of the skull boys descends on him, and Hernandez is just aware enough to throw up his hands as the assailant bears down with a syringe.

Within the same beat, I'm confronted by the second guy and staring into the hollow sockets of a skull, my entire body rioting with the desire to commit carnage.

Destruction will serve more than one purpose today.

As I lunge toward him, he meets my sluggish attack with an elbow to my face, thoughtlessly knocking me aside like an afterthought as he stays on his course.

Going straight for Halen.

Hellfire licks my viscera as I lurch to my feet. Seconds before he reaches her, I tackle him to the uneven terrain and pin my knee between his shoulder blades. I look up in search of Halen, finding her with the bagged knife held in her grip. *Good girl.*

I wrestle him onto his back and brace my forearm against his throat, taking note of his wiry frame. He's a spry motherfucker for his average size, and curiosity has me bashing the skull off his face.

"Shit, I know him." Halen's voice is shaky as she steps near.

The local officer glares up at me, eyes wide, pupils blown, mouth gasping uselessly for oxygen as I press down on his larynx. I vaguely recall him from the night of Alister's assault on Halen.

"You were there," she accuses him, her tone low, but I hear the threat banked behind her deceptive calm. "Were you following me?"

I don't let up on his throat. There's nothing he can say that will change his damned fate. His singular focus on Halen gives me the only answer I need.

He will soon be a dead skull boy.

I direct my gaze up to Halen, where she's still clutching the knife. "Remove the bag," I tell her, my words grit between clenched teeth.

She's trembling from adrenaline, still shaken from the wreck, an accident not unlike the one where she was driving, or the hit-and-run that took her parents. The difference is, this time, she has someone she can punish.

As her emotions climb, she toes the edge of that terrace all over again, her hair as wild as her eyes, her fear tearing through her logic. She's an aphrodisiac hitting my bloodstream.

God, she's fucking hypnotic.

She fears the terrible things we're capable of, the loss of control.

She fears *us*.

Little Halen is frightened over so much about herself, terrified to face that part of herself she lost control of once before. But it's not a door that can be sealed off once it's been opened.

Fuck, she blew the hinges right off.

Both hands still gripped to the bagged knife hilt, she cages her emotions and levels me with a tapered gaze, and I swear I've never been punched harder by a fucking look.

If she removes the knife, evidence is lost—*my* evidence. My fingerprints and DNA on the weapon.

It only lasts a moment, but her doubt detonates inside every single one of my cells, the destruction catastrophic.

"I can't loathe you, Kallum," she says. "There are more emotions on the spectrum than lust and anger. I'm hurt. I'm...heartbroken." She swallows hard, and the pain in her eyes impales me. "Leave him alive. I can't help you otherwise."

The guy beneath me is fading, his struggle all but forgotten as I watch Halen lower the knife. She avoids my eyes as she tosses the weapon on the ground, her decision made.

Without a backward glance, she pushes her hair out of her face and starts in the agent's direction. A white-hot coal of rage burns in the pit of my stomach.

My muse might have a death wish, but I won't let her so much as break a nail for Hernandez.

The guy falls unconscious beneath my arm, and I lower my mouth near his ear. "You're lucky I have some groveling to do." Then I send my fist into his face. The wet smack of his blood is satisfying as his head drops sideways.

Once I'm on my feet, I prop the heel of my boot on his shoulder and give him a hard shove, sending him toppling down the sloped ridge. Unconscious, he settles near the totaled SUV.

Then my entire focus is on Halen. She stands at the edge of the fray between Hernandez and his attacker, where the agent is losing his fight.

I could let Hernandez die right now. A more selfish, *smarter* version of myself would do exactly that. Whatever he suspects of me would die with him, and while Halen would mourn his loss, it would be one less obstacle.

But my obstinate muse strips me of my free will once again when she launches herself onto the guy's back.

"Fucking hell." I shrug off my suit jacket and toss it to the ground. My muscles band painfully tight around my bones as fire gathers between my sinew and flesh.

Teeth gnashed together so hard my jaw aches, I watch as Halen grabs hold of one of his spiked antlers. For a suspended heartbeat, anticipation for the kill collars my throat in an arousing chokehold. The marshy air crackles with her volatile shift. She's a fierce, unstable element that holds me breathless.

With a desperate cry, she flings the skull away, her fucking logic derailing her course once again. Halen digs her nails into the guy's eyes and succeeds in diverting him away from Hernandez. He drops the syringe, but only so he can latch on to her forearms. He groans and slings her off his back.

Halen hits the ground hard, and the pain that explodes across her face covers my vision in a pulsing haze of red.

My gaze narrows down to a pinhole on hoodie guy. Fury seethes from my pores, my nostrils flared and teeth bared as I stalk toward him like a predator scenting its prey.

A growl tears free as I deliver a ruthless punch to his face, relishing in the *crack* I hear as his nose shatters, and the resulting blood that stains my knuckles. I drop another hit, and another, intent to demolish his features.

The harder we deny our nature, the more painful our existence.

I stopped resisting my demon the moment my muse entered my world. I surrendered to the primal violence that wanted to dominate my atoms when she called out for me, when she *needed* me. Hell, I became the villain for her. And I owned the bloodthirsty monster who fed on chaos and carnage, like I own that monster now.

No longer able to stand, the guy chokes on his own blood as he crumples to the ground, my fists following him down as I submit to the wrath. Balance is lost under my unhinged blows, and we slip farther down the embankment.

Only when I glimpse Halen on the edge of my vision do I slow my assault.

"Kallum—" She's breathy as she comes to a halt at the bottom of the ridge. "He has answers."

In the same way Halen needs me to harbor her darkness, I need her to offset the violence that wants to consume. Without her, I'd be utterly lost to it. My muscles aflame, I hold back the next strike that wants to annihilate the last remaining shred of this fucker.

I haul him up by his hoodie collar and glare down into his ruined face. Deciding he's coherent enough, I step in behind him. As he's unable to hold his head up, I dig my bloody fingers into his hair and wrench his head back, forcing him to look at Halen.

One arm braced around her midsection, she stares at me with that cute, worried divot between her brows. In her other hand, she wields the carving knife. She won't let it out of her sight.

I spit the taste of copper from my mouth, unsure if the blood is mine or his. I crane his head back farther, earning a lethargic groan. "Get your answers," I grit out.

Anxious, she paces a few steps, then turns my way. "Did Devyn send you after us?" she demands. "Where is she?"

He refuses to talk in his thrashed state. I lower my voice into a menacing rumble just for him. "If you have no use for your voice, I will tear your throat out."

He nearly chokes on a cough, and I allow him to spit a mouthful of blood to the ground. Then his swollen eyes latch on to Halen. "He wants her."

A feral rage takes hold. I hear nothing but the roar

inside my head, feel nothing but the pulsing demand beating inside my veins to destroy.

He wants her.

I sniff back my fury and tug his head harder. "*Where is he?*"

I can feel the mix of panic and uncertainty stirring within Halen. Despite her convoluted morality, she knows how this will go. That's why she's looking at me and not him, those fearful eyes blinking too fast, her lips trembling.

"Kallum, he bit off his tongue." She covers her mouth with her hand as the guy in my grasp begins to convulse. A gurgled choking sound fills the air as I shove him to his back.

Blood trickles from his open mouth as shock cords his spasming body. I spot the discarded mass of flesh on the ground.

"An offering that won't save him." I roll my head along my shoulders, then wrench him to his knees and hold him upright by his collar. "Maybe he can provide a written statement," I say, and oh, I love the seething glare she gifts me.

Halen embodies every emotion on the red spectrum, her vitriol so eloquently lends to passion to inspire an array of shades in her color pallet. I feel like she'd be impressed with my psychology reference.

I lower my gaze to the knife gripped in her hand. She knows what has to happen. We've been here before.

It's just us on a darkened stage, hidden within the spindly copse of trees, the threat of the storm our backdrop, the ink-swollen clouds casting her eyes in the silver hue that cracks right through my sternum and makes the dead muscle beat.

Halen gives her head a firm shake, clearing the white streak of hair from her vision. "This isn't the same as Landry," she declares, pushing back against her rampaging emotions. "I'm not in immediate danger."

My smile is dark, my predatory gaze on her stating otherwise.

"That's not why you drove a bone into his jugular, sweetness." Nor was she in immediate danger when she tore a hack professor's face off.

All the dirty little truths I whispered in her ear, she can't deny any of them, not when I felt her shatter in my arms. She can't hide the blaze I see raging in her depths, the storm brewing darker than the electric atmosphere around us. The elements are all hers, the charge in the air building with her ferocity as she tries to rein in her rioting emotions.

She's so beautifully torn as the dark chasm opens wide beneath her.

She looks away, unable to maintain eye contact around the mutilated man in my grasp as he sputters blood and saliva. "Hernandez called for help," she says. "Backup will be here soon."

My disappointment in my dark muse might as well be a tire iron to my face.

She hugs her arm tighter around her waist. Blood stains her sleeve where her stitches have once again been torn. She clutches the knife, protecting the evidence.

I exhale the discontent from my inflamed lungs. "I should've just tried to eat you," I say, not masking the disdain in my tone. "You would've forgiven me a whole lot faster for that, apparently."

Like a crack of thunder, her anger strikes the air between us, and I love the wild flicker in her eyes. "You want to talk about Devyn?" she says, contempt lacing each word. "All right, let's talk. You wanted her dead for no other reason than to protect yourself. It was never about any threat to me."

I lick the blood from my lips, savoring her venom. "If you have something to accuse me of, sweet Halen, then just come out with it."

She tips her chin up defiantly. "You were communicating with her while at Briar. You manipulated her—" She grits her teeth, the hand at her waist curled into a tight ball. "You used her to get to me, and now she's in danger because of you, *the alchemist*."

I swipe my free hand over my mouth, working the aching tension from my locked jaw as my eyes track admiringly over the bruises along her face. "You wear your violence so beautifully." My sigh is anguished. "I'd say it's a shame we have to go to extremes to bring it out, but honestly, the deviant in me finds it so fucking hot." I tighten my hold on the guy's head. "If I'm going to be punished like a bad boy, then I might as well do something to be punished for."

Her wary gaze drops to the convulsing man in my grasp, and panic flares within her. "No—" She grips her hair, shaking her head. "This isn't who we are. This *can't* be."

I cock my head. "And why is that?"

The dejection that touches her eyes almost caves my resolve. "Because killers eventually get caught."

Her grief bleeds between us in a river of blood and denial. She's lost everyone in her life, and I read the anguish in her lovely, distressed features.

If we fear a thing too much, for too long, it is inevitable that we manifest it.

She takes a hesitant step forward. Then another. Coming to stand at my side, she touches my cheek, her gaze pleading. "You didn't lose me in the wreck. I'm right here, Kallum." Her words are a gentle whisper as she gives voice to the destructive fear annihilating my mind.

Hung on her watery gaze, I say, "I won't lose you."

"Then don't lose me." Fear brims her delicate features.

There's an undercurrent of threat there, and I can taste her heartbreak as she delivers that threat. It stings my lungs, the sweetest, aching pain as I breathe her in.

"The man who supports his madness with murder is a fanatic," she quotes Voltaire, trying to seduce me with her reason. Then she places her hand on my arm, an urgent appeal to release the man in my clutch.

"The lover's whisper, irresistible—magic to make the sanest man go mad." Homer's words cleaved from my soul. "You are my madness, Halen. I am maddeningly, fanatically in love with you."

"Kallum…" Her voice cracks, a tear falls free, and I see it in a matter of a blink, all that is being torn away, all that is being lost.

A dangerous man is a mad one with nothing to lose.

"You've always known who I am," I tell her. "You just

prefer the illusion." I choke up on his head. "Sometimes, we just need the sharp snap of clarity to awaken us."

I keep her teary gaze trapped in mine, then deliver one hard, fast twist.

The bone-snapping *crunch* of his neck breaking echos through the chasm before his body falls slack to the earth.

Halen's emotions clash in a vortex stronger than any storm, and I lick the saccharine remnants from the air, tasting her, whetting my appetite.

"You killed him," she says, shock infusing her breathy words.

"If you didn't want him dead, then you wouldn't have said so much that he couldn't know."

I cast a glance down at his unmoving body. I should've torn his spine from his neck to really send a fucking message.

He *wants* her—and I'm making damn sure he knows I won't let that happen.

She tears the plastic evidence sleeve off the knife and points the blade at me, and my blood is fire. "This is what you want. Madness, mayhem. Chaos—"

"Those are listed on my résumé." I step over the body as I pry my necktie loose.

Homer understood the struggle in having a muse. Once invoked, our muse is free to use her vessel however she pleases, and we are but empty and fallow as we wait to be inspired, unable to even take a breath until graced by her divine beauty.

Halen retreats another step, her foot placement slipping farther down the steep incline. "Kallum, please. I have to get help. You can't come with me." She looks pointedly at the ankle monitor.

"Fuck, you really do lie so pretty."

Dr. Keller is long gone, hauled ass to the next town by now.

Hernandez is injured, maybe even dead.

The backup feds are still another five minutes away, if they were even called.

With a deep grunt, I kneel and snap the pin on the GPS monitor wrapping my ankle. The strap falls loose, and I fling the tracking device out across the ridge.

As I rise to my feet, I lock Halen in my predatory gaze. "If you run from me this time, sweetness, you better run fast."

The rush of her fear nearly levels me.

Every twin flame gives chase at some point, and my muse doesn't disappoint.

She runs.

I roll my sleeves up my forearms and trace my fingers over the sigil branding my flesh, then ritually spin the ring around my thumb, giving little Halen a head start before I pursue. I've been chasing her for a long, long time.

It's about fucking time I catch her.

Homer knew one other truth: *We men are wretched things.*

12

PRIMAL MAN

KALLUM

T he lust for the hunt always rivals the kill.

At my base core, I'm a primal beast that relishes the chase.

And Halen is by far my favorite prey.

Gazing into the dense thicket of marsh grass and trees, I breathe in deeply, pulling Halen's intoxicating scent into my lungs. Her emotional arousal is goddamn delectable.

My inner beast is salivating.

The liberation I feel from the tracking monitor stirs my blood into a frenzy. My heart rate climbs with each second that passes. The farther away she gets, the hungrier I become, the deeper the desire to bring us together.

The low rumble of thunder builds slowly, drawing out the tantalizing buzz in my veins until all I can feel is her dark elements tangled with mine, a sinfully wicked seduction as the kill heightens my arousal—how I know it heightens hers.

That's what my fearful muse is truly running from. Halen is always trying to outrun that darkness whispering in her ear. But today, there will be no escape.

I relent to the carnal demand to give chase and bound toward the tree line.

My feet pound the earth in pursuit as I track Halen's clear footprints. Adrenaline surges the chambers of my heart, dopamine floods my neuro pathways, and I swear if I catch her too soon, I'm going to make a mess of my meal.

Crossing into the deep brush, I swipe the viny branches to clear my path and push into the coppice of pines and willows. The leafy sprays give off a trace of wintergreen as I brush past, my steps light now as I strain to hear the sounds out of place in the marsh.

My little twin flame will give herself up, because deep down, she wants to be caught.

Plato may have framed the origin, but the terminology is relatively novel—a mystic belief in the union of dual flames and their stages once reunited.

While I spent the vast majority of my time in the yearning stage, made obvious by my years of pining for my muse, once Halen and I were thrust together, we accelerated through the others, raging hotter than a holy fire.

The chase and surrender stage might as well be written in our stars. As the chaser, it's my sole purpose to pursue my little runner until she's thoroughly exhausted, where she's forced to face her fear before she ultimately surrenders.

Fuck, her surrender will taste so sweet.

I don't have to adopt a new age theology in order to appreciate the symmetry. Being open to new ideas is how one prevents repeating historical mistakes.

Like the day I yielded to my weakness and handed Halen the means to lock me away in a psychiatric hospital. Now, I'm much more cautious with what I let slip past my lips.

Her allegation of lies, while demoralizing, does little to deter my purpose. I have but one desire, one obsession, and I've sacrificed *everything* to obtain it.

The distinct *snap* halts my movements.

There's a rustle of reeds, the telltale squelch of soggy earth being shifted, then Halen's small gasp.

That's all it takes, just the breathy cadence of her fear whispered through the canes, and I'm feral.

"You know what happens when the prey runs from the predator," I say as I duck under the low-hanging sprays. "Are you provoking me on purpose? I'm hard just thinking about how you begged me for the pain, Halen."

My gaze sweeps the high grass. I hold my breath and wait, my body humming with anticipation.

The alluring scent of her arousal invades my senses, and I close my eyes to taste her. Honeysuckle and clove settles at the back of my throat, the burn so good.

I undo the buttons along the placket of my black Oxford, the desire to feel the natural elements on my skin as demanding as my need to feel her skin against mine. My ethereal fairy creature is well suited here in this secluded wood, hiding from the hunter that wants to devour her.

The sound of her careful steps sinks into my skin, and like a pop of kindling in the open air, my body heats with kinetic energy, and a twisted smile hooks the corner of my mouth.

I take off after her.

From the corner of my eye, I catch a glimpse of her white streak as she rounds a gnarled tree and dips into the thick underbrush. She's fast. So damn fast. The thrill to catch her heats my blood to molten as I gain on her. The faint sound of her sharp breaths touches my ears like the moving notes of a classical piece. Decadent, affecting. Erotic.

The deeper we verge into the wooded landscape, the denser the canopy above, the darker the terrain below. The storm hovers on the brink of the field, as if waiting for Halen to break before releasing the torrential.

I'm already soaked in her desire.

The charged current cracks the air between us and electrifies my body, shrinking the distance between us as I'm drawn to her like a moth to its fiery goddess of flame.

"Why are you even running, Halen? Do you know?" My boots punch down on the soppy ground. "Are you running from me, or how turned-on you were when I snapped his neck?"

The captured still I have of her in that moment flares hot and tantalizing, the silver flecks of her eyes ablaze, her sultry mouth parted, the exquisitely pained expression creasing her features—the same way she looks right before she peaks in pleasure.

My groin throbs in painful demand to deliver her that release.

A clearing breaks up ahead, and I stop before the array

of thin willows. Controlling my breathing, I wait to see if she's brave enough to try to outrun me in the open.

"Your heightened emotions are telling, little Halen. I can *feel* you."

The eerie stillness thickens around us. Then, like the defiant muse she is, she breaks the silence. "You knew it was Devyn," she calls out. "Right from the start, you knew who the suspect was. When I asked if you knew it was her, you lied to me."

I could tell little Halen the truth, that the only lie I've told her has nothing to do with the priestess or this case. I could pour my proverbial heart out and beg for forgiveness —but I've been telling her the truth since our eyes connected across that quad.

"It's not what you think," I say instead as I sweep my hand over the top of the reeds. "As cliché as that sounds, it's not as if I went to diabolical lengths to keep my petty manipulations a secret."

"Secret," she echos, her tone low and mocking as her voice carries through the marsh. She's itching to fight. "At the hunting grounds, you told me a detail like the chalk used on the victim's face would only be known to the officials working the case. You knew it was her and you were fucking with me."

"Oh, sweetness. I love fucking with you. But your logic has you all twisted up." I settle my shoulder against a tree and pull the necktie from around my unfastened collar. Leisurely, I loop the tie around my hand.

The movement of the reeds snags my attention, and I imagine little Halen crawling along the muddy earth, using the high grass to shield her. She's so clever.

I rub my thumb over the cashmere tie, aching to feel her soft skin. "I could have sat in that institution, day after excruciating day, waiting, hoping you'd come to me on your own. But I'm not very patient."

"So you used her—a *dying* woman—for some twisted game with me. I trusted you. More than anyone...even before my memories resurfaced, I trusted you." The tender undercurrent of her heartbreak wraps around me. "That's the worst betrayal."

I wait for her to continue. While I'm not so patient, I do understand Halen. I know what she needs, and how she has to logically digest her reality. I can take her lashings for a while.

But then it's my turn.

I continue to spool the tie around my hand, tighter and tighter. "It's only betrayal when you don't have all the pieces."

Her laugh is sharp and derisive. "I'll never have all the pieces with you, Kallum."

Her responses are becoming shorter, her voice coming from farther away. My runner is trying to creep around the clearing.

"Somehow, from the very first moment, I knew you had a hand in it. God, Devyn even quoted Chaucer to me. I mean, she misquoted it...but now I think she did so on purpose not to appear obvious." There's anger, but there's also raw hurt and vulnerability leaking through. "Then the eyes. Of course you orchestrated the scene. You took your own father's eyes. The scene has you all over it."

I breathe through the constriction in my chest as I flex

my hand, tightening the ligature. "Devyn was already on her course. She didn't need much of a push from me."

"Bullshit. For five years, she harmed no one. Then she interacts with you, and in less than four months, there are blood rites and organs and—"

"Her situation was already taking place," I shout, unable to curb the increasingly impatient edge in my tone. "The outcome was unavoidable. I know how you just love to revel in your guilt, Halen. But Devyn is better because of us, because of *you*. Where would she be right now otherwise? Strung up in that room by chains? Locked in that cage?"

The silence prickles my nerves, and I clench my jaw. "Will a confession satisfy my fuming little muse? Then yes, the eyes were me. Because I knew the scene had to be something unique. It had to draw you there. But even then, I didn't think it would be enough. So I made sure your director gave you the case."

And for good measure, I charged a sigil using a thumbtack, of all lame things. My desire to have Halen on the case got every piece of metal removed from my room. A small sacrifice.

Paying a ridiculous sum of money to have CrimeTech hacked and ensure their problematic criminologist was assigned to Hollow's Row should have been what got me caught. But damn Torres and those emails. Having access to exchange email was the only reason I agreed to his fucking case study and let him wade around in my head.

Not only was he a risk, he was a liability. It was only a matter of time before he lost the last of his faculties.

"Unbelievable." She's barely audible beneath the

insects stirring to life, their habitat disturbed. A rumble of thunder rolls in the distance, and the vibration flows along the ground.

"The whole theory around the case...your obsession with the duality and Dionysus." Her breaths come faster, and I lock on to her general location in the reeds. "Every bit of it was you."

"While my ego enjoys being stroked, I'm not omniscient. I didn't create the circumstance, I only seized the opportunity." I tear a hand through my hair in frustration. "I told you, it's the universe, little Halen. Nearly every philosophy is steeped in paradox." I push off the tree and stealthily creep through the reeds, staying hidden behind the tree line. "All schools of thought adopt some form of 'opposites attract.' If not Nietzsche's doctrines, it could have been Nicholas of Cusa's *coincidentia oppositorum*, or *Logos*, or hell, there's no limit with Jung. Take your pick. History repeats itself, remember? It's just our turn to observe it."

After I was remanded to Briar, I pored over emails for weeks in search of very specific qualifiers I could utilize on the outside. As an authority in the occult, who has a somewhat notorious reputation, I receive all kinds of interesting messages.

One such anonymous message with an encrypted address held promise. The author had reached out to establish a foundation for explorative shamanic rituals in connection to the higher self through alchemical practice. Again, this could have been any philosophy at play. The options are limitless.

After three emails, I provided a starting point for their

experimental pursuit, steering them toward an awakening with a specific sacrifice. But it wasn't until the news aired of a ritual crime scene involving eyes that I knew this person was committed to their pursuit. Then Halen walked into Briar, and our fate took over. When I discovered the symbols carved in a tree near the hemlock, my exhilaration was legitimate.

I couldn't have designed a better game board for us.

I took all the risk. Because while the author knew who I was, I didn't know their identity. Yet they couldn't reveal me without revealing themselves. A real conundrum for them. So it stands to reason that Devyn would try to have me removed from the case by framing me for murder. That, and she wanted unobstructed access to Halen.

After I realized I was being framed for Jake Emmons' murder, I started to narrow the scope on suspects. While I had some suspicion about Devyn, there was no certainty she was the author of those emails until that moment in the cave when she sank to her knees and confessed her failure.

I could have driven that antler into her and ended the threat to us right then.

I glance down at the ink on my knuckles, every selfish desire marked on my flesh. My opposite, Halen could never be as selfish.

That's why I had to be the one.

My sacrifice had to be astronomical.

Silence descends over the marsh. It stretches until the screech of insects competes with the drumming of my heart. I push farther into the willow sprays, a violent energy coiling my spine as I realize my clever runner is using their strong scent to mask her own.

"Run out of accusations?" I call out to her.

I stop walking, becoming as still as the reeds while I wait for her voice to lead me in her direction.

"Come on, Halen," I shout. "Don't leave me in suspense."

"I want the truth," she says, her voice breathy. "Were you ever going to tell me?"

The truth.

I rub my fingers over the inflamed crescent on my chest, feeling the truth of us deep down in the rotten marrow of my bones.

"Yes." My voice carries across the clearing. "But timing is everything when it comes to us, muse."

"So you wanted to make sure I was good and seduced before you sprang it on me."

A dark chuckle slips free. "Are you angry that I seduced you, or that you wanted to be seduced?" I goad her, fanning that flame.

At her prolonged silence, I say, "Six months was already too long. I made a promise to you sealed in blood. I couldn't risk you being alone if it all came crashing back. I admit, fear ruled me...the fear of what you might do to yourself while I was trapped inside that fucking place. That fear will drive a man to extremes, Halen." I swallow past the burn in my throat. "Tell me I'm wrong, that the guilt wouldn't have destroyed you."

There's a distinct rustle in the grove of willows, and a devious smile curves my mouth. "I tried doing this the nice way, but that's never worked for us, has it? I'm going to catch you. Not *if* but *when* I catch you, Halen, I'm going to bind your wrists, then I'm going to fuck you until you're screaming, tears smearing your beautiful face as you finally submit to the goddamn inevitability of us."

She rises up in the middle of the clearing and darts through the reeds.

Blood hot and adrenaline peaked, I bound out of the gloomy coverage after her.

Her hair is loose, dark tresses whipping behind her as she streaks through a field of tweed and gray, her feet finding solid purchase to push her farther ahead. I stay close behind, my breaths chopping the air, muscles on fire as anticipation to wrap my arms around her batters my skull in ruthless demand.

I've let her escape too many times. Felt her slip through my fingers like sand sifting too fast through an hourglass. This time, I won't give her any chance for escape.

Her steps grind to a slog as she hits the field boundary of swampy marsh, but she fights her way through the mud. A gray skyline appears through patches of dark storm clouds, the reflection shimmering off a winding watercourse.

When Halen realizes she's running straight toward a channel of water, she tries to change direction. She slips and slides across the beach, but claws her way back to her feet, keeping hold of the knife. Her feet slap the hard-packed dirt as she stays close to the shoreline.

Slowing my pace, I don't follow directly in her path. Instead, I stay in pursuit from behind the spindly trees that line the marshy beach. She appears in flashes from between the trees as I keep my gaze locked on her.

The next break in the tree line is close, and I pump my

legs harder to gain ground ahead of her. As the opening appears, I push through and grab her around the waist. She releases a tiny yelp as her feet come off the ground. Arms wrapped around her slight body, I secure her arm down by her thigh, bracketing her wrist to keep the knife held firmly away.

Chest heaving with each breath that tears free, she struggles against my hold.

Her back crushed to my chest, I band my arm tighter and press my mouth to her ear. "You want me to chase you like an animal, then I'll fuck you like one, too."

I take her down to the ground.

The lust for the hunt always rivals the kill—but our primal passions are fiercely hungry. Once the beast traps its prey, it must devour its kill.

13

DUAL FLAMES

KALLUM

As her delicate scent infuses my senses, her rioting emotions arouse the bestial craving to unleash every unhinged desire. We are all animalistic when provoked into a powerless state, and Halen doesn't just threaten my willpower, she obliterates it.

Like a shameless fiend, I revel in the maddening friction of her hot body squirming against mine. Our knees dug into the mud, I push her onto her elbows and seal my hand around her wrist, knocking the knife from her grasp against the marsh floor. I then unravel the tie from my hand and secure it around her mouth, tugging the knot tight against the nape of her neck before I flip her onto her back.

Mud covers her front, and it's such a beautiful, dirty sight, Halen covered in filth. Her breasts rise enticingly as she drags air into her starved lungs. She tries to talk around the gag, and I latch on to her jaw and place my mouth right up against hers to taste her desperate breaths that slip past.

"You vilified me from day one," I say harshly over her mouth. "I have half a mind to let you go on believing your lies just because it makes you so goddamn wet." I shove my hand between her thighs to feel the proof. "*Hmm.* I can feel how soaked you are through your jeans, Halen."

The violent flutter of her pulse beats against my fingers as I grip hard to her jaw. She bashes her tiny fists against my shoulders, and with a growl, I push back and straddle her thighs. I grab hold of her shirt hem and tear her top and bra over her head, using the material to bind her wrists together.

One hand fastened to her bound wrists, I pin her arms to the sodden ground and anchor my other to the waistband of her jeans. "I feel it coiling beneath your skin, that sick, needy ache. Your body is begging me to scratch it to the surface."

As she groans around the tie, I let my gaze track greedily over her body, admiring her perfect pear-shaped tits, the scars from her accident that blend beautifully with the marks I've branded on her skin.

"God, you're so fucking sexy like this," I say as I hover closer, my shirt falling open above her. "I'm dying to tear into you."

I lower my mouth to her breast and tease the peaked nipple with my tongue before sucking it hard into my mouth. Her body bows beneath mine, and I palm the curve of her waist to hold her against me, relishing in her reactive shiver.

"You're going to listen," I say, my heated gaze drifting

up to lock on to hers. "Every time you interrupt, I get to touch you, taste you, and make you as dirty as I want." I yank the snap of her jeans open in forewarning, savoring the way her belly flinches.

Her eyes narrow on me in seething fury as I tow the tie down her chin, and she immediately says, "I don't want to hear your delusional excuses."

A devilish smile slants my mouth. "But you obviously want me to ravish this body."

Her thighs squeeze together beneath me to give her away.

Pressing her rougher into the muddy ground, I use my knee to part her thighs and grind down heavy against her before I seal my mouth over hers. I kiss her with ruthless need, swallowing her furious cries. My cock throbs at the abrasive feel of her body fighting against mine. I kiss her until she's breathless, sparking a riot of savage hunger.

As I break away, I slip the black tie away and tenderly caress her neck. Some of her fight has been drained, and I'm absorbed in the tantalizing labor of her breathing, the motion of her body as it rises and falls in time to the gentle lap of water along the beach.

"While I love tasting you, I keep my word." I collar her throat and slap my hand down on the muddy earth, then smear the mud over her breasts, earning a delicious moan as the cold, gritty dirt slides across her skin.

Her body struggles beneath me as I work my palm over her skin, streaking the mud between her breasts and over her belly, so fucking close to coming undone at the salacious feel of her slippery and dirty under my touch.

"You look so breathtaking covered in filth, sweet little

213

Halen. Keep interrupting. I'd enjoy nothing more than rolling around in the mud with you all night." I back my claim with a dollop of mud dribbled over her tits as I hike an eyebrow, insistent.

After a few strained breaths, where I swear her glare might actually ribbon the flesh from my bones, she concedes with a single nod.

Freeing my grip on her throat, I covetously run my thumb over her cheek to clear away the specs of dry mud from her bruised skin. Her lips swollen from my kiss, she turns her head to force my hand away.

"I'm not offering any excuses, delusional or otherwise," I tell her. "And I'm only saying this once. I didn't lie. I didn't know it was Devyn. At the visitation table, when you mentioned a crime-scene analyst quoting Chaucer, I never asked who that tech was. Whether or not they were connected, I didn't want to know." I expel a lengthy sigh. "I wanted, selfishly, as much time with you as I could get on this case."

I wait for her to argue, to interrupt. Selfishly, again, so I can slather her body with mud.

"But you had that same information," I continue. "You refused to see Devyn through the blinders you have for her. I may have orchestrated the first scene and set the game board, but you're the one who decided how the game was played."

She blinks up at me, her lips pressed together. Breathing heavily through her nose, she drops her gaze— and I see it in the slightest flicker of her eyes, the doubt of her own convictions.

"Your turn to tell me the truth. Would locking them up

have been enough?" I ask her, my tone a degree more gentle than my touch.

Her soft eyebrows crease as she meets my eyes with uncertainty.

"If you could've found that person, would watching them get sentenced in court have been enough?" I demand to know. "They might've gotten ten years…possibly more. Hell, even if they'd gotten a life sentence, would imprisoning the person who killed your parents have satisfied your need for retribution?"

Her breathing quickens, her gaze slit as her raging fury ignites. "I don't know. I never got that chance."

My jaw tightens in dissatisfaction and I smack my hand in the mud. "Lies earn another mud bath."

She shakes her head against the ground. "Fuck you for even saying this—"

I cup her breast with my mud-caked hand, effectively cutting her off. She bucks beneath me as I coat the grainy sludge over her nipples, the coarse texture making her just as ravenous as she clamps her thighs against my hips.

I lower my body, feral at the feel of her muddy breasts slipping against my bare chest as I whisper my demand in her ear. "I want the truth, Halen."

As I rise up, angry tears brim her eyes, and she furiously blinks them back. "No," she says, the word delivered on a shaky breath. "It wouldn't have been enough."

I wet my lips, tasting her, a glutton for more. "If that person was here right now, what would be enough? Could you smash their face in? Could you paint the reeds red with their blood? Would that be enough?"

Her body trembles seductively beneath mine. "No... But it would be a start."

My gaze roams slowly over her features, captivated by the raw pain I find there. I make a low sound of agreement, my heart grazing my rib cage as the muscle races to match the staccato beat of hers.

"And after..." I dig my fingers into her hair at the base of her neck and tip her face up. "Would you have asked for forgiveness?"

She fastens her eyes closed to deny me the fierce emotion banked there. "Never."

A tendril of hope unfurls. She has a darkness inside her that she taps into to see beneath the veil—but it's only ever a peek, enough to work the cases that call to her as she masks herself in the killer's persona. Her fear always shuts it down.

Bound beneath me now, she's Nyx to my Erebus, night to my darkness. A goddess who spawned the very brutal entities that still torment her soul. Death, Strife, Pain.

Her parents' killer was never caught, and that first tipped domino set off our sequence of events that, when she finally tears through the veil, will part the sands of time like a tidal wave.

But I have to make my own concession that she might not ever uncover this fragment of memory. This is the reality of us that tortures me, forced to accept that this—right now—is as far as we come.

If this is to be our story, then I want her to see the monster. I need her to look into the eyes of the fiendish villain and glimpse every atrocity attached to my soul.

Then I need her to accept me.

"I won't ask for forgiveness," I say, flaying my soul wide between us. "Not ever, Halen. There's no ecstasy in the celestial planes that can ever tempt me to atone. You're the only heaven I want to be in. Don't damn me, sweetness."

The shrouded sun casts the marshy shore in muted grays, an echo of the tormented demon clawing at my mind as the sky is torn apart to unleash the rain.

No amount of rain can rinse me clean. Only *her*, that fire raging in her depths.

"Then we're both devils," she says, her voice so soft she's nearly drowned out by the fall of rain pelting the water. "We're monsters who've done monstrous things, and we should both burn."

I expel a harsh sigh and lower my forehead to hers. Our chests touch, heart to heart, the dirt between our bodies a conduit for that purifying burn.

"You want me to tell you placating things and make this easy for you. I won't, because it won't ever be easy for us." My thumb travels over her delicate jawline. "But I will paint the whole fucking world red for you. I've tasted enough of your grief and regret to haunt me a hundred lifetimes. If you're torn away from me, I won't seek retribution after the fact—I will eviscerate the fucker before they ever get the chance, Halen St. James."

A torn sound escapes her, and she bites into her lip to fight it back. The dark fringe of her lashes sheen with unshed tears as the rain falls harder. I tug her lip free of her teeth and sweep my thumb across, lost in her fragile softness.

"Christ, you really are a genius. Just so fucking smart,

Professor Locke." The vitriol in her tone halts my movements. "You say you don't want to lose me, so your plan is to burn the world down with us in it? Your arrogant, reckless actions will force *me* to lose *you*."

I swallow hard as what she said on the ridge comes back in startling clarity: *Because killers eventually get caught.*

My hold on her wrists loosens, and she seizes the chance. She brings her balled fists down on my chest. Her hands slip against the rain and mud slicking my skin before I capture her arms and restrain her again, dropping my full weight on top of her.

Halen struggles for a second longer, then gives up the fight as those fierce orbs of silver alight on me. "The guilt I'm suffering isn't for Wellington. It's because of you, for what I've done to you. What I've made you. And now I'm complicit—you *make* me complicit in putting Devyn in danger, in every life that you've taken since that night together. Do you understand you could be put to death? You killed an FBI agent. God, I loathe you for making me care…for having someone to lose all over again. Fuck you to hell and back for that."

The fire rages into an inferno behind her gaze, and goddamn, I'm entranced with my fiery siren of fury. "Fuck."

"Did you hear what I fucking said?" She's a vortex of wild emotions churning out of control as her gaze aims to pulverize me. "You're already locked in a mental institution—"

"Because you put me there—"

"And you manipulated a dying woman—"

"That I didn't know was ill." I secure my hold on her tighter. "But I would do it again. In a fucking heartbeat. To have you just like this beneath me, I would do it again and worse. I'm that sick and evil and twisted. Whatever label you want to slap on me, I will be that goddamn devil. You will always come first."

The boom of thunder provokes fresh tears, and I trail my thumb down her lips, letting the pad taste her delectable melancholy. "You will never lose me," I vow to her. My elbows dig into the mud as I palm her face, gently coaxing her eyes on me. "Look at me, Halen. There is nothing in this universe that can tear me away from you, not even death."

A racked sob escapes her chest. "You can't know that."

My tongue glides over my bottom lip, tasting her riled emotions that threaten to consume her. That's my job. I was made to consume her sweet heartache.

"Let me take the pain," I whisper. "Let me take it for you."

The softest sound escapes her, a sigh so gentle and sweet it aches. "We can't do this. It's madness." She licks her lips to further torture me, then she lowers her arms to strike me with her fisted hands.

This time, I'm prepared, and I catch her forearms and link her bound wrists around my neck. "I promised you we'd talk until our breath gave out, but I'm entirely too famished, and this devil is going to feast."

My mouth crashes against hers, and I hold her bound to me, kissing her deeply as I drain more of her fight.

As the storm darkens the sky, I unlink her arms from my neck and draw to my knees above her. I shed my soaked shirt, letting it drop to the ground as I stare down on her filthy, half-naked body. Before she can try to squirm away, I grip the waistband of her jeans and yank her pants down her thighs, tearing them to her ankles.

Her sharp cry travels straight to my groin. "God, you're fucking crazy—"

"You haven't seen the bounds of my crazy, sweetness." I bring her restrained ankles over my head and latch on to her hips. "We're just getting started."

Hoisting her hips off the ground, I lick a hard seam up her pussy, a damn deviant as I relish the divine taste of her. A low groan rumbles out as I breathe over her, a crooked smile stealing across my face at how wet she is.

"Tell me to taste you," I demand.

"Not like this. Go to hell—"

"Then you can curse me while you come in my mouth." I suck her clit into the hollow of my mouth and flick my tongue over the sensitive flesh before I surround my mouth over her, and her back arches off the ground.

My fingers dig into her skin with bruising force as I hold on to her writhing hips. As the steady drizzle of rain patters our bodies, I indulge on her, my tongue a fiend invading her as I lap at her sweet arousal like a starved beast.

Untamed lust fires through my veins as I feel her already so close to shattering against me. "Do you still despise me?"

Struggling to capture a full breath, she says, "Yes."

I smile against her. "I'm going to fill you so deeply, there's no room to hate me."

With an impatient groan, I shuck her boots off one at a

time, then I have her jeans wrenched off her ankles and tossed to the mud. I spread her thighs wide, my fingers leaving bruising imprints as I hold her pinned to the earth.

I plant my hand in the center of her pelvis as her thighs clamp against my head, as if that will stop me from devouring my dirty girl. Then I eat her sweet pussy.

Twisting her arms, she successfully fights her wrists free of her shirt. Her dainty hands find my hair and she digs her fingers into the roots, her nails scraping at my scalp as she tries to escape. I let her tear her blunt little nails into me, savoring the delivery of her pain.

My hand fastened to the underside of her leg, I turn my attention to the sigil on the inside of her thigh. I sink my teeth into the mark, and the coppery taste of blood spills over my tongue. A feral growl works free as my inner beast demands to devour her until she's thrashing against my hold.

"Do you still want to hurt me?" My tone is gruff as I restrain myself from taking her closer to that shattering edge.

She's shaking, furious tears mixing with the rain as the droplets slide down her temples. "I want to claw your skin off."

With one last selfish taste of her sweetness, I push to my knees. A wicked smile carves my face as I grab her ass and haul her forward. "Claw my fucking skin off, baby."

The fiery venom in her eyes says she's either about to fuck me or kill me. I'm obliged to let her do both, as long as she doesn't deny me her touch.

The carving knife lay discarded in the mud, and I grab the weapon in one hand before I secure her wrist in my other. I press the hilt into her palm and close my hand around hers, our heated eyes locked.

The gray sky hangs over us like a threat, falling a shade darker than our desire as we kneel in the mud, bound by the charged current strung between us.

Stripped naked and trembling, Halen braces her free hand against the hard wall of my chest. "Kallum. You have to stop—"

I latch on to the back of her neck and draw her face up to mine, my mouth descending on hers before she can crucify me with the lethal words poised on her lips.

The flat of the blade crushed between our bodies, she keeps her palm welded to my chest to hold me at bay. Her fingers skim the crescent, and I can feel the violent storm within her fragile walls.

"You know how to make this stop." My nostrils flare as I grip her wrist tighter and move the tip of the knife over my sternum. The sharp point draws blood. "Aim for the heart. If you miss, I won't ever stop coming for you."

A tear streaks her abraded cheek, and I want to lap the salty wetness with my tongue, to taste her confronting that terrifying fear. It's easier to run from the monster in front of us than face the one within.

Her fingers inch higher to cover the sigil, her desire charged so deeply into me I feel it with every aching breath. "That's not what I want," she whispers.

"What do you want?" I've asked this of her countless times, desperate for her answer. "What the hell do you desire, sweetness?" I cup my hand over hers, anchoring her to me. "God, please fucking tell me."

The tears fall freely now, and when her silvery eyes

flick up to capture mine, she might as well drive that knife through my damn heart.

"For you to have found me before my life fell apart," she says around an uneven breath. She's shivering, from the chilly air, her cresting emotions. "Before the death and the tragedy and the pain, and the endless void that I can't find a way out of. Before I became...*this*. Why didn't you find me *before*?"

Because then, maybe then, she could have let herself love me.

Before I became the goddamn devil of her nightmares.

A crash of thunder recoils through my bones, cracking as violently through me as her words. Because I have failed her so immensely, this is my punishment.

"And this is our descent into madness, the *what if* of us. It will ruin us, Halen." I trap the lock of white framing her face. The strands are covered in mud, and I rub her hair between my fingers affectionately like I did that night. "What you are, to me, is so fucking lovely, sweetness."

Her watery gaze connects with mine as I utter the words I whispered to her once before, when she revealed the basest side of herself to me. I mean them now as I did then. *This*—the darkest part of her nature; what terrifies her—is my haven.

The fierce desire to work the ritual and spin my ring tears through me—but there is no magick powerful enough to influence this outcome.

Only her.

I can't harbor her darkness forever, though I might try. There's too much danger in keeping one side repressed; it will find an outlet. And by then, it's a magnitude ten quake and a man's face is mutilated by a tire iron. Halen can't sustain that level—her humanity, her logical nature, will always punish her.

My conflicted muse has to embrace this part of herself.

I lick my lips, tasting the rain water, desperate for that hit of pure decadence that comes from her mingled with it. "Fuck, we could love, Halen, if only you'd let us."

Her smile is fragile, so achingly beautiful it chars my throat. "I don't think we're capable."

"If I ripped my heart from the cavity of my chest, I'd still feel you, and that is the painful reality of my existence. Tell me I'm heartless, and let me prove it to you." The tip of the blade digs deeper into my flesh with each strenuous breath. A rivulet of blood travels down the ridges of my abdomen.

Expelling a shuddering breath, she eases the blade away, but doesn't release the weapon. Tentatively, she raises her other hand and caresses the reliefs of my chest in the same fashion she did as we stood before the fire. Her fingers reverently map the inked stag skull, mixing blood and rain with her heartache like her own form of alchemy.

"I knew who you were." Her voice is as faint as her touch. "I remember…I knew you, and it wasn't that I recognized your tattoos, that I'd read you. I felt safe. Everything that was bad and wrong would dissolve, and it did as soon as you kissed me."

From my periphery, I watch her raise the knife. For a strangled heartbeat, I fear she'll try to send that blade into herself. My muscles gather tight in anticipation.

"You're beautiful, Kallum," she continues. "Terrifyingly beautiful. Like a strike of lightning, arresting and awe-inspiring when first glimpsed, but soon the fire rages out of control and sets the whole forest ablaze."

"Without you, that's bound to be my doom." Knelt over her in the mud, I lock the base of my spine, my gaze trained hard on that knife.

As her other hand gradually dips lower, my stomach flexes beneath the sensual feel of her fingers trailing past my abdomen. She takes hold of my belt, and every nerve in my body thrums as she yanks the leather free of the buckle.

"You're chaos and destruction incarnate and, god... you're the only one," she says, her words guiding my eyes back to hers.

Halen brings the point of the knife to her palm. She drags the blade across to open a seam, and hematic red beads against her flesh. A visceral yearning stirs down deep in the pit of my stomach, like a fucking aphrodisiac injected right into my bloodstream.

With my fading willpower, I shackle the beast that wants to maul her beautiful body—and fuck, I'm rewarded with the wicked sight of her licking the line of blood from her hand.

A flash of lightning charges my soul, and she's there in the flicker, my goddess of the moon to illuminate the dark.

She drops the knife to the shore. As her gaze lifts to mine, a hard shiver rocks through her, caught by the carnal beast dangerously close to ravishing her. She rises higher on her knees to kiss me softly, in direct contrast to the thrashing beat of my heart.

The saccharine taste of her melds with the sharp tang of blood, so fucking intoxicating. I grip her shoulders, my sanity wrecked as she proceeds to lower my zipper and take me out.

"Jesus, fuck." My muscles cord tight at the feel of her hand surrounding my rock-hard erection, the hot and wet feel of her blood stripping me of control. Jaw tensed, I groan against her lips. "Goddamn, Halen. You are trying to kill me."

Her soft breath teases my mouth. "I'm claiming you as mine."

A roar rushes my ears, all sounds of the marsh muted beneath the resounding crash of my heart through my chest. As she strokes the length of me, she gathers the leaked pre-cum at the tip, and the feel of her blood combining with the fluid sends me into a blind lust. She strokes me with her slick palm, and my cock jumps, throbbing at the way she fists me tighter as she works her hand back down to the base.

I tunnel my fingers into her hair and grip her to me with ferocious need, restraint fucking annihilated. With my other hand, I collar her throat, shocking the breath in her lungs. "Touch yourself," I command, my words grit from between clenched teeth.

Her swallow pulses enticingly against my palm as my predatory gaze tracks her slow descent down her body before she pushes between her thighs. She swirls her fingers over her clit, eliciting a breathy moan that sinfully curls around my spine. The scent of her desire scorches the blood in my veins.

"Don't stop touching yourself." My gaze fixes to the apex of her thighs, where a thin layer of red coats her silky skin.

My hunger builds into an unbearable pang until I'm forced to grab her waist and haul her up to her feet so I can drag her leg over my shoulder and bury my face against her pussy. I'm ravenous at the taste of her arousal and blood, like the first delectable taste of her during the ritual.

"Kallum—god." She grabs my shoulders for balance.

"That's the right order." I lick and suck until she's shaking, the wild fury of my little muse cresting like a rising tidal wave, ready to pummel me. She rakes her nails through my hair and rips at the strands, urgently compelling me to my feet.

And I let her attack.

I let her claw at my chest until she draws blood. I let her thrash and flail and shove, taking her fight as I'm claimed by my dark muse. I let her pound her fists against my body, a deviant begging for every one of her frantic lashes as she unleashes her excess of emotions. All her fear. All her anger. I will always take it for her.

I let her push me until my back hits the tree. The rough bark scrapes my skin with satisfying pain as her nails puncture my shoulders, her fingers gripping as she climbs my body.

I grip her ass as she locks her legs around me. She uses her feet to push my pants down until she can dig her heels into the backs of my thighs. Her chest crushed to mine, I splay my hand along the curve of her lower back as the rain drenches our filthy bodies.

Halen peers right into me. A dark flame ignites amid the silver embers of her eyes to hold me captive, then her mouth crashes against mine.

As her body slips down my chest, her perfect pussy

sheathes me, drawing a fervent curse past my gritted teeth at the feel of her arousal coating my cock. Her soft moan taunts me to swallow the sound as she grinds down harder, taking me deeper.

Our atoms slam together, a fusion of energy so fucking combustible, we threaten the very stars with our untamable fire.

Her nails dug into my shoulders, she rides me with wild, erotic rolls of her hips, fucking me against this tree like a sexy little nymph. I bury my mouth in the bruised joint of her neck as I fist her hair, my hips thrusting in furious, relentless need to meet hers.

"Fuck. You feel so goddamn perfect." The ungodly obscenities and coarse grunts she works from me rise above the rain. The explicit rock of her hips is maddening, my legs strained to keep us held against the tree, the bark tearing at my back.

I trail my lips across her heated skin, scrape my teeth over the bites I've branded there, the heady, consuming taste of her blood still lingering on my tongue. A torn sound catches in her throat as she works her pelvis in desperate undulations to speed my thrusts, her core pulsing tighter around my cock as she grinds lewdly against me in demand for more friction.

Every gritty, abrasive rub of dirt between our bodies demands more—our flesh striking together over and over to set us aflame.

As she arches her back to ride my cock, I groan long and hard at the salacious sight as feral lust threatens to unhinge me. I circle her wrist and drag her palm to my mouth to taste the purest hit of her, becoming deliriously ruined, before I push her hair back to capture her face, driving my cock deeper, harder, just to feast on her throaty cries.

"Goddamn, you're a vision. *My* vision," I say, my tone guttural, my words punctuated by each unrestrained thrust.

The debased way in which we fuck is divine only to us, and I revel in her sin and sanctity. Reaching a higher plane within her. Covered in mud and blood, sweat and rain, a debauchery that would invoke the god himself.

She bites into her lip to draw a bead of red as her inner walls clench around me, daring to hurl us both over the edge.

"Hold on to me." I push off the tree, my entire body rebelling against the desire to take her back down to the mud and fuck her like the depraved demon within craves.

"Kallum...ah...I'm close—" Halen breaks off, her climax denied.

"Not yet."

She glances over her shoulder to see the reserve of fresh water. "Why—?"

"Because I want to drown in you."

As we reach the edge, I fight free of my boots and soaked pants, keeping Halen held to me with one arm. I wade in, and the cool temperature elicits a delicious shiver from her.

Still deep inside her, I submerge us beneath the surface. Her legs tangle around my waist as her fingers lightly trace the scratches along my back, her touch more soothing than the balm of chilly water.

Hands fastened to her hips, I dip her backward, rewarded with the alluring sight of her arched body, her breasts peaked above the glassy surface. Temptation thunders through me, and I caress her chest, hand dipping between the valley of her breasts as I clear the mud away.

As I bring her forward, her hair wet and smoothed back, so fucking sexy, I'm lost to her.

"I could…" she whispers over my lips. Just a hint, a glimpse of a future where she could let herself fall.

And it's enough to destroy me.

"I'll wait." I cage my arms around her and sink inside her so deeply, it tears the sweetest cry from her in response. I'm there to capture that sound, kissing her with the fiery yearning blistering my soul.

As I pull back, I say, "I'll wait, but I need you to fight, to want to live, Halen. I have to serve the rest of my time, and I can't do that unless I know you're going to be there when I get out."

I watch the hard swallow drag down her slender throat as the fall of rain ripples the water around us. "I'll be there," she says.

Her movements slow and tender, the gentle rise and fall of her body guides us into a slow-burn pace that tears at the last remaining shreds of my sanity. I use the momentum to thrust deeper as I bring her hips down, driving inside her as the waves lap over our bodies, washing away the dirt.

I find her eyes. "Hold your breath, sweetness."

Then I take her under.

Completely immersed in the tranquil water, I wrap my arms across her back and cup her shoulders, bringing her down against me as I seal my mouth to hers.

I hold her below, drinking the last dregs of air right

from her lips. My chest burns from the pressure. The lack of air and build of the climax is an erotic combination. I glide my palm down the backside of her thigh and pull her harder against me, the water slowing every movement, setting an excruciating but arousing pace.

I've never made love before—not like this. With Halen, every touch is addictive, every kiss electrifying. I hold us underwater until we're both deprived of oxygen. Her eyes flash open as the impulse to fight for air grips her.

I kiss her with the desperation searing my lungs.

It's not that I don't want to breathe without her—it's that I can't. The crushing pain in my chest is how I've felt every day waiting for her, and I aim to make Halen need me with the same desperation that she needs air, the way I need her.

And as I feel her contract around me, her sweet moan breathed into my mouth, breathed *through* me, I grind against her clit and thrust deep, denying her that vital oxygen her organs crave. I'm fucking ruined as she begins to shatter.

It's pure catharsis while feeding our monsters, sating our darkest cravings, reaching for that elusive taste of ecstasy while the water cleanses the filth.

We burst above the water, gasping to fill our aching lungs, and her shattering orgasm grips me so fucking hard, I release deep inside her, clinging to her the way she clings to me, obscenities falling fierce between us.

She buries her face in the crevice of my neck as she pulls in air, her body still locked around mine. Her hand cups the back of my neck. "You're the only one," she whispers.

In the aftermath of our lovemaking, I'm the one shaking.

The architect of chaos magick wrote: *The discovery of one's true will or real nature may be difficult and fraught with danger, since a false identification leads to obsession and madness.*

When the chaos magician attempts an extreme metamorphosis, he cannot deceive himself, no matter how dark the soul he encounters.

For her, my muse, my sweetest epiphany, I strove to alter my nature, to be what she needed.

But she's the seer. I only exist when observed by her. My nature was never mine to determine.

Man. God. Devil.

The choice has always belonged to her.

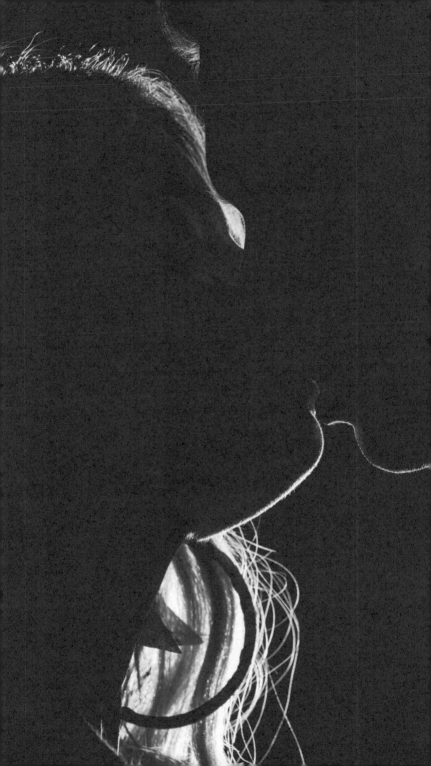

14

DARKER SIDE

> 66 Everyone carries a shadow, and the less it is embodied in the individual's conscious life, the blacker and denser it is. Let these harmless creatures form a mass, and there emerges a raging monster.
>
> — CARL JUNG

HALEN

I f you fall far enough into the void, there is no longer an up or down. It's the loss of equilibrium that impairs us. We become trapped in the darkness, suspended in the shadow.

It's not the falling part that scares me.

It's the never coming up.

This dark silhouette of our psyche has different names, such as the repressed self, the alter ego, the id. As we delve below, we tend to describe our confrontation with our darker side metaphorically: Journey to the underworld. Overcoming our demons. Dark night of the soul. Or my personal favorite: Wrestling with our devil.

Which explains how these dark aspects of ourselves can morph into complexes.

Essentially, complexes are splinter psyches often caused by trauma or emotional shock. Complexes can inhibit our purpose and even our memory. When one is overpowered by a complex, it's referred to as archetypal possession.

Before Jungian psychology achieved recognition, Robert Louis Stevenson penned a story about Dr. Jekyll and Mr. Hyde, carving a figurative scalpel through the psyche as the author wrote: *man is not one but truly two.*

An internal war waged between the good and evil of Jekyll's character as the repression of Hyde fed his shadow side until it consumed. Thus paving a dark and disturbingly accurate portrayal for Jung's shadow self.

The archetypal shadow is, at its core, a source of wicked.

Sometimes, just the attempt to draw a breath is painful, like gasping for air beneath the iceberg, my lungs filling with frigid water.

Sometimes, I wonder if I've already stopped breathing. My reality is disfigured, and I want to look to the people who love me to find my way up, to see my reflection in their eyes.

My demon found me at my worst; that's who I am to him. A dark muse. Seeing the reflection of myself in Kallum's eyes is a terrifying loss of equilibrium.

I fear falling too far into the void.

I'm clawing my way up as the painful reminder of experience comes rushing back, and with it the sounds of violence.

Warmth touches my face, and I fight to stay in this serene place right on the fringe where those blissful few seconds of peace remain. But too soon, I'm wrenched out.

Against the dense backdrop of night, the crackling flames of torches cast a misty glow over the marsh shore, then the sickening sounds of pain crack the calm illusion.

Kallum's pain.

Darkly cloaked figures attack with brutal force from all around. Kallum is in the heart of the ambush. Adrenaline rushes the chambers of my heart at the sight of him, shirtless, feral, every defined muscle tensed, a dark god bathed in the light of the torches as he swings wildly at his attackers.

Panic fuels my shaky movements as I try to reach him. My mental fog is further cleared by the press of cool steel under my chin, and I'm suddenly made aware of the threat hovering from behind. There's no verbal command, but the order not to move is clear.

The blade digs into my neck as my hair is snatched in a firm grip, and I'm forced to watch six skull-masked figures strike Kallum with torches. With each strike, fiery embers rain the open air as his enraged growl rips through the night.

He's a force of fury and chaos.

Until his fierce gaze touches mine, and his fight stops.

They descend on him.

Two of the horned men wrench Kallum's arms back and force him to his knees. He doesn't break eye contact with me. His inked skin sheens with blood and sweat. Dark red stains his mouth. He turns his face to spit a trail of blood, giving me a better view of the fresh bruising.

I make Kallum weak.

The moment I'm in danger, he loses his own will.

His eyes anchor to mine before he drops his gaze to assess me, slowly wandering over my body in critical study—his black dress shirt that clothes me, my mud-caked jeans—and stopping when he reaches the blade held to my throat. Features hard, a muscle flexes along his jaw, flames of malice lit behind his clashing eyes.

"I'm all right," I assure him. I swallow down the ache past the pressure of the blade.

The crackling pop of fire infuses the marshland as our attackers swipe their torches through the dark, their movements frantic but focused. One of them binds Kallum's wrists with rope as I'm made to stand.

My chin is set free, then the sharp tip of the knife prods my back in warning. Forced to walk barefoot, we're silently led into the woody marsh. Everything is wet and smells of earthy rain from the downpour.

I steal a backward glance at Kallum. He prowls behind me, a caged animal biding his time. His inked skin gleams in the torchlight, his dark hair unkempt, his eyes just as wild. Rough wounds lick his skin. His seething fury is thick and heady like the smoke in the air, an intoxicating pheromone to rouse the beast.

My body identifies the scrapes and bruises from the wreck and my sliced palm, but most of my pain stems from the brutal physicality that is Kallum and I together.

My body is a tapestry of marks, a fusion of pleasure and pain from Kallum's desire.

Wrestling with my devil.

We verge deeper into the marsh away from the reservoir, and Kallum's kept at a distance so he can see the threat aimed on me. While Kallum is chaos incarnate, he won't risk any attempt that endangers me.

Pale moonlight slants across dripping moss from the sickly marsh trees in eerie beauty, overlaying the dense reeds in splashes of tweed and slate green, the same vibrant color as the green I see when I look into Kallum's eyes.

A fire blazes in the center of a clearing where rocks with white markings have been stacked around the perimeter to form a circle. A giant black willow tree rises up from behind the flames, its thick roots clawing out of the muddy earth. The bone-white skulls of stags hang from its willowy branches. Runes and alchemical glyphs chalk the bark.

The sizzling roar of the fire dampens all other sounds of the marsh, the crickets a distant chirp. The fine hairs along my nape lift away as I glimpse the others dotted around the clearing, their cloaked bodies tucked into the darkness of the marsh, the spines of antlers rising above the thin reeds.

But that's not the most unnerving part of this scene.

Between the tree of bones and the fire, a tan parchment covers the ground. A sketched *ouroboros* rings the sheet. Other symbols have been drawn both within and outside of the tail-devouring snake. And in the center, the body of the man Kallum killed, his broken neck evident.

The body has been stripped of clothes. His eyes crudely removed, the bloody sockets exposed. His ears are shorn off. His torso sliced open and his stomach disemboweled, his organs harvested. Glass jars border the parchment, the contents gruesomely unmistakable.

On reflex, I touch my stomach, only comforted once I feel Kallum beside me. "I made you leave him alive," I say, referring to our other attacker on the ridge. "He's how they found us."

"Actually, nothing happens in my fields that I don't know about."

Her distinct, melodic voice travels over the crackling flames.

Dressed in her headdress of antler bone and ivy, Devyn emerges from around the tree. She's once again adorned in her sheer, flowing skirt and armbands, but she's also donning one other item: a corset made from a human rib cage. The bones are woven with twine, showcasing her expert technique in all its macabre glory.

I'm gripped by the otherworldly sight of her as she finds my gaze past the fiery sparks licking into the night, and for a fraction of a second, I glimpse a touch of softness before her features adopt the hardened mask of a priestess.

Our silent abductors toss their torches into the fire before they nudge us onto the fine cloth parchment, closer to the mutilated body.

Kallum coughs to conceal a groan of pain as we're forced to our knees. "This scene was already set. They were coming no matter where you were," he says, an attempt to reassure me. "He wants you." I look up into his face, pained at the dark bruises forming beneath his beautiful eyes. "I won't let him have you."

"Don't do anything reckless," I say.

His devilish smile carves the dimple in his cheek to squeeze my heart as a drum strikes from somewhere behind us. I stay locked in Kallum's heated gaze, the fire dancing amid the flinty shadows.

Then Devyn breaches the circle to break our connection. Her movements are fluid despite the constricting bones shaping her torso in stiff posture. As she reaches us, her dark gaze travels over my appearance. Kallum's shirt fitted loosely, strands of my hair matted with dry mud. My body itches as the heat of the fire bakes dirt into my skin.

A fragile smile lifts her mouth. "I see you've made peace with losing your mind over the sexy expert consultant."

"I'm hard to resist," Kallum says, sarcasm heavy in his gruff tone. "Unhinged women can't seem to keep away." The baiting remark is directed toward her.

Devyn *tsks*. "Remarkable how that male privilege affords you so little fear," she says, offering him a bright smile. "I soon realized Halen was your agenda. Once I saw you together, so much made sense." They trade a look before she aims her attention on the masked man standing at Kallum's side. "Prepare him. I want to speak with my sister."

Her order is eagerly obeyed, and Kallum is hauled to his bare feet and taken to the other end of the parchment. "What are you doing to him?" I demand.

Devyn leisurely lifts her gauzy skirt and kneels before

241

me, her spine forced to keep perfect posture by the bone corset. "Don't worry," she says, collecting a stick of white chalk from the cloth. "Nothing too heinous."

Fury pricks my composure, and in the same way she struck me in the cave, I slap her cheek. My palm stings from the impact, and I instinctively dig my nails into the cut on my left hand to balance the pain. "That's for trying to eat me."

Yet it's for so much more. The emptiness I feel for trying to keep my promise to help her—for failing her. Knowing now there was nothing I could do to save her.

She gingerly touches her face, concealing a faint smile. "You have a sick fetish with pain."

"Why am I here, Devyn? Am I going to end up like him?" I jerk my head in the direction of the mutilated corpse near the fire.

"I wanted to introduce you to my brother," she says, delicately grazing her fingers over the bones encasing her chest. "I keep Colter close now. Since birth, we were always together, rarely apart, such as twins are. And now that I've been deprived of my family, he's the last that remains."

Appall roils in the pit of my stomach as I stare at the twined bones. "It's probably a bit difficult to be on the run with a gang of people who have no eyes." I manage a partial shrug. "Just saying."

A smile brightens her pretty features. "You've gotten feisty, Halen St. James. Hot, dirty sex with the professor suits you." She grips my chin and brings the chalk to my forehead. I control my breathing as she begins to drag the cool stick over my skin.

Early on in the case, Kallum claimed the Overman suspect chose Nietzschean doctrines because of the artist's soul, attributing it to the *rausch*. Devyn is an artist. Her art allows her to break free of her stringent perfectionism and obsessive compulsive nature. Her artist's soul is why she connected to Nietzsche over any other philosopher. And despite the ghastly nature of her corset, I'm choosing to believe that, in her own artistic way, it's a sign she's still connected to whatever remains of her humanity.

I swallow past the thick ache of grief in my throat as she tilts her head, turning pensive. "But wait," she says, "it's more than that."

I try to look away, but she keeps hold of my chin, proceeding to scrawl the chalk across my cheekbones. "Something's changed," she says solemnly.

What Devyn sought to connect to within me was my grief, the pain. Kallum said the suspect was seeking unity in their opposite, but honestly, that was Kallum's agenda, never Devyn's.

I wanted to leave, and she wanted to stay.

An even trade.

"You want to live now," she says, studying me intently.

Aware Kallum is listening, I say, "Yes. I want to live, Devyn. But I know you're dying."

"I had no doubt you'd figure it out." Some of the woman I knew from before shines through. She appears more lucid than the last time I saw her. Certain medications can help control the unusual movements caused by her disease. They can also help offset any delusions or hallucinations that might present. I have no idea if Devyn is medicated, or if her devout belief is merely overriding her regression.

"I am dying," she says. "But really, I think I died the moment I lost Colter. Without those we live for, are we truly alive? You know the answer to that, Halen."

She discards the chalk and spins away, severing the connection.

Alarm flares in my veins. I no longer have any delusion of reaching her, but I have to keep her talking.

"Devyn, wait. Listen. Someone in your life made you feel inadequate," I say, stalling her. "I profiled this, remember? At first, I thought it was your brother. But it wasn't. It was him, wasn't it. This man in authority over you."

A flash of uncertainty tightens her features.

"He killed Bethany with hemlock," I say, not letting up. I realized it wasn't Devyn when we were attacked by the men with syringes. "You cared for her. You wanted to help her—to help them all. But this man...he's obsessed with you. He can't let you go."

I felt the dark obsession in that chamber. I sensed the malice, the vile desperation.

Devyn leans in close to whisper. "He won't even let me die."

As she pulls away, a chill blankets my skin at her words. Keeping me snared in her solemn gaze, she snaps her fingers. "It's time."

At once, the surrounding marsh comes alive with the rustle of reeds. The figures masked in skulls move in from the high grass. Those closest to the flames place a beveled black plate over the fire. The beat of the drum rises, the rhythm climbing and accelerating my heart rate as they converge around the circle.

A sordid energy tangles my senses, and I seek Kallum across the parchment. His face is chalked with alchemical symbols. The philosopher's stone marks the center of his forehead—darkly ironic, as it's the same symbol he scored into Alister's skull.

He watches the scene unfold as if he's studying an ancient text, unlocking its code. As if he came here by choice.

Once they're all gathered around the fire, they remove their masks. No longer anonymous dark figures, they become people. The officer who attacked us, his face bearing the bruises from Kallum's wrath. Mrs. Lipton, her diamond earrings catching the firelight. Most of the others I place as family members of the locals that went missing.

What's curious is that there are far less of them than what's expected of this society. There were thirty-three missing locals. Yet there are only thirteen of their relatives present.

Devyn clasps my hand, making me startle. "I told Bethany to run," she whispers near my ear. "I told her to run, Halen."

I angle my face to meet her dark eyes. "I don't understand—" My words are clipped short the moment I see him.

Shirtless, his broad chest adorned with glyphs, Riddick removes the skull from his face. He strides in Kallum's direction, and I push past Devyn to reach him first.

Wrists still bound with rope, Kallum squares his

shoulders and matches Riddick's sinister glare. "You got my message."

Riddick hangs the skull on his belt, his features carved in a sneer. "I did, and since we still need a tongue —" he glances down at the body "—I'll just take yours. And I'll really fucking enjoy it, too." He rests his hand on the hilt of the dagger strapped to his belt. At Kallum's silence, he chuckles. "What? No final, smart-ass quips, professor?"

Kallum's mouth curves into a menacing smile, baring the blood staining his teeth. "Aristotle said, evil brings men together." He glances around. "Looks like we're all here. Untie me, and let's have a real fucking party."

Riddick drops his fist into Kallum's face.

Kallum takes the hit, his head canted to the side as he swipes a bead of fresh blood from his lip with the back of his hand.

Emotions soaring, I lunge at Riddick, making a reach for the knife.

He expertly catches my wrist in a firm grip, then pushes my sleeve up. His narrowed gaze lowers to my forearm, to where the wound has long since torn open. "You really should have let me stitch you up, Halen."

As he says this, I realize I was too focused on him at the ravine, on his suturing skill in connection to the suspect. "Where's your superior?" I ask him, snatching my arm free.

Riddick doesn't wear the antlers. He doesn't have implants. He's the second half of a partnership, the one who had to go undetected. I missed the obvious point Riddick made to replace this person's police hat after he lost it during his fall down the ravine. Riddick did so to make sure to hide the implants from view.

As the fire snaps and burns hotter, Devyn materializes in my periphery. Staring into the depth of the marsh, she announces, "He's here."

Pulse firing in my veins, I look to the shadows where the immense figure emerges from the high reeds. Clothed only in black jeans and a skull, his stature is every bit as brawny as Landry, but he's less defined. The years spent excelling at sports still shape his physique, but time and his current profession behind a desk has worn him.

Detective Dean Emmons lowers the menacing skull from his face, but the antlers remain, sharpened into spears atop his head. Letting the skull hang from his hand, he opens his arms wide. The drum surges.

While there was suspicion surrounding Detective Riddick when he stepped in, it was only so Emmons could operate behind the scenes.

Emmons advances into the clearing, his gait still slightly hindered by his injury. Devyn meets him halfway, and he clasps her by her nape in a show of ownership.

"Guess Emmons has the bigger dick," Kallum remarks and cuts his gaze to Riddick, provoking him.

Riddick's jaw tightens as he widens his stance in front of Kallum. "You flayed Alister," he accuses in a hushed tone. "Wasn't me or Emmons. So that means it had to be you. You're one twisted fuck."

"You're so sure," Kallum questions, turning his sharp gaze on the couple. "Maybe you just weren't privy to their plan."

It's only a flash, but doubt registers in Riddick's

features, anger quickly taking its place. And I realize there's a fracture in the society. From Riddick's doubt of Devyn to the small gathering here, trust has been broken among them.

Riddick looks over Kallum smugly. "What did the fed do, Locke? Look at her too long, touch her like this…"

He seizes my throat in his thick hand, his other reaching around to grab hold of my ass. I struggle against his clutch, nails raking his arm, only to earn the back of his hand to my cheek.

A violent charge cracks the air. Kallum's wrath is a blaze of lit kerosene racing through the darkened wetland right before he slams into Riddick and takes him to the ground. He braces his forearm across Riddick's throat with crushing force.

Emmons moves into the fray and, with a low, controlled command, orders his lackies to haul Kallum off.

My bruised cheek smarting with a painful throb, I face Riddick once he's on his feet. "He's going to kill you," I say in a low tone, and not as a threat, as a warning. Riddick should run.

Riddick's smile is crass as he licks his lips. "Worth it, *sweetness*," he mocks.

Hot rage sparked deep in my chest, I seek out Devyn, finding her watching me with a curious tilt to her head as she caresses the bones of her deceased brother along her chest.

"If the feds aren't already combing the marshland, they will be soon," I say, easing toward Kallum.

Emmons rolls his broad shoulders, his eyes flaring wild. "Soon it won't matter." There's no inflection in his tone. The man I first met on the case has seemingly deteriorated.

He claps his hands together, the crack reverberates through the clearing. "You know your places."

Moving in front of me, Kallum grabs hold of my shirt, his fingers bunching the fabric until I'm pulled closer. Then he covertly lifts the hem and slips an object into my pocket. "When the time comes, don't hold back."

I swallow hard at the tender feel of his fingers grazing my waist before his hand falls away and we're prodded toward the fire's edge.

Heart clutched in a vise, I outline the object in my pocket. The fierce, rhythmic drumming fades to a muted thump in my ears as I recognize the distinct shape. I've held an object like this before. I used it to take a life.

I glance at Riddick positioned across the fire, my gaze dropping to the skull hooked to his belt—the one that now has a broken antler.

As the flames heat my body, Kallum drops his tied wrists around my neck, his sole focus on me. The chalked symbols swirl over the blood and bruised skin of his face, in direct contrast to the dark tendrils of ink along his neck. The combination is stunningly beautiful.

"You know what's about to happen," I say, catching sight of Mrs. Lipton as she selects one of the jars. "Tell me."

Kallum's tongue darts out to catch a drop of blood, trailing the cut along his lower lip. "The above is of the below, and the below is of the above," he says. "You're standing on the formula for gold, sweet Halen."

I look down at the cloth parchment, at the markings within the *ouroboros*. "Now's not the time to be cryptic."

As the drum swells higher, the beat increasing to a frantic cadence to match my firing pulse, the members surround the pit of flames and chant those very words. They proceed to empty the contents of the jars—blood, organs, flesh—into the plate positioned above the fire.

"A prominent alchemist once compared the creation of the philosopher's stone to the resurrection of pharaohs," Kallum says, his breath falling over my lips. "A parallel in which both the stone and the body were subjected to a violent process to purify, transform, and resurrect a perfect form."

Emmons commands them to: "Fill the cups," and Riddick circles the ring, filling the empty jars with a cloying red liquid that turns my stomach.

"First, the blackening," Kallum continues. He glances at the gore roasting in the center of the ceramic. "Ingredients cleansed to a black matter to purify."

Bile rises to the back of my throat as the stench of cooking organs permeates the marshy air. "This is what you lied to Dr. Markus about."

"Not lied, just a purposeful oversight," he confirms with a twist to his mouth. "That wall of glyphs was meant to mislead. If I had said—"

"That the prominent alchemist was a woman, then no one would take him seriously," Devyn interrupts. "Though prominent is quite a stretch, seeing as she was wiped from history just for *being* a woman."

Regardless of her claim, the reason Kallum didn't identify the contradictions in that chamber was for me, because I asked him not to point to Devyn. My ask was high; my own self-deception.

A dark gleam ignites behind Kallum's eyes. "In you, Cleopatra the Alchemist, is hidden the whole terrible and strange mystery." His arms tighten around me as he regards her. "You've advanced, priestess."

"I was given little choice," she snaps. "Will you be displaying your wings tonight, demon of fate? Or was that merely a flashy distraction, like quoting Ostanes now?" She wags her finger and sways to the pulsing rhythm of the drum. "Nietzsche was so close to ascension, if only he had been strong enough to devour his sun in the end. Instead, he just went mad."

Kallum straightens his spine, towering over me protectively. "The same fate awaits your boyfriend."

"Did you miss the part about the ego?" Her smile stretches. "You cited the master sorcerer of the dark arts himself. You're so good at dropping hints, like little riddles. Tell me I'm wrong, that I'm still unworthy."

Some understanding passes between them, and her gaze narrows on Kallum with disdain before she turns my way. "The sacrifice of a human was never intended to sever humanity, Halen. You got that wrong. Not only is a blood sacrifice the most powerful, it's the only way to keep the mind intact. You can thank your boyfriend for that insight."

Kallum cradles the back of my head, his fingers speared into my hair possessively. "While I sympathize with Emmons' lovesick heart, only one of us gets the girl," he says, firm resolve in his deep baritone.

Devyn raises her chin, her antlers casting a tall shadow behind her. "Love makes us all sick, professor."

The flames cast Kallum's features in striking relief, his gaze on me just as feverish. If given the choice, he would sacrifice himself for me in this moment. I see the truth in those clashing eyes that smolder hotter than the burning coals.

This close to Kallum, his bare skin humming with an electric current, our eyes fused on each other despite the watchful gazes all around, we're always connected. The only two people in existence as the rest of the world falls away.

I raise my hand to his face and trace the arresting contours, the chalk smudged beneath the press of my fingertips. How lost has Kallum gotten in his own obsession?

"Don't do anything reckless for me," I tell him again, stressing my desire to keep him safe.

He lowers his mouth to my ear. "I will bathe this ground in blood, sweetness," he whispers, eliciting a shiver over my skin. "Every star in my universe burns in the silvery pools of your eyes. An infinity of wishes cast there, and I only desire one thing, *lunam deam.*" He presses his forehead to mine, his voice a coarse plea as he says, "Stay with me."

I seal my eyes closed, feeling only the heat of his body against mine despite the raging flames, hearing only his shallow breaths as the drum fades into the background, just like the night of his ritual when he implored me to remember, to face the fear pressing at me from the shadows.

In analytical psychology, Jung states there is nothing more terrifyingly frightening than the mind. Repression of the id's desires is where our shadow is fashioned. When an internal struggle is not made conscious, it happens outside as fate. The world is forced to act out the conflict, and thus we're torn into opposing halves.

Our shadow side is born.

Once only the dark, destructive grief remained, my shadow was a raging monster. The night I set off after a killer, it took mass.

And like in the cautionary tale, when Jekyll realizes he's losing the battle to his monster, he makes the choice to end his own life in order to stop the fiend from taking over. Not only did I crave that escape, I pursued it. I wasn't supposed to survive that night. I leapt into the void and never planned to resurface.

It's never been the question of whether or not I killed —it's whether I can stop.

Can I know without fail that I will never take another life? I can't—because I felt it in my blood when Kallum kissed me during the ritual. I felt it when I fought Landry, and when Alister attacked me.

I feel it now as I pull back and stare into Kallum's captivating eyes, the pain I want to unleash, the punishment I want to deliver as I caress his chest with my wounded palm, gently touching his battered skin.

Vengeance.

My shadow archetype craves retribution.

The pit of the fire burns hotter, and I have the compulsion to reach into the coals, to feel the soot. It's a part of me.

Pushing up onto my toes, I capture Kallum's full lips in a tender kiss, sealing the promise I made months ago before a crackling fire to stay with him.

He brushes his thumb along the nape of my neck, then his form tenses, and I sense the threat behind me like a resinous sludge traveling through the veins of the marsh.

Emmons splashes the blackened, boiling organs with a clear substance, and a noxious gas releases into the air. A crazed gleam flashes in his eyes as he looks at Devyn. "Lead them," he commands her.

I tighten my hold on Kallum as Devyn sways toward us, her hips rolling in sync to the rhythm, her hands sweeping through the air as if she's weaving a pattern through the atmosphere. The antler spine in my pocket digs into my hip in reminder. This time, I can't hesitate.

As she comes to a halt near our locked bodies, Devyn reaches up and unfastens one of the slender antlers from the implant on her scalp, then she removes the other.

"Sex is the most potent energy source," she declares, raising her arms, the antlers casting trembling shadows against the ground. "The bestial craving for blood and sex is our primal desire, and it must be fed."

Dread floods my bloodstream as I tip my head back to search Kallum's fierce gaze, those intense flames burning with a truth he can't hide.

"Oh, god." The words fall from my mouth as I latch on to his forearms resting along my shoulders. He remains silent, his features a hardened mask.

Devyn pitches the antlers into the fire. "*Ekstasis* commands us, rules us," she cries. "We submit to the divine pleasure."

My heart thrashes the cage of my chest as realization dawns. Before we're to become one with the elements in a madman's alchemy dish, we're first required to reach *ekstasis*, the height of ecstasy.

From my periphery, I see Devyn dancing. The corset of bones moves with the flicker of firelight, the sheer material follows her elegant movements. She weaves around Riddick, and I feel his tarry eyes on me. His sick lust crawls beneath my skin.

As Devyn returns, she walks a slow circle around us, now holding Riddick's dagger in one hand. She reaches with her other to touch us, prompting. "As they looked upon her, she lectured on the great work, and they declared they'd fallen into ecstasy at her revelations."

Kallum clenches his teeth, a muscle tics against his tight jawline. "Misinterpreting seems to be your only specialty," he admonishes her.

Devyn stops her progression, coming to a halt at his side. "Fuck her, sorcerer, or I'll let Riddick do the honors."

A dangerous growl rumbles from deep within Kallum's chest. His body vibrates with the strike of the drum as it rises in unison with the chanting. His hold on me tightens painfully, as if he can feel my desire to flee.

"This can't be happening." I shake my head against his forearms, then I look up to find the sky. The gnarled trees climb within a helmet of branches and moss like gods overseeing their offering, the moonlight their seduction.

The masks once again cover their faces, and the figures move like the reeds sway. The people are shadows in the marsh, taking on the elements themselves, the bones of

255

stags that tramp the ground like bloodthirsty animals, awaiting the kill.

"Say the words," Devyn commands of Kallum. "Speak Cleopatra's words and transmute the elements to the divine substance."

Savage fury lit within the depths of his eyes, Kallum slowly removes his arms from around my neck. He drops his bound wrists between us, where he gently takes my face between his splayed fingers. "For he who fled entered into the one who did not flee, and he who controlled entered into the one who did not control, and they were united with each other."

An ache burns at the back of my throat, my body trembles uncontrollably. I feel the vulgar press of their eyes on us as their chant climbs into an urgent entreaty, calling for *ekstasis,* rapture, frenzy.

I curl my fingers against the solidness of Kallum's chest, trying to fight the fear as it becomes tangible, suffocating. I turn to escape, immediately caught as Kallum drops his bound arms around me, welding my back to his chest.

"You can't run yet," he whispers in my ear.

"They're watching us..."

He captures my jaw with rough fingers and tilts my face up, forcing me to stare into the fierce intensity of his eyes. "Don't look at any of them," he says, his voice gravel. "Eyes on me—look only at me, sweetness."

He lowers his hands, his thumb traveling down the center of my body until he reaches the clasp of my jeans. He flicks it open, summoning a hard shiver from my body.

Then his descent resumes, his hands roving below my pelvis and pushing between my thighs.

A dizzying sensation sweeps over me, and I shut my eyes against the onslaught.

"Stay with me," Kallum commands. "I need you to stay with me, Halen." His fingers touch the sigil on my inner thigh, snatching my breath. Compelling my eyes back on him, he anchors me with the seductive cadence of his voice.

Emmons breaks the protective haze with a command to drink from the cups.

As I sink into Kallum's strong embrace, I feel myself tunnel under, losing equilibrium like I'm in that torture chamber all over again, hearing the flutter of the moth's wings, seeing the flicker of the firelight like the swaying bulb against my eyelids. Then the erotic feel of Kallum's hand stroking between my thighs envelops me in torrid heat to tempt me to the surface.

The seductive rock of his hips against my backside urges me to push back, lured into him. "Don't slip away," he says, his breath a heated caress over my neck before his lips find the throbbing pulse point. Then he's kissing, tasting, and I'm fading under his spell.

"I trust you," I tell him—but I can't be present for this, my mind already delving below.

He unleashes a dark groan as his teeth sink into the soft curve of my shoulder, brutally awakening me from the trance.

My eyes open to chaos.

A shrill scream splits the air. Jars drop from their

hands, murky glass rolling over the stomped reeds. The cloaked figures around the fire fall to their knees.

And amid the disorder, Devyn stands before me, her hand gripped to the hilt of the dagger.

My chest heaves, the wick of fury lit within me as I drag air into my constricted lungs. Kallum tenses around me as she raises the knife, her threat clear—but I don't look away.

"Is to die what you want?" I ask her as I slip my fingers into my pocket.

"We all die eventually," she says, her voice soft, her words meant just for me.

Anticipation threads my muscles as I grip the sharp antler, and my fingers brush the pendant of my necklace. My heart stalls.

He won't even let me die. Devyn's words fill my mind.

In the fraction of a second that hesitation costs me, Devyn brings the knife down.

The steel blade cuts through the rope binding Kallum's wrists.

"But not today," she says. Her eyes flash wild as she shifts her gaze to Kallum and presses the dagger into his hand. "Don your wings, moth. The doomsday is upon us."

15

PURSUIT RITUAL

HALEN

Three things happen at once.

The drumming stops. Several people around the fire collapse. They convulse, seizing with juddering spasms as a foamy substance leaks from their parted mouths. The few who didn't drink from the jars tear off their masks as Devyn shouts, compelling them to escape.

Emmons stands stock-still, his arms stationary at his sides, betrayal carved deep into the lines of his hardened features as he watches Devyn deceive him.

Riddick is already in furious motion before the last person hits the ground, his target decided as his steely gaze zeroes in on me. Kallum pushes in front of me to block his path, and they clash in a violent impact. I'm knocked to the ground, my fingers digging into the crushed reeds.

The aggressive sounds of their fight assault the air. The

dagger is held aloft in Kallum's grip as Riddick uses his forearm to evade the strike.

A hand surrounds my bicep, and I'm yanked farther out of the fray. "Halen, we have to run," Devyn urges me. She sheds the bones encasing her chest to reveal a nude bralette beneath.

"I'm not leaving Kallum." I twist my arm free, spinning to find him.

Bare chest heaving, he drives his fist into Riddick's face. The mist of blood is caught by the firelight like tiny red flares amid the darkness. With a deep groan, Kallum pitches his opponent sideways. Then his gaze captures me.

It's only a second, one spared glance, but that's all it takes. I see him across the grassy quad, a striking professor in an all-black suit, and my heart constricts when his beautiful eyes connect with mine and I feel the weight of my ring on my finger.

Something inside me fractures and slips into place all at once.

Hurled back into the present, I watch as Kallum faces the threats moving in. Spurred into motion, Emmons bows his head and charges forward like a bull. Riddick careens toward Kallum from the side, the collision inevitable.

And the knife rests near Kallum's feet.

Adrenaline singeing my veins, I break away from Devyn and lunge for the weapon. My hand shaking, I repeatedly grasp at the handle, securing it too late.

With Kallum's back to me, I rise up to witness the horror unfold as if in slow motion.

Kallum cages his forearm around Riddick's neck and wrenches him forward, using Riddick's body as a shield right before the sharpened spears of Emmons' antlers impale his sternum.

A broken sound escapes my mouth.

Kallum anchors his hands to Riddick's shoulders and, with a ruthless grunt, thrusts Riddick's torso farther onto the horns. He then tears Riddick free and lets his body fall to the earth, ensuring he bleeds out. No mercy is offered with a quick death.

And I see it there in the manic gleam of Kallum's eyes, his satisfaction with the kill.

Riddick chokes on the blood pooling in his mouth, desperately and uselessly pressing his hands over the wounds. Emmons stares down at the carnage, his large arms corded with tension, the spiked bones fastened to his head covered in blood, the dark red gore dripping down his face.

Devyn grasps my face, her eyes clear and imploring. Her voice is muted beneath the pounding of my pulse before she breaks through. "We *have* to leave," she's saying. "They will die. All of them. The whole town."

Past the shock and adrenaline fighting for dominance, I take in the death all around, the poisoned bodies lying motionless—and I envision the bare canes at the hemlock grove after it was raided.

"Oh, my god," I mutter, my fingers tearing through my tangle of hair.

On instinct, I lift my eyes to Kallum. His gaze fuses to mine, holding me within the fierce blue cinders, the slate-green of the eerie moonlit marsh. My gaze pans over the sigils carved in his flesh, all the desires longed for by a chaos magician.

And I am terrified to lose him.

You will never lose me, I hear his voice intone, a promise I have no choice but to trust.

I inhale a shuddering breath as he easily pries the knife from my clenched grasp before he says, "Run."

Then his focus is on the unhinged detective barreling for him.

Devyn takes my hand, and like the raving ones, we run.

My bare feet hit every divot and bramble trying to slow my pace, the roots reaching up from the muddy earth to grab at my ankles. I refasten my jeans, ignoring the way they stick to my skin as sweat leaks from my pores.

I follow Devyn as we track parallel to the reservoir, using the sparse coverage of the marsh trees to shelter us amid the swampy wetland. "Where the hell are we going?"

"Up the mountain," she calls back to me. "We have to make it to the top."

For one petrifying second, I fear I'm succumbing to her delusion, or that I'm delirious from dehydration, because I see the hulking forty-foot structure coming into view against the dusky skyline.

Blinking red lights mark the concrete and slate-black stones of a dam rising up from the reservoir.

"Oh, hell." The curse is sawed from my lungs. The horrid truth hits me in an instant, what Emmons has done.

Ignoring the pain searing my muscles, I push my legs harder.

A white light cuts across the barren branches ahead of us, and a sharp twinge of panic slows my pace. I glance back once to see the beams slashing through the shadowed trees, hear the footfalls beating the ground.

We're being chased.

I follow Devyn into the thick brush where we're out of sight, yet a fence barricade of mesh wire halts our advance. Gripping my side, I bend at the waist to pull in a shot of crisp air. Devyn climbs over the top and offers me her hand.

I hesitate as I stare at her outstretched hand. Then I glance over at the ladder leading to the top of the stone dam. A manic laugh slips past my lips, and I swallow the raw burn in my dry throat. "But of course it would be heights."

The sounds of the pursuit grow closer to propel me past my fear, and I latch on to her hand.

In direct opposition to the wild beat of my heart, the body of water is still and tranquil. The moonlight reflects off the glassy top of the reservoir, placid despite the dangerous current swimming through the air.

Defying my instinct to turn back, I anchor my hands to the cold ladder and hike my body up the rungs, breathing through the constricting fear.

Wind whips at my hair the higher we ascend. I try to pretend it's just the library ladder, and that Kallum is there below. The thought causes a pang of regret to flare inside my chest, and as a shiver attacks my muscles, I miss a rung. Muttering a curse, I find purchase and pull myself close to the bars.

Don't look down. Keep your eyes right there.

Hearing his voice, I tilt my head back and open my eyes to the stars dusting the midnight sky.

To further distract myself from the anxiety threading my nerves, I mentally link the details. "You told me Jake Emmons was already dead," I say to Devyn, my voice shaky. "But it wasn't from his illness. I read the ME's report."

There's a lengthy pause where I think she won't answer, then: "Emmons killed him."

His own brother.

"That was his trade," Devyn says from up above me. "His sacrifice. For me." This last part barely reaches my ears, her voice as passive as the body of water below us. "I wanted to believe he did it to offer mercy. I *had* to believe that. But when I found out there was a new treatment option for Jake, and that Emmons knew this..." There's a tense pause. "I only discovered this before I took you to the mine."

As we reach the concrete platform, I hold my hands out to gain balance. The drop to the rocky stream below is so far down, the world tilts. I reach for the secure feel of Kallum's arms surrounding me as his comforting scent envelops me from his shirt, preventing me from toeing too close to the edge.

In the distant marsh, the beams of light flicker through the trees. A mix of hope and dread swirls my bloodstream, unsure if I'm comforted or not by the presence of the feds.

I don't know what Agent Rana will find when she reaches Kallum—the man or the devil.

Devyn hovers in front of me like a specter, her loose layers fluttering around her soft frame. "Colter wasn't supposed to die first," she says, anguish hitching her voice. "He took his own life."

I swipe my hair out of my vision. "A symptom of the disease is hopelessness," I say, offering some form of logical comfort.

She holds up a hand. "Colter's will was the strongest. He was never hopeless. I knew then, right fucking then, when I found him in the ravine..." She averts her gaze and drags in a sharp breath. "I'm the one who became hopeless. I'm the one who lost the will. And by doing so, I drove Emmons to this end. When Colter died, it was as if he just snapped. My brother's death made mine an unavoidable reality."

I nod slowly, gaining more of my bearings. "And you thought Professor Locke could help you."

A knowing smile stretches across her lips. "He did," she says. "He brought me you."

Leaving it at that, Deyvn spins toward the building sitting on the elevated bluff that overlooks the reservoir. A blend of gothic and industrial architecture, the original masonry stacks faded bricks two levels high, with a dark cast-iron water tank housed on top.

I lift my face to a gust of wind, just to feel it brush my skin before I follow behind her.

"After each failed ascension into the alchemical overman, Emmons disposed of them with hemlock," she says as she pulls the glass door open. "Once the bodies have all been recovered, they'll find traces of it, just like with Bethany."

I tilt my head, studying her. "Why are you telling me this?"

"Because you want answers." She swings the door wider and steps inside. "When the FBI arrived, Emmons knew it was only a matter of time before we were exposed, and he became desperate."

As I wait for her to say more, I glance around. The track lights overhead are dimmed, as if the emergency lights kicked on afterhours. The renovated interior is a stark contrast to the worn exterior, complete with updated concrete flooring and monitors displayed on whitewashed walls. Reinforced steel beams cross the ceiling alongside galvanized air ducts.

"The hemlock was never intended for mass destruction," Devyn says as she rounds a corner. "You got that wrong, too. It was given as an option for self-destruction, for those who personally chose that means. But Emmons saw it as a way to take it right back to your profile."

"I don't understand." But even as I say this, a revolting awareness washes over me.

I theorized that if the divine wisdom was rejected by society, the Overman would incorporate the hemlock into their delusion. Only Emmons did the opposite of Socrates —he contaminated the whole town's water supply.

"I gave him the idea," I say, a sickness roiling my stomach.

"He said it would be a convenient way for us to have a new start," Devyn says, confirming my thoughts. "Force the skeptics to drink the poison. Wipe it all clean." She looks back at me. "Starting with the inner circle."

Devyn halts, touching the wall to catch her breath. She stares at the floor. "I didn't know he laced the wine. I didn't know he was going to do that back there. You have to believe me, Halen."

I'm not sure what I believe, but I study scenes, the evidence. The logical story that is revealed beneath the mystery. That's what I know. And if I was investigating the scene we left behind tonight, I would uncover intent with a cold malice.

"You made Bethany a shrine because you loved her."

She pulls herself upright. "Instead of letting her become just another one of his failures to be sacrificed, I gave her to you." She meets my eyes. "I offered you a scene only you could decode. I wanted you to stop him."

"Because if I was the one, then you wouldn't have to betray him."

"Even after what he's done, I didn't want to hurt him. Not after all that he's sacrificed for me." Her vibrant brown eyes sheen with banked moisture. "But there just wasn't enough time."

The mention of our limited time raises the hairs along the back of my neck. "We have that time now."

Her smile is crestfallen. "Only because I abandoned him."

Without another word, she navigates the hallways, our steps echoing against the emptiness. The silence is unsettling. My bare feet slap the cool floor as I glance around in search for security or a shift employee—coming to a sudden halt at the wet feel beneath my toes.

Instinctively, I look down. Dark red pools on the concrete. I follow the blood to a discarded body, the neck slashed.

Emmons has reached the height of desperation, removing anyone who stands in his way, even the people he swore an oath to protect in his town.

Farther ahead, Devyn pushes through a door, and I speed my steps, tracking a trail of blood behind, feeling just as desperate. I match her quick pace once we enter into the main water filtration and treatment area—the system that feeds the town's water supply.

"Christ, Devyn." The warren of pipes that line the space feels impossible. It's not just everyone in Hollow's Row that will be affected, but possibly the neighboring towns as well.

The species of hemlock that was cultivated in the marshland grove, once ingested, results in extreme nausea, convulsions, and then death. All within minutes.

I shove my hands through my hair. "Shit. Where do we start?" I ask, trying and failing to follow the maze of pipes to a source. I straddle one of the blue pipes and grab hold of the valve lever. It's impossible to turn. "Why are you just standing there?"

With a calm countenance, Devyn walks to a wall panel with a red alarm light mounted on top and flips the cover open, the panel having already been unlocked. My heart thumps painfully in my chest, the sounds of the facility muffled by the roar in my ears as I watch her run her finger down the row...then push a button.

She turns to face me. "Done."

Licking my dry lips, I climb off the pipe, my burning gaze hung on her. "Explain," I demand.

She hugs an arm around her trim waist. "The backup water supply was contaminated," she says. "Emmons bypassed the main distribution pipes, like when the pipes need repair. I'm sure he also had Sammy out there disable the sensors—"

"Before he killed him—"

"—so no monitoring alarms would go off when he contaminated the tank with hemlock," she pushes on. "So all we needed to do was enable the central pipes again."

I hold her calculating stare. "And alert the task force of the contaminated supply." I bite down on my lip, not sure if I'm feeling an overwhelming sense of relief or anger. "I'll find a phone."

She nods once, but before I disappear around the corner, she calls my name. I pause long enough to listen. "I knew if you came with me, then it would be all right. I knew this."

I hover a moment longer, torn between debating logic over her belief system. "I need to make the call."

Finding a landline in one of the offices, I grab the receiver and punch in the only number to the FBI I have memorized. After I leave an urgent message for Agent Rana with an operator, I reenter the room where I left Devyn, only to find her missing.

As I search the area, a sense of unmistakable dread settles deep in my stomach. This was all too simple, too anticlimactic to have been her design.

My thoughts cease when I catch sight of her through a tall casement window.

Standing on the crest in the center of the dam wall, Devyn stares out over the stream, the reservoir at her back, the sheer material of her skirt and armbands whisked around her by the wind.

I push the window open and tuck the loose hem of my shirt into my jeans before I ease onto the ledge of the platform. Then immediately close my eyes as the dizzying sensation sweeps my head. "Dammit."

With deep inhale, I force my eyes open. "Do you always have an ulterior motive?" I call out to her.

She doesn't acknowledge me, but I can hear a hint of a smile in her voice. "If it means anything at all, the only way I could've gone through with it back in the mine was to drug myself."

"It's good to know you couldn't dine on me sober." I try to keep her talking as I crawl onto the crest, my fingers gripped to the graded surface. While the width is a good bit over eight feet, the drop-off over the spillway makes it feel like a tightrope. An inappropriate laugh escapes as I think about the symbolism. "Couldn't just keep walking a metaphorical tightrope over your abyss," I mutter beneath my shaky breath.

"I thought…one life for the many," she shouts, her voice cut by the wind. "I wanted them to be saved, to finish what Colter and I started before it all became corrupt."

The choice to either take a life or sacrifice your own. Devyn said this to me in the cave as I held a weapon above her. I took her words to heart. Only now, I realize she was talking about her internal struggle with Emmons.

She's trying to reset the balance, to correct what he's done by trading her own life.

"I know you didn't mean what you said in the mine. None of it. You were angry, confused. I know you really care for them." My body trembling, I stall a quarter of the way onto the crest. "Devyn, please don't make me come all the way out there."

Her bare foot eases closer to the edge of the downstream slope, and I force myself to stand. "You're right," I say. "I need answers. I can't leave before I have them. You owe me that."

After a tense beat, she slowly takes a step back. "I thought you could be the answer. At least, to buy time." As she turns my way, she smiles. "They say when you get closer to the end stages, stamina kicks in. You can have bouts of clarity, where you don't feel sick, where you're symptomless." She strains to hold her smile, forlorn. "I just…needed more time."

A heavy layer of heartache bears down on my chest, and I blink away the sting of the wind behind my eyes. Devyn is in her late stages. She believed she could use this burst of stamina to convince Emmons that she ascended, that she was recovered.

"And then what after?" I ask, chancing a step closer. "Once you started to show signs of the disease again?"

"Maybe I wouldn't." She offers a small shrug. "I was really ill for five years, then I was better. What do doctors know? Nothing of the mind. I believed I could reach that higher state, if only Emmons would have trusted me." Her shoulders rise as she pulls in a breath. "But I destroyed him. You saw that room. You saw what he's done. The man I knew is gone, driven too far over the edge."

As she says this, she drapes her arm out over the literal edge, stopping my heart.

"I saw the room," I say, leaving only a couple feet between us, where I can reach out and grab her. "I also saw the cage. You were the one he trapped inside those bars, Devyn. And you're still locked inside."

Devyn angles her face toward me. "So let me be free."

I frantically clear my hair from my eyes. "Madness is welcomed over suffering and death," I say. "That's the escape, right?"

I'm speaking to her delusion, but I just have to get her off this fucking dam.

Her smile is shattering. "I'm already dead, Halen."

As she creeps closer to the side of the crest, panic flares within me. "I don't believe your brother lost hope, either," I blurt desperately. "You said his will was the strongest. I think he sacrificed himself for you, so you could be the one to ascend. Colter understood what Emmons didn't. He knew that there is no greater destruction than one of self, no catalyst more powerful to wield in alchemic creation." I use Kallum's words once again to reach her.

"Destruction isn't an end, it's a beginning," she says, her voice whisper-soft. Her eyes sheen with shimmery starlight reflected off the water as her gaze connects with mine.

"When Emmons sacrificed his brother, his act was selfish." I keep going, stoking that frail ember of hope.

"But your brother gave his life for you, Devyn. He gave *you* the gift."

I see it the moment she surrenders, the flicker of clarity that sparks in her eyes. "I miss him so much," she says.

A tear tracks down my cheek. "I know. I miss them, too," I say, referring to my family. Then I take the final step toward her. Reaching into my pocket, I bring out my necklace. I open the clasp and gently slip the chain around her slender neck, fastening the back.

"But we'll be connected forever," I tell her, the same words she said to me in that dark moment. "Two halves made whole through primordial unity, where we transcend beyond our pain."

Tentatively, she touches the diamond sitting in the hollow of her throat before she enfolds her arms around me. I embrace her, hugging my friend who I know I will never see again. Not in this lifetime.

The distinct sound of feet hitting the ladder rungs echos against the concrete, and I pull away. "Devyn, just go." At the worried draw of her features, I say, "I'll tell Agent Rana you went over the dam. They'll dredge for a body, but they won't find you."

He won't find you.

Understanding crystalizes in her dark eyes, and I see her suffering, the despair—knowing she'll be alone when she dies, but she also won't be locked away. It's a sliver of hope that I cling to.

Before she escapes, she embraces me once more, her mouth near my ear. "The Harbinger saw an omen, Halen. You'll figure it out."

I seal my eyes closed, not wanting the delusions to be

my last memory of her as I hold her close. I feel her pull away, and when I open my eyes, Devyn is gone.

With a shuddering breath to fill the aching cavity of my chest, I allow myself to feel the pain of her loss while I listen to their approach on the crest. Then, as I turn around, my gaze collides with his.

Blood stains the sharp spears of bone projecting from his head. His face bears deep cuts and contusions, the evidence of a fight to the death. His brawny chest is covered in streaks of blood and soot and mud. His eyes blaze with an unhinged, crazed intensity that steals my breath.

As I stare at Emmons, the horror of what his presence means crashes through me with a devastating violence.

Kallum.

"Where is she?" His words are delivered in a controlled manner.

Yet I hear nothing. Not the roar of his follow up demand. Not his enraged growl as he limps forward across the crest. The thundering beat of my heart cancels out everything. I'm drawn inward to some dark recess as the world descends into shadow.

The sigil on my thigh burns my skin as adrenaline pours into my blood.

Hand trembling, I touch the sleeve of Kallum's shirt, swallowing the painful ache as I drag the cuff up to feel the defaced script on my forearm. The sticky heat of fresh blood coats my skin.

Emmons comes to a halt before me, his massive frame towering over mine. "Where the fuck is Devyn?" he shouts.

My palm coated in red, I dig my nails into the wound and then rip the remaining stitched threads from the flesh of my arm. The pain is a sharp relief to the debilitating ache encasing my soul as I tear through each layer, ripping my wounds wide open. I let the blood flow, the pain bleeding out of me and igniting a furious frenzy.

I bring my fingers to my face and trace the contours along my cheekbones, smearing blood under the hollows of my eyes in a horrid depiction of the killer I once hunted.

I was Kallum's muse, although I never felt like one, especially after I killed the Harbinger. No, muses aren't supposed to inspire death. In that moment, I shed the layers as a victim of loss and became a huntress like Artemis, the goddess of the hunt and moon, a vengeful deity.

As the drums surge through me, I embrace the violence that wants to reap retribution. If Kallum is gone, then there's nothing left to inspire.

I wear the face of a killer as I go to meet the Harbinger in that abyss.

Slowly, with methodical, deliberate ease, I cast a look over the side of the dam, giving Emmons his answer. "She's down there."

"*No—*" he roars. Teeth clenched, he strikes quick. His hand snaps around my neck and he drags me closer, my toes scraping the rough surface of the dam. "Goddamn bitch…"

His words slash through me, and Wellington's mutilated face flashes across my vision. The pool of blood spreads, coating everything around us as his sinister voice rises up from the trenches of my mind: *I'll show you, bitch.*

The vise choking my throat tightens.

It's just a snatch of memory, but the overpowering deluge that comes with it leaves nothing in its wake but wild fury.

My throat constricted in the vise of his hold, I gasp around the crushing pressure. "I can't let the killer get away."

The words are plucked from another moment in time, an echo of the past. Delivered right now, they're vengeance personified.

Balanced on my toes, I sink the nails of one hand into his strained forearm and dig into my pocket with my other.

Emmons has two weaknesses: his blinding obsession, and his injured leg.

I use both to my advantage as I curl my fingers around the broken piece of antler in my pocket. "She's not a killer," I manage to whisper, my lungs burning for oxygen. "Not like us."

He pushes his face close to mine, where I can see the blown pupils of his eyes, the maniacal desperation. He's lost everything—and he's going to choke my life away.

I recognize this feeling, because it surges through me now with the strike of the drum. My lips curl into a manic smile as I jam my heel in his leg right above his knee. On reflex, he drops my feet to the concrete, and I drive the sharp point of the antler through the fleshy submental under his chin.

Stunned and off-kilter, Emmons releases my throat. He

stumbles back and claws at the bone. I don't give him time to recover.

"You'll never find her," I tell him as I brace my feet against the concrete and push off.

I crash into the solid wall of his chest to send us both over the dam.

The moment I go over the edge, arms band around my waist—the strong, familiar arms I recognize as he crushes my back to his chest.

A racked sob escapes as I twist in his locked embrace, needing to see his eyes, to know that he's really holding me now.

Against the darkness, I meet the striking blue and green embers of his gaze.

Kallum looks past the blood and tears as he swipes his thumb across my cheek. "I will never let you fall."

16

NIGHTS IN WHITE SATIN

KALLUM

The moody, smoky ambience is absent from Pal's Tavern, the pool tables vacant, the curved bar top abandoned. The establishment has been closed to the public in order to accommodate the FBI's task force unit now that the Hollow's Row Police Department is under investigation.

Seated under the softly lit lamp of one of the round tables, I prop my forearms on the lacquered walnut and spin the ring around my thumb, my gaze cast on the front door of the townie bar.

Slow and melodic folk music drifts from a jukebox along the far wall. The rising, emotive chorus competes with the news broadcast currently playing on the widescreen above the top shelf liquor bottles.

It appears that a doomsday has been averted in the small town of Hollow's Row, where just yesterday the FBI reported an end to their investigation of thirty-three missing residents and two suspects wanted in connection to ritualistic crime scenes incorporating human remains that resulted in the murder of a federal agent.

One of the suspects was confirmed to be police detective Dean Emmons, a native to the town and once beloved member of the community. Emmons died during a procedural pursuit that led authorities to the town's water treatment facility, where earlier the source had been contaminated with a fatally toxic strain of hemlock.

The facility was shut down when authorities arrived in time, preventing a disastrous event that could have ended in tragedy with a fatality rate in the thousands.

It's also being reported that a minor concentration of hallucinogens was discovered in the town's water supply, alleging its residence were under the influence of a highly susceptible substance. We'll be following this story closely as more information develops.

At this time, it's still unclear as to how many of the missing residents have been recovered alive. There is no update yet on the second suspect who evaded capture, but who is presumed to be dead. The whereabouts of the Harbinger killer have not been determined. A pending investigation into the offender's connection to the town is underway.

This case has many people questioning if this was the prophesied doomsday the Harbinger killer foreshadowed at the start of their killing spree. As it does seem Hollow's Row has in fact escaped a disastrous fate, maybe this town owes gratitude to not only the authorities, but the Harbinger, as well.

Next to me, my lawyer makes a sound of derision.

"Fucking serial killers and government cover-ups," Crosby mumbles before taking a swig of bourbon. "Locke, next time you decide to chase a girl to a small town, don't get me involved with the feds. Also, try for an island with white sand and blue water. Something tropical."

A wry smile tips my mouth. "Duly noted."

The FBI's press statement declaring hallucinogens in the water is one of the sloppiest cover-up attempts on their part. Of course, how else were they going to explain that the simple and good people of this town suddenly decided to dance naked around fires, mutilate animals and people, and bore implants into their heads to don antlers?

It also helps excuse the FBI's many missteps during the investigation.

The task force uncovered more houses with hidden crawlspaces that connected to the shafts of the mine. That, along with occult artifacts and secret living areas, solidified that most of the families of the missing locals were involved. Agent Rana's sub team had been closing in on Emmons, but before one brings in a law official for questioning and declares them a prime suspect, one really needs hard evidence. Unfortunately, the detective went MIA shortly before the torture chamber beneath Mrs. Lipton's house was uncovered.

After an intense twenty-four hour interrogation, Mrs. Lipton was the first to offer up details. The society started small, select. Devyn and Colter hosted gatherings and experimented in the first Dionysian rituals. Then as the society progressed, Colter declared thirty-three higher men was the number necessary to attain their ascension.

With the support of the Liptons, that goal was

achieved by recruiting people with incurable illnesses from within and outside of the town to be a part of their movement.

When the town reported the missing people five years ago, the fact they were sick was kept from the media. The families feared search efforts would stall once it was revealed they were terminal. Colter realized the families had to become a part of the movement, and shortly after, the town went silent, with more and more members being initiated to support some faction of the society. Like Tabitha the waitress, with her tiny antler nubs, earning her way up the hierarchy ladder.

When you have an affluent, influential family like the Liptons leading the charge, it makes it easier to go along with. And sometimes, all it takes is the tiniest spark of hope in a void of hopelessness.

Once Colter died, however, their society took a dark turn. While Devyn kept to her core belief system, Emmons verged into more extreme rituals, delving deeper and darker, risking the lives of members to attain the unattainable.

A sharp spasm of pain grips my side. I grunt as I adjust my position in the seat, trying to find relief for the tight dressing bandaged around my torso. I took one of Emmons' antlers right to my flank, resulting in two fractured ribs and several stitches, but sparing my major organs.

The door swings open, and all pain is forgotten as I look up, anticipation seizing the air in my lungs until I see Agent Rana walk through. I expel a heavy breath, not masking my disappointment as Hernandez hobbles in on crutches behind the group and takes the vacant seat next to me.

"She'll be here soon," he assures me, leaning his crutches against the table. The agent's leg was broken when he was hit by the truck. "She's getting discharged from the hospital."

I nod once. "Thanks."

"Sure." His faded brown eyes meet mine briefly, leaving something unsaid between us, before he flags down Pal to get a bottled water.

Whatever issue the agent had with me appears to have been resolved when I saved his life after the accident. As I sit here without an ankle monitor, I decide he also covered for me during his debriefing when he went on record to state Halen and I were abducted by Emmons' crew at the accident site.

I'm not sure how much Hernandez witnessed while he was drifting in and out of consciousness, but as there was no dead body when the task force arrived—only a wounded fed and discarded ankle monitor—the incident report basically wrote itself.

Coming face-to-face with death does have a way of clarifying one's existence. It's possible Hernandez has some plan for me later, but until then, I'll consider him a friend.

Across the table, Dr. Markus seats himself beside my field psychologist, who has annoyingly not left my company since she was recovered on the side of the road after the wreck. Though Dr. Keller was thoughtful enough to take her phone when she escaped the SUV before impact. As such, she was the one who placed the call to

Agent Rana, which in turn got the task force promptly canvasing the wetland.

I rotate my glass of bourbon on the table three times, my desire to will Halen through that fucking door becoming a compulsion. I need to lay eyes on her before I walk out of this bar.

A stack of paperwork slides into view, and I shift my focus to Rana opposite me. "Your account of events," she says. "And the renegotiated contract." She regards my lawyer with a sharp side-eye. "I just need your signature, then you're released."

She sends a pen my way, and I slap my hand over the felt-tip, keeping my palm flat on the tacky surface. I can feel Crosby's impatience rippling off him, ready to abandon this town.

I flip to the first page of the report summary and scan the fabricated details, our account of events a forgery of the finest fiction.

Halen and I fought off our abductors and fled to the facility to shut down the water supply. We were trailed by Emmons and Childs. Sheltered inside the facility, we both witnessed Emmons follow and attack Childs on the crest. Childs defended herself, resulting in them both going over the side of the dam.

Simple. Precise. Unemotional.

While the lie wasn't necessary to protect Halen—she had a legitimate claim to self-defense—she'd already underwent heavy scrutiny for Landry, and the story was necessary to declare Devyn deceased.

Most conveniently, the carving knife was recovered at the newest marsh ritual site—wiped clean of prints and DNA—backing the theory that someone on the inside removed the murder weapon from the evidence room. As Jake Emmons' crime scene was staged to replicate one of the Harbinger's scenes, it's being documented by Agent Rana that either Emmons or Childs was the perpetrator who killed and mutilated Agent Alister.

It will be released in an upcoming press statement that the Harbinger was never in Hollow's Row.

Case closed.

I tap the pen on the table in rhythmic beats to the music, drumming up the memory of Halen bathed in firelight, swirled symbols smeared by the tears on her beautiful face, right before I told her to run. I had to let her go to protect her in more ways than one. An unselfish act that spared this town its damned fate.

Unselfish. Something I once thought I could never be with her.

The truth is, if all those innocent lives were lost, Halen wouldn't be able to sustain that level of guilt. Not when there was a chance to save them.

For her, I've played by the rules for the FBI and this town. Well, for the most part. But I'm officially done with being a good little leashed consultant.

I scrawl my name across the bold line, then slide both the pen and documents over to Rana.

"On behalf of the Federal Bureau of Investigation, we thank you for your service, Professor Locke." She tucks the binder away in her leather case, then looks me in the eyes. "Don't take this personally, but I hope to never see you again."

285

A smirk hitches the corner of my mouth. "I would think it would be the other way around, agent."

Her smile is genuine. "As I'm officially off the clock, I'd like a drink."

Crosby plants his hands on the table and rises from his chair. "Well, everyone, while it's been eventful, it's time for me and my client to depart—"

The door opens, and for a suspended heartbeat, all sounds of the bar fade away. I touch my chest, my heart knocking painfully against my sore rib cage as my gaze connects with hers.

Crosby groans and reseats himself. He then lifts his hand to summon Pal. "I'll take another."

"I second that," I say, my gaze not wavering from Halen as she walks toward the table. Still so breathtaking despite her wounded appearance. Rather, with the bruises dusting her face, I find her even more alluring, strong. A bandage wraps her forearm. Her hair spills in loose waves over her shoulders. She carries her tote in one hand, a notebook tucked under her arm.

"I don't think you should drink while medicated for pain," Dr. Keller admonishes me with a stern glare.

Halen rests her bandaged hand on the doctor's seat-back. "He's not medicated," she says, holding my gaze. "Professor Locke doesn't like to dull his senses."

My smile stretches. My little seer is starting to see right through me. Anticipation to get her alone nearly has me upending this table, but more than ever, the next sequence of events requires patience.

For now, seeing her here, looking into her hazel eyes and knowing there is a next has to be enough.

"Can I get you a drink, Halen?" Rana asks, her address informal.

As Halen carefully eases into a seat, she shakes her head. "Uh, no, but thank you. I am very medicated."

Hernandez offers Halen a friendly nod as drinks are delivered. Conversation strikes up around the table, a customary tension breaker at the end of the case. My gaze falls to the notebook Halen sets on the table, noting the town name and date. The Harbinger killer's third crime scene.

After half a beer, Rana lets it slip that Tabitha revealed the bodies of the deceased missing locals were being stored in the diner fridge units until the organs and other parts could be utilized in the ritual offerings.

"Jesus, we ate there," Hernandez says, expression horrified.

"That was the least appalling thing uncovered," Rana says. Placing the amber bottle on the table, she picks at the label with a tight frown. "Mrs. Lipton stated that Emmons killed his brother while aware there was a possible treatment for him."

A tense silence thickens the air at the revelation.

"He had to make an exchange," I say, my gaze falling on Halen. "A sacrifice isn't a sacrifice unless it causes you pain. He chose to sacrifice one person he loved to save the other."

Halen's glassy eyes fix on me before she swallows and says, "It explains why Emmons was so dejected, becoming increasingly mentally unstable. Killing an innocent person can attribute to that."

I watch her closely, observing the way she traces her

finger over the notebook cover, her speculative thoughts turning inward.

"Murder of any kind can do that," Hernandez states, his tone gruff, his gaze purposely aimed away from me.

Halen releases a soft sigh. "When I first came here, I swore this town felt evil. But there are only evil acts. Imperfect people using knowledge imperfectly. Intent to protect the person you care for is harmless, until it's not."

I lower my glass of bourbon. "You can be a saint, but you still have the potential to be the devil."

Halen's gaze flicks up to capture me as I quote Jung for her sake. A measured beat stretches where we stay locked together, the stirring music rising around us, her sweet, addictive melancholy aching within the core of my chest.

"Carl Jung," Dr. Markus announces, effectively interrupting the moment. "I always took some issue with his doctrines in college." This garner's my attention, and I lift an eyebrow. "Now Nietzsche said, 'Man is the cruelest animal'. Fittingly stated, I think, for this case incorporating his philosophy."

Smugly, he takes a sip of his drink. Halen tilts her head, eyes flared wide, as if sending me a warning not to engage. How can I resist?

"Christ," Rana mutters. "I can't believe I'm looking forward to the next case that doesn't involve philosophy."

Unfazed, Dr. Markus barrels forward. "Now I am still curious about the philosophy of the town as a whole. Mrs. Lipton didn't have the body modifications to indicate she was a part of the society. How many others like her still reside here? It's impossible to know how many of the residents were involved."

"In retrospect, Mrs. Lipton's penchant for parties is very Dionysian." I grab the knot of my necktie and straighten my spine, earning a little sprite glare from Halen. "I said in retrospect." I smile, giving her a pop of dimple to distract her, because I know it melts her a little. "And I don't know, Dr. Markus, the folk music playing around this town might give us some indication as to the level of involvement."

He pushes his glasses up the bridge of his nose. "I'm sorry, I don't understand, Professor Locke."

"Nietzsche associated folk music with Dionysus, saying every period rich in folk songs has been most violently stirred by Dionysian currents."

While all eyes slowly shift to the jukebox, Halen's gaze remains trained on me, a charged current snapping between us. I send her a wink before I glance over at Pal to give him a small nod.

Then I drain the last dregs of my bourbon and set the glass down with finality, having made peace with my disdainful relationship with Nietzsche.

Halen once asked me whether or not I believed the man truly went mad. I can't claim to have deciphered any shattering insight from his works, but it was there in his personal letters, the ones he sent to his friends, family, colleagues. The coded message of his life, and his quest.

In a letter, the troubled philosopher once wrote: *Unless I discover the alchemists' trick of turning this filth into gold, I am lost.*

I do believe Nietzsche sought the philosopher's stone,

and I do believe he lost his mind in the process. In the end, what ultimately drove him past the brink wasn't his descent into his depths. It was his isolation, his loneliness. If he'd had some sort of touchstone, he might have been able to pull himself out.

That is our human condition, our great wound, our need to be connected. Even the greatest minds suffer this affliction.

A chiming ringtone sounds from a phone, and Halen retrieves the device from her back pocket and taps the screen. "My lift to the airport is here." With a wan smile, she stands and says her goodbyes. I watch her, spinning my ring, my chest on fire until she turns my way.

"Goodbye, Professor Locke."

"Safe travels, Dr. St. James."

As Halen retreats toward the exit, Rana follows after her, stopping her at the door. The agent speaks to Halen in private, setting my senses on alert. With a groan, I reach over and offer my hand to Hernandez.

He looks at it with a raised eyebrow before he accepts the gesture.

"Thoreau said, the language of friendship is not words, but meanings," I say to him, able to produce a tight-lipped smile. "Actually, I just don't have shit to say."

"What-the-fuck ever, that's a first." He grips my hand tighter. "You better take care of her, Locke."

I nod once with sincerity before I turn to my lawyer. "Call my FBI escorts. You can meet me out front."

Crosby audibly sighs. "About fucking time."

Passing Rana, I push through the door in chase after Halen, finding her standing with her suitcase on the sidewalk, wearing an expectant expression as she looks straight at me. Then a beautiful smile curls her lips.

I touch my bandaged side, then drive a hand through my hair. "What did Rana say?"

Halen shakes her head. "Nothing important." The SUV idles behind her, and I swear to god, watching her take that small step toward the vehicle feels like she's being severed from my sternum.

"Halen, wait—"

She turns my way again. "I will be. For three months."

I let a smoldering, lopsided smile grace my mouth.

A feverish blush sweeps through her skin as she tucks her notebook under her arm. I look pointedly at the journal before I eat the remaining steps between us and feather the defiant streak of white behind her ear.

History repeats itself. Before I walked off the ritual ground, after Halen began to recover her memory, I told her I'd wait for her. What I didn't tell her was for how long I'd already been waiting, and that I'd never stop.

As I trace her delicate jawline, I let the pad of my thumb taste her lips. "You'll be there."

"I'll be there," she says, then she disappears into the depths of the SUV.

It's the connection of the twin flame. Once your other half is found, if divided, it will consume and devour everything in its path like the fires of hell to be reunited.

It's the course.

17

MOTH TO A FLAME

HALEN

O bsessions die hard.

For the past three months, I've been meticulously linking the Harbinger's victims to Percy Wellington. The connections between the Harbinger killer and his victims weren't obvious, unless you knew where the first domino toppled, then the rest of the tiles started to fall into place.

It took time to uncover Wellington's dealings with the victims, but there is always a rational, logical explanation for the unexplained.

The first Harbinger crime scene: Oxford, Maine casino location. The victim was a loan shark who had a reputation to "do away" with his defaulted clients. A deep dive into Wellington's financials uncovered that he owed the victim a substantial amount of money for a gambling debt.

The second Harbinger crime scene: New Haven, Connecticut recovery center location. The center owner was notorious for extorting patients. During Wellington's private stint at this facility for his alcohol and gambling addiction, the owner blackmailed Wellington with a threat to ruin his reputation with the university.

The third Harbinger crime scene: Medford, Massachusetts university location. The victim turned out to be a high-end drug dealer Wellington played poker with, and who'd had an affair with Wellington's wife.

Notably, Wellington's victims were not the best of society. But without a prime suspect to investigate, none of these connections could be linked. The Harbinger letters left behind at the scenes offered no clues to the suspect. The foreshadowed "doomsday" now appears to be little more than Wellington ridding himself of the people who posed a threat to his life, his career, even his marriage.

The solved mystery, oftentimes, is less enthralling and fascinating.

The case will never officially be closed. Not without a suitable scapegoat to take the fall for Wellington's murder. There may still be a way to offer some form of closure, but to do that, I need to enlist the expertise of a particular professor.

I stand outside the entrance of the Graystone Institute, my arms tucked close to my chest, shivering despite my thick coat and gloves. It's been ninety days since Kallum and I parted at Pal's Tavern and he refused visitation, adamant that we'd never again meet inside an "asylum," though the mental health and wellness hospital is more of a country club compared to Briar.

When the glass door slides open and Kallum emerges,

I realize the reason I'm shivering has nothing to do with the frigid Massachusetts weather.

Dressed in a heavy wool overcoat, his sophisticated suit beneath clashing strategically with his combat boots, Kallum is smoldering desire wrapped in designer attire. Immediately, I'm rendered defenseless against his devastating smile. As his striking blue-and-green eyes sweep over me, I feel him all over, igniting a hot ache between my thighs.

"Dammit." While we have spoken over the phone during the length of his stay, it's easy to forget how affecting Kallum is in person. How when his long strides close the distance between us and he drops his bags to bracket either side of my face, I'm lost to him all over again.

He says nothing at first, choosing instead to touch his lips to mine in a tender, familiarizing kiss. His mouth coaxes mine into a more demanding caress before his tongue glides over my bottom lip, tasting me, owning me.

His soft lips track across my jawline, where he nuzzles his face into my hair and breathes me in. "Just as sweet," he says, the baritone of his voice sparking an electric current beneath my skin.

I swallow hard against the pressure of his palms. "I still don't understand why you refused to see me."

He straightens to his full height, forcing me to crane my neck as he locks me in his sure gaze. "Having you right in front of me and being unable to touch you... That's a torment I choose to no longer bear, Halen." He flashes me a crooked smile. "Come on. You're freezing, and I'm anxious to get the stench of this place off me."

We load his bags into the back of my Rav4, which I specifically acquired to make the climb up the Berkshires. I click the fob to close the rear lift-gate, my gaze lingering on the boxes wedged between my luggage.

The drive to Great Barrington takes just under two hours. As I turn off the highway, I can feel the press of Kallum's stare. "Did you decide if you're going back?"

The president of the university offered Kallum his previous position. As he was never found guilty of murder, and he did aide in an investigation that helped save a whole town, I suppose Professor Locke is just too much of an academic commodity, making his time served in a mental institution easily overlooked.

"No," he says evenly. "Not sure I want to return to a lecture hall."

I nod knowingly. After watching Kallum work a case, I find it difficult to picture him in a classroom setting. Especially now that he's had a taste of danger.

"Are you working a current scene?" he asks, angling his body my way.

I shake my head and glance over at him in the passenger seat. "I just wrapped one up two days ago. I'm kind of between places."

"What case?"

Since the news out of Hollow's Row, I've been contacted by police departments, the feds, private investigators, and even one psychic medium to help solve cases.

"A cold case, actually." I grip the steering wheel tighter. "I find I like helping to solve the cases that would otherwise languish without answers, being able to give closure."

He makes a sound of acknowledgement, his gaze drifting over me deliberately.

While the scenic drive up the mountainside comes with breathtaking views, I was hoping for the stunning oranges and reds that blanket the peaks and valleys during the fall. Instead, it's the bleak winter sky with tufts of white and barren, leafless trees that remind me too much of the marsh.

Nestled high in the Berkshire Mountain range amid rocky outcroppings and tall trees, the renovated chalet comes into view. Both rustic and elegant, Kallum's home is like a modern work of art banked on the side of the mountain incline.

Once inside, the interior is awe-inspiring. Stained black cedar contrasts with natural wood tones. An open floorplan with window walls wrap the home, surrounding us with frozen nature and views of the ridge.

"God, this is impressive, and intimidating." I shed my coat as I spin in a circle, taking in the leather mixed with delicate textiles. A double-sided stone and metal fireplace anchors the space of the first floor. Alongside it, a vertical firewood rack stacked with logs ascends the wall.

"I thought about stealing you away here more than once," he says, capturing me with a devious smile. Then he has me in his arms. The perfectly right feel of his body enveloping mine triggers an ache deep in my chest. "Take a shower with me."

I lick my lips, and his gaze drops heavy on my mouth.

"I want this part over, done," I say, my eyes flitting to the fireplace.

We had agreed to do this together. The issue of trust wasn't raised, but since discovering Kallum kept an article of my clothing from that night—which he had his lawyer relocate here after the search of his residences was concluded—I decided it's important for both of us to be present.

He releases a lengthy sigh before he places a kiss to my forehead. "You're right. Give me five minutes." He disappears down a side hallway, leaving me with the silent fall of snow from all around.

I expel the trapped breath from my lungs before I get to work. After I've lugged the boxes from the vehicle and stacked them near the raised stone hearth, I open the screen and use a remote to light the fire. To ensure the flames burn hot enough, I wedge additional tinder between the artificial firelogs.

This feels strangely ironic, as the last time Kallum and I were preparing to destroy evidence, I was the one in the shower while he built a fire. Kallum would say history repeats itself. At the thought, a chill prickles my skin despite the warmth.

While I wait, I walk to the backlit wet bar and debate between water and liquor. "Fuck it," I mutter and grab an expensive-looking bottle of bourbon and pour a shot into a rocks glass. Then I kneel before the fireplace and set the glass on the hearth.

As I drag the first file box toward me, the second box vies for my attention, the contents within where I need Kallum's input. But first...

I tow the lid off and remove the evidence of Alister's assault on me. I withdraw the torn shirt I was wearing at the time and toss it on top of the logs. The skin cells I scraped from beneath my nails I sprinkle in next.

I watch the flames lick higher, the smell of smoke mentally luring me back to the marshland. Filling my lungs, I look through the window at the veil of snow glittering beneath the moonlight. Then I drag over the second box and lift the unlocked lid.

The sweatshirt Kallum gave me rests on top. I touch the sleeve, my thumb rubbing the soot stain absently as the firelight dances in my periphery to transport me back to that night.

My spine straightens at the sound of Kallum entering the room. Resigned, I push the box aside and toss back the whiskey to steel my nerves. Then I stand and face him.

The beat of my heart scales to a frantic pulse in my veins as I absorb the sight of him in only a pair of black joggers. I track the shaded blackwork tattoos covering the sculpted contours of his chest and arms, the healed-over scar along his side, down to the defined V-shaped abdominal muscles that descend beneath his waistband.

In one hand, he holds the shirt I was wearing the night I killed Wellington. In his other, the obsidian knife he used to sever the head.

Alcohol burns through my bloodstream, bolstering my steps toward him as I sweep my thermal over my head and let it drop to the floor.

His gaze devours every exposed inch of skin, his nostrils flare as I come to a stop just before him. I place my hands to the solid plane of his chest, his skin still warm from the hot shower, his hair wet and dark, his scent of spicy sandalwood heady and so overwhelmingly *Kallum* that a broken sound escapes as my hands wander over the scarred sigils carved in his flesh.

A muscle jumps along his tense jaw. "What about the evidence disposal?"

"Later," I say, my voice as raw as my hunger for him. "I want you to make love to me, Kallum."

A rough groan sounds from deep in his throat. "Fuck."

Letting the objects in his hands fall to the floor, he slips his fingers beneath the straps of my bra and tows the garment down until I'm bared to him. The caged beast unleashed, he lowers down to grasp the backs of my thighs and lifts me against him. His mouth covetously seals over mine as he carries me toward the fire and sinks to his knees, where he splays me out before him.

He prowls over my body like a starved animal prowling over its prey. The empty black eyes in the skull of the stag look right into me, and I stare back into those hollow sockets as I drag my hands across Kallum's inked skin, nails raking in hunger's wake.

Kallum makes love to me on the rug near the fire. And it's violent and passionate and tender, every touch branded to own, to possess. He buries himself inside me, his hips heavy between my thighs, the weight of his body a familiar comfort. A fierce growl is torn from the cavern of his chest as he rolls his hips and slams inside me.

Yearning and heartache are so similar in nature, the fiery ache of one easily exchanged for the other. I cling to his shoulders, consumed by the inferno as our bodies reconnect.

We're both at the brink too soon, his thrusts increasing with force. He allows me to roll on top of him and straddle his hips. I shove his hands over his head and bear down on his wrists.

"Goddamn…" His tone is coarse, his thrusts driving up against me in desperate need.

This is the only time Kallum drops his guard enough not to see my next move.

I lower my face close to his, my eyes holding his bound as I say, "You never asked my name."

As I stare into his intense gaze, I watch as it slowly registers, the understanding of what I'm saying.

"That night, you never asked my name, Kallum."

Two things happen at once: I reach under the box and grab the handcuffs, latching one steel shackle around his wrist and the other to the metal bar of the wood rack. Kallum gets one arm banded around my lower back and drives his hips up to slam inside me with vicious, decimating thrusts. I seal my eyes closed.

"Look at me," he growls.

My eyes instantly open, and an orgasm grips me, tearing through my body as I clench around the hard length of him. His muscles contract, and I feel him release deep inside me, his groan rumbling against my chest as I tremble through the peak of my climax.

A cruel and beautiful smile slants his mouth. "There you are, darkness."

I pull back, slowly slipping farther out of his reach. The snow continues to fall in a hushed tone outside the windows, further insulating us as I quietly pull on my clothes.

"You said when the case was closed, you'd reveal every dark truth to me." I toss Kallum his joggers. "It's time to honor our deal."

He sits up against the fireplace, his wrist handcuffed to the rack, his back to the flames. "I never asked, because I knew your name already, Halen St. James."

I blink and nod, my thoughts churning as I cross my arms. "Question everything," I say, my voice low, "the chance of our meeting, how you came into my life, even how long I've known you. Question everything...even the first time we met."

"Oh, how I love the story of us." He studies me closely, trying to gauge just how much of my memory I've recovered. "I might love it even more that you're finally carrying handcuffs."

"The longer I questioned, there were things that I just couldn't reconcile," I say, a shiver still clinging to my body as I let my thoughts tumble out. "In the university parking lot, you said, 'come back to me.' After you found me covered in blood, you said it just like that. The way you did when you carved a sigil in my thigh during the ritual, and in the SUV after the wreck—but it was then when it struck me, how odd of a thing that is to say to someone you've only just encountered. Then on the terrace, you said the first time you saw me was in the setting sun. Yet it was night when Wellington attacked me. So if I question everything, even the timeline, then all the hints you arrogantly dropped during the Hollow's Row case start to paint a different picture."

Kallum rattles the handcuff against the bar. "You know I'll get free of this."

I nod again, swallowing hard. "A magician with a bag of tricks. I'm well aware of your skills, Professor Locke. But first, I'm going to get what I came here for."

I rub my thumb over the slashed scar on my palm, feeling the recurring pang in my chest. This has become a compulsion, like touching the verse on my forearm used to be.

As I remove the sweatshirt from the file box, I again touch the soot on the fabric. Then I hold the gray garment up to Kallum.

"Another detail that kept bothering me was how I managed to get soot on the sleeve. I would've had to reach into the fire, but why?" At his intentional silence, I square my shoulders. "Then I remembered seeing it drop to the bottom of the fireplace. I reached in, but it was too hot. When I stood to grab the fire poker, there was a cufflink sitting right there on your mantel. Not the one that I brought with me from the crime scene. Not the one that I had put in my pocket before the attack, that was then burning through my bloodstained jeans. But the *matching* cufflink to the pair." I take a breath to fill my lungs. "And I realized as I stared into the flames...in a solitary moment of terror...it was all too convenient. How easily you went along with the staging of the scene. How you spurred me on to kill him. How you made me an accomplice."

I knock over the box. The contents of the third Harbinger crime scene spill across the rug.

"I asked you if you were the Harbinger killer," I say, my chest rising and falling quickly. "I looked into your eyes, past the blood and mask of a killer, and I said you weren't the Harbinger. You never corrected me."

He tilts his head to the side. "You didn't want me to."

I huff a derisive breath. Kneeling down, I pluck out the one piece of evidence that, the moment I spotted it, stopped my heart. Angling the printed picture toward Kallum, I point to the foreground. "You were framing Wellington as the Harbinger killer."

The picture was taken that same day while I was photographing the scene. In the background of the image —once zoomed in—is a man dressed in a stylish, all-black suit with distinct, identifying tattoos marking his hand.

"You were there," I accuse him. "First you stole Wellington's cufflinks, then you planted one at the third crime scene. It had the college insignia and his initials. Once discovered, it would've been easy to trace the evidence back to Wellington and name him the prime suspect of the Harbinger killings."

Kallum licks his lips, and a faint smile twists the corner of his mouth up. "I'd offer a slow clap but—" He yanks at the handcuff to emphasize his bound state.

"The best I can figure, you were on your way to plant the other cufflink in Wellington's car when you stumbled across me being assaulted in the parking lot. But that raises another question: why not just leave the cufflink behind after the murder in the first place? Why chance returning to the scene of the crime later?"

He doesn't look away, waiting for me to string the connections on the figurative murder board.

"The evidence couldn't be recovered too quickly," I say, reasoning. "You had to make sure that investigators were on the scene first. Specifically, one person you wanted to find that evidence. Only, I wasn't supposed to go to the campus alone. I wasn't supposed to show up at night, ruining your scheme."

"That did throw a tire iron into the plan." Kallum smirks arrogantly. "Luckily, the universe had a far better plan for us."

"Ha, yeah. The universe." I nod slowly. "The universe didn't do any of this, Kallum. You did."

He shrugs a shoulder. "Sometimes the universe needs a little help."

"Where is it?" I demand. "Where is the cufflink? The one that I left behind in your fireplace when I ran out of your townhouse after I realized I'd killed an innocent man."

"Innocent is a stretch for Wellington."

I clench my hands as I try to control my rapid inhalations. Eventually, I did recover most of my memory from that night. By the time I made it back to my hotel room, shock and sleep deprivation wreaking havoc, I buried everything into a filing box, thinking I could bury my guilt. It wasn't that I had killed a man that shattered my mind; it was that I had killed an *innocent* man.

And I had done so with the Harbinger.

"While you never cease to impress me, sweet Halen, you're still missing a key piece."

I lift my chin defiantly. "And that's exactly what I came here to get."

But first, I have to understand the madness of the man.

I sit in the leather chair across from him and look over into the fire. "Wellington was always a part of the equation, just not as the actual killer. He was supposed to be the scapegoat. You always have to have a scapegoat. So in order to solve the equation, we have to have the unknown variable." I lock with his severe gaze. "Me."

He captures me with that irresistible smolder, and I hate how it affects me, how my heart squeezes. I stand and pace the room, my gaze cast down at the floor, letting my thoughts take me back to that moment with Kallum in the killing fields when he brought up the Harbinger case.

"Atropos, Lachesis, and Styx," I recite. "Three species of the death's-head hawkmoth. All from the Greek mythos, and all associated with the underworld, with death. When I said the species of the moth was irrelevant to the Harbinger case, you made sure to point this out to me, that the Acherontia moth is an omen of death." I glance up at him. "I didn't understand what you were trying to tell me at the time, but I do know you never say anything randomly. There's always a reason."

As his gaze roves over me, a sly smile brightens his features. "God, you're brilliant. No one else could've put this together, Halen."

"I keep trying to understand why you chose the moth, why you devised such elaborate, macabre scenes, how they connected to Wellington. I just couldn't understand your reasoning, so I went back to the Harbinger letters. They were too vague, some obscure riddle. At first, once I linked the victims to Wellington, I thought they were only meant to denote his doomsday. That's what the authorities were supposed to glean from them, right?"

The setup looks like Wellington was killing off people who could hurt him financially and career-wise. Kallum is, quite literally, a genius. His victim selection process was meticulously tailored to Wellington, a gift wrapped package for law officials to make their case.

"Care to elaborate?" I prompt him.

"Only if you whip out the sharp objects so we can put these cuffs to good use."

At my refusal to be baited by his charm, Kallum shifts his gaze to the flickering flames. "It was like it was predestined," he says. "Percy Wellington set himself up the first day he walked into my lecture hall. He laid the foundation for the Harbinger in that room, with his ideals and talk of doom." He smiles to himself. "Percy was already a monster. I just gave him a moniker."

I shake my head. "But that doesn't explain the letters, Kallum."

He reacts to my use of his name, his throat working to force a swallow.

"What were the letters—?"

"They were love letters." His gaze snaps to me as his words compress the tense atmosphere to a point.

My throat tight, I swallow past the torrid ache. "To me," I say to clarify. "They were love letters to me."

He nods once.

My thoughts drift back as I recall what Kallum said to me that night in the marsh, when he opened himself up about his fear of losing me: *All risk poses a threat of ruin. If you want to destroy me, don't take your next breath.* His wording was just similar enough to the phrasing in the Harbinger letters.

"You were always trying to tell me," I say as I swipe my hair from my vision. "The letters were about me, an omen for my future doomsday. My death."

Devyn said I would figure it out—and I thought she was the delusional one.

"To prevent your death, Halen," he says, offering further clarity.

"I still don't understand how—"

"Yes, you do."

And somehow, I do. Because to follow that lead, we have to go all the way back to the very first moment I laid eyes on Kallum Locke—to the moment we *almost* met.

A year prior to that fateful night, in the university courtyard, as I stood there laughing with my parents, I glanced across the quad and my gaze connected with his.

As was their tradition, my parents always visited their *alma mater* on their anniversary. And that day, I came with them. I was having doubts about marrying Jackson. We'd had another argument. Always about my job. He hated what I did, had confessed that it frightened him, but I knew I couldn't *not* work the cases.

And as I spun my engagement ring around my finger, my fears cresting, my desire to escape mounting, I looked over and right into the strikingly beautiful blue-and-green embers of Kallum's eyes.

It was only an instant—one suspended moment in time —but something in the universe, in me, altered.

I would later forget about those fleeting seconds when my world fell apart the very next day at the news of my parents' death. But somewhere in my unconscious, that memory was imprinted.

Kallum uses his index finger to spin the silver ring around his thumb. "It was your laugh that first captured my attention," he says. "I was spellbound. Then when I saw you, I fucking swear, you upended everything I ever thought I knew or believed. *He whom love touches not walks in darkness.* It might be arrogant of me"—he flicks his gaze up—"but I would amend Plato's *Symposium* to, he whom love touches not walks in darkness alone."

The ache in the center of my chest becomes almost unbearable. "Kallum, please…"

"Because there will always be darkness," he continues, undeterred, "there will always be pain, and suffering. But it's not bearing it alone that makes life endurable. Because of you, I now understand that."

He rests his forearm on his drawn knee, a vein tics in his neck. "I was addicted from the first sweet, melancholic hit of you. I wanted to keep breathing for the first fucking time in my life. I wanted to walk right up to you, to talk to you—"

"Why didn't you?" I demand.

"Your ring." The slight pull of his mouth is almost bitter. "Trust me, I've been punished endlessly for my weakness in that moment. I know I failed you, and I've been trying to make amends ever since." The dejection in his tone tightens my chest. "But right then, I thought we had all the time."

I nod knowingly. "Keep going."

"When you returned to the campus the next day, as you walked the grounds, retracing your parents' steps, trying in vain to find the culprit of the hit-and-run, I watched you and your fucking pain choked the goddamn air from my lungs and I knew. Because I could *feel* you—" He breaks off with a sigh. "The only lie I've ever told you is that I never thought of taking a life before you. I have. My own.

That's how I recognized it in you, that same destructive desire. Yours tore through me with such violent force, I had little choice in what I did next." He tilts his chin up, his eyes darkening. "Out of my fear, the Harbinger was created."

Unable to hold his eyes, I bow my head, hearing Kallum in the night-cloaked marsh all over again, seeing him look right into my depths, flaying the darkest part of me wide open, as he confessed his fear.

"You want me to believe that, because of your fear that I'd take my own life, you started a killing spree."

"Not a spree. Three murders. My gift to you," he says, and my stomach dips. "Performing the ritualistic killings to stave off a future doomsday. An event to wipe out humanity." His eyes bore into mine. "Your humanity, your life, Halen."

The truth unfolds like a gruesome crime scene layered with blood, and violence, and twisted shadows.

Unable to stare directly into that vile truth, I turn toward the wet bar, desperate for a drink, an escape.

"More than any light, you needed that darkness to chase." His voice halts my steps. I keep my back to him as he continues. "You needed a reason to wake up, to keep going, to keep breathing. You needed the hunt. The obsession. And it had to be special, a case worthy of you." I spin around to meet his eyes. "You needed a villain to punish."

I shake my head slowly, as if I can make him stop.

But he doesn't. "To keep you alive, I didn't just sell my soul, Halen. I became the goddamn devil himself for you."

Fury gathers my muscles tight. "And in making me an accomplice, I became just as wicked as you."

His smile is sinful. "What do you think the muse of the devil looks like, sweetness?"

A tremor of fear lifts the fine hairs away from my skin. I will my erratic pulse to calm. "Where is the cufflink?" I demand, more adamant this time. I need this proof—this tangible piece of evidence to know that I haven't lost my fucking mind. "Tell me, Kallum."

With deliberate, slow movements, keeping his gaze fused to mine, Kallum brings his left hand to his right. Then he removes the silver ring from his thumb.

I watch, my heart punching through the cage of my chest, as he places the ring on the stone hearth.

The crackling fire is muted beneath the roar in my ears as I carefully hedge toward the gleaming object. I pick up the ring and turn it over in my fingers. The inside of the band is worn, the silver plating dull and faded to reveal the gold hidden beneath.

I'm pulled into my memories, thinking back to my first conversation with Kallum. Standing together on the campus grounds, the setting sun falling behind him, the crisp smell of fall and his woodsy cologne imbuing the air. And I recall, with a startling realization, that he wasn't wearing the ring.

"I had it melted down before the trial," he says, answering my unspoken question.

Shaken out of my reverie, I lift my gaze—and my blood runs cold.

Kallum stands before the fire, the handcuffs discarded

311

on the rug. A dangerous current charges the air as he drops a piece of metal to the floor.

"You seem to always forget that I can feel you," he says, his expression void of emotion. "I felt you outside the institute and the whole way up here. That vortex of conflicting emotions. Thought I might need a few things in my pocket just in case."

Chest heaving, air escaping too quickly to catch a breath, I take a step backward.

He moves in sync, one daring step toward me. "You know the rule about running—"

"Run fast." The words have barely left my mouth before I dart in the opposite direction.

The house is dark. The moonlight reflecting off the snow casts the interior in an eerie glow, yet not bright enough to light my path through the hallways. I use the wall as my guide and dash into a room, immediately slamming the door shut behind me.

Kallum catches the corner of the panel. I retreat as he throws the door wide. He advances on me, his steps eating the small span of distance in three long strides.

We've been here before.

Only this time, there's no monitor wrapping his ankle. No agents to burst into the room.

No one to stop him.

My back flattens to the wall, and Kallum pushes into my space until he's towering over me. He secures my wrists and pins my hands above my head. His nostrils flare as he traps me in his heated, predatory gaze.

His mouth descends on mine, kissing me with bruising demand, before he breaks away. "You want the truth so badly, yet you're always running from it, little Halen. That sweet, sweet fear so goddamn tantalizing." His claim is delivered in a low, deadly tone to rattle my heart.

Pulse crashing against my veins, I breathe heavily through my nose. "You let Emmons attack me," I accuse around a ragged breath. "Just like Landry, when you watched him strangle me."

He presses his ring into my palm. The scar flares hot at the feel of him closing my fingers around the cool object. "Every time, you get a little closer to unlocking that truth."

"Just tell me the *truth*—" I shout. The threat of angry tears stings behind my eyes. There's still one piece missing —the final connection that needs to be made—and Kallum is the only one who can give me that. "Why don't I regret killing Wellington?" I hold his lethal stare. "Even now? Why? Am I a fucking monster?"

Kallum drags his thumb down the inside of my wrist, and I clench the ring tighter.

"Because I have to be," I say, the words torn through a racked sob. "Because even after everything you've done... god, I'm still in love with you."

For the briefest second, his expression shifts. The subtle groove between his brows deepens. A hard swallow tenses his jaw. Then his heavy exhale traces a path down the contours of my throat in the wake of his heated gaze.

He links my wrists together in one hand and drops his other to my collarbone, his touch branding. "Trust me."

That's the only warning I'm given before his hand collars my throat. The sudden pressure ramps my heart rate. My eyes flare wide. "Kallum—"

"Think back." His tone is a gruff command. "Go back

to that moment right before he attacked you. Wellington said something to you. What was it that set you off, Halen?"

He squeezes, his grip on my throat constricting my airway, and adrenaline pours into my bloodstream.

"What did he say that made you swing that weapon?"

Crushing pressure builds in my chest until my vision darkens. Like a reel flicking between past and present, the features of the man before me harden into the face of another—his dark, furious eyes seething with rage, his teeth gnashed and his breath as vile as his twisted features.

During Emmons' attack on the dam, something was triggered. There was a fragment right on the periphery, a tease of a memory that felt within my grasp—and as Kallum seals off the air from my lungs, that moment in time crashes to the surface

Then suddenly, it's Percy Wellington strangling my neck.

"I'll show you, bitch."

Blackness rims my sight as I gasp for air. I'm tunneling under too fast. As desperation claws my insides, I kick out, trying to break free, but the vise around my neck only cinches tighter. Then I feel the anguish take hold.

I was ready to stop fighting, to give in and let go. Until…

"Are you an investigator?" The man's breath reeks of alcohol. "Did that slut send you?" His callous laugh elicits a spark of anger. "Are you here for that couple? That fucking wreck?" he seethes through clenched teeth, his hands closing tighter around my throat. "It was an

accident. You'll never prove anything. I'll make sure of that."

"*Oh, god.*" I merely mouth the words, frantic for air that won't come as bile burns like acid at the back of my throat.

The reel won't stop flipping. I see my thumbs mash his eyes. I feel the heaviness of the tool in my hand. I feel the iron reverberate off his skull.

I see the blood.

My vision blurs as tears well in my eyes, and I'm pleading for the images to *stop*.

With a fierce groan, Kallum releases me, freeing my throat and wrists at once. I fall against his chest and swallow down air into my deprived lungs, hungrily breathing in his scent. He presses his mouth to the top of my head, our heavy breaths the only sound in the still room.

Wellington killed them.

Critical mass is reached when the gravitational force of matter halts the expansion of the universe.

Everything grinds to a halt.

Still struggling for a breath, I curl my fingers over the warmth of Kallum's skin, the ring clasped in my fist. "It was him," I say, my voice raw, throat enflamed. "He was the one who hit my parents and just left them to die."

Kallum's strong arms enclose around me, where I'm comforted by the solid feel of him before I'm lifted up against his chest. I drape my forearms around his neck, buried in the pocket of his shoulder as he carries me into the living room.

"Wellington thought his wife had hired me," I say as he

deposits me in front of the fireplace. "That I was there to investigate him. Because I had been following him...he'd seen me. He thought I knew about the hit-and-run."

After I'm draped in a fleece blanket, Kallum sets a glass of water on the hearth. He then kneels before me, his beautiful features cast in sharp relief by the firelight. My gaze travels over him, taking in the inked sigils and scripted tattoos as if for the first time. I'm rocked with a shiver, unable to deny the truth as my eyes sweep up to find his.

"Synchronicity," I whisper.

"Everything connects."

The history lesson Kallum gave me in the killing fields our first night on the case wasn't really about the case at all. It was about me. About us—our history.

Everything connects.

History repeats itself.

Three is the magic number.

A shared, hidden wisdom.

"Shit," I mutter. With a shaky hand, I drop the ring next to the glass, then lower my face into my palms. I suck in two deep, sobering breaths to cleanse the lingering ache from my lungs.

Delicately, Kallum hooks his finger under my chin and forces my face up. "Keep going," he says, an echo of my own words.

"You knew," I say, the accusation clear. "You knew it was Wellington who killed my parents. How?"

His eyes catch the blaze of the fire as he tenderly strokes my jawline. "I saw Wellington's car," he admits, lowering his hand. "It was something petty I did, slash his tires just to fuck with him." He shrugs, indifferent. "But on that particular morning, I saw the dents, the smashed headlight. The silver paint deposit. The evidence of an accident. Then the news hit campus of a couple—Silvia and Darrin St. James—who had lost their lives due to a hit-and-run and their daughter who was seeking information. It didn't take a genius to link the pieces together."

I swallow hard and touch my throat that still flames. "Kallum...I... Why didn't you just tell me it was him?"

He releases a rough exhale. "Wellington had his car towed within an hour to repair and hide the damage."

I shake my head. "But there was still a record of him doing so, it still could've proven—"

"Would it have been enough to give you his name?" He cuts me off, his intense gaze hard on mine. "To arrest him? See him imprisoned? If he even would've been. Would it have been enough, Halen?"

The same question he asked of me once already. Only now, I understand why he needed the answer from me.

"No." I blink away the remaining tears. "I wanted him dead."

The confession tumbles out easily now, no resistance. No guilt. Maybe because I was primed, or maybe because it's simply the truth. When I made the connection to who Percy Wellington was that night—right in that blink of a moment—I swung that tire iron with one intentional outcome.

To end his life.

"That fury in you needed to punish, and it would have eventually, in the most destructive way to destroy you," he says, his tone of voice somber now. "So I gave you a killer to chase, a villain you could punish. I created the darkness that you needed to feast on, sweetness."

The Harbinger.

The serial killer spawned from my pain, Kallum brought into existence. Resurrected like a shadow monster from the darkest abyss.

And I didn't just chase that darkness, I immersed myself in it. My obsession with catching the Harbinger became my reason to bathe, to get dressed, to eat. *Breathe.*

Until my wreck.

Kallum doesn't need to voice what transpired afterword. I barely lived through it. Who was behind the wheel that night—me or my shadow? No matter what the accident report cited, I was the one driving. I was responsible. My guilt tore through me, annihilating. I might have never resurfaced.

The only thing that awoke me from my catatonic state was the Harbinger's next murder.

"I had to keep you alive." Kallum's clashing gaze searches mine. "Three murders, three crime scenes. Designed for you. On the anniversary, I was giving you what you needed, letting you catch their killer. Even if you never made the association to Wellington, you would feel the totality. I had it all planned out—"

"But then I showed up at the college." Disrupting the course and opening Pandora's fucking box.

"It wasn't all you." A mild dejection touches his expression. "I was supposed to trust the course, no matter where it led. Selfishly, I made demands." He traces a finger over the scarred sigil in his pectoral. "I just craved you too badly."

The blanket slips from my shoulder as Kallum takes my hand in his. The pad of his thumb caresses the scar on my palm. "The design was flawless," he says. "After you caught your Harbinger, I'd approach you like I should have that first time, and the goddamn planets would align. If they didn't, then I was prepared to leave this world in a blaze of glory and escape to the next, where maybe—just fucking maybe—I wouldn't fuck it up that time."

"Kallum—"

He pushes forward and captures my face between his palms. "But my design wasn't flawless. It was your design. Always yours. When I saw you in that moment, a goddess of the moon harnessing all your dark fury... Goddamn, you were utterly breathtaking. You delivered your violent retribution and brilliantly scapegoated the murder."

Yes, I scapegoated it right onto Kallum. But then he evaded the murder charge with a plea of insanity.

A testament to his genius—or the proof of his psychosis.

The twisted irony of accusing the Harbinger of the murder I committed is a paradox that threatens to shatter any rational mind I have left.

"I can't be a muse," I say to him, shaking my head against his hold. "Muses aren't supposed to inspire death."

He sweeps the tangle of white strands behind my ear affectionately. "Muse, goddess, huntress. From every fracted angle of light to the depth of your darkness, I'm inspired by all of you, Halen St. James."

I feel the atoms in the room charge. The night Kallum found me, I became his muse, his inspiration for the darkest acts of violence. That truth still remains, just on a longer timeline.

What frightened one man, the dark stirring of my soul, the thread of violence woven just beneath my surface, enraptures another.

His execution of the Harbinger was, in fact, flawless. The design skillful dark artistry, the synchronicity that's intwined into every intricate facet of us eloquent genius.

Kallum is frenzy. Kallum is mania. Divine madness and sanity cannot coexist in the same mind.

The price is too high.

A self-sacrifice that's cost him his soundness of mind.

Without a tether, with no counterbalance, he will be lost to his tortured mind, to his abyss. He will eventually be caught.

As his captivating gaze sears into mine, I'm standing on the precipice of the void.

Claw to the surface—or sink further.

My hand trembles as I gingerly touch the crescent sigil I sliced into his flesh, my desire for Kallum and I to have met before my life spiraled. I know he feels what I'm feeling, how badly I wish I could take us back to that moment.

With a heavy exhale, he reaches into his pocket and retrieves a silver ring. The simple band is fashioned similarly to the one he wears—and it's unmistakable.

The second cufflink.

He slides the band onto my finger and turns my hand over, where he delicately kisses my palm, the place I bled for him, claiming him as mine.

"I had this one made at the same time," he says, "because you were made for me, sweetness."

An ache burns in my throat as I first glance at the ring on the hearth, then the one circling my finger. "Double rings," I say, thinking back to that dark chamber. "A full circle."

A snake devouring its tail. Consuming us over and over.

"The double *ouroboros*," he confirms, his gaze lit with a mix of praise and hope as he laces our fingers together. "The balance of the upper and lower natures, the joining of opposites."

I focus on the solid feel of his hand, the sureness and comfort of his touch.

"For all the darkness and pain we've forged in this life to be together, for all the depravity and suffering, there is another space in time where I walked right up to you, where I held on tight, where we existed in the light, and it was so easy...like breathing, Halen. But because that beauty exists there, we can have it here. It belongs to us. We just had to wade through hell to find it."

A broken sound forms at the base of my throat as he offers me the desire of my heart.

There is no greater destruction than one of self...no catalyst more powerful to wield in alchemic creation. Destruction isn't an end, it's a beginning.

Our beginning.

Some cages, we design for ourselves. This one, I designed for us both. To deny him would be like caging a beautiful moth. He'd break his wings to get to the light.

Maybe he already has. But I have the power to repair the damage. I've always had the power.

I crawl into Kallum's lap and wrap myself around him. "I will never let you fall," I swear to him. Whatever cage is waiting below, I will never let Kallum fall. This omen is mine to prevent.

I kiss him with the passion we're barely able to contain between us. I make love to him furiously, the only way our souls connect, the most violent, heated parts of us destroying each other before we're healed with cleansing fire. The alchemy of our dark souls.

There is beauty in the darkest art, genius in the fault, the imperfections. The very substance that makes us bad and violent and wicked, when broken down to our divine state, makes us lovely.

We were designed for each other.

18

DARK MATTER

KALLUM: TWO YEARS LATER

Nietzsche once said: *To live is to suffer, to survive is to find meaning in the suffering.*

Nietzsche and his great pain. His tortured path to the philosopher's stone. Not to insult the renowned philosopher (more so than I already have), but fuck survival.

Who wants to merely survive this life?

That's like settling for being a god.

Let me explain.

Once upon a time, as a bored, egotistical professor of occult sciences, my only suffering was a meaningless existence. A chaoist without a madness of his own.

Then like a strike of lightning, my muse illuminated my dark sky.

My utter, divine inspiration.

My beautiful madness.

While the *rausch* enraptures us in an artistic

outpouring of pure frenetic ecstasy, for those who see through the veil, it can also be an affliction.

The mind is what is sacrificed for our desire.

The frenzy makes us feel as if we're reaching a higher plane above humanity and becoming godlike. But the gods could never feel as we do, be as passionate as we are. Because they bear no pain.

Our great pain inspires our great art.

Without the capability to descend to the depths of suffering, we are never able to experience the sheer, transformative ecstasy of pleasure.

There are no high and low notes.

Without my muse of heartbreak, I would have never experienced this deep pain, because I was not designed to feel this alone. I would have coasted through this life, unfeeling, unmoved. A callous, reviled rock of mediocrity.

What she brought me was something so ineffable, a love so divine, I would insult it just by trying to describe it.

So while it's true that to live is to suffer, we also have the ability to ascend to far greater heights than mere survival of this life. Look for the symbols. Follow the course. Seize your madness.

It's been two years since Halen and I destroyed every article of evidence from the Harbinger's last scene at our mountain home. Two years since my beautiful muse submitted to her dark flame that binds us together. And not a single day passes where I don't acknowledge that a single flutter of a wing could've deviated our course.

Like the gnarled trees of the marsh, without her, I would have become one of them, twisted and decrepit, trapped in the seventh circle of hell by my own violence.

Hope is such a frail and flimsy emotion to hang our desires on.

While I hoped Halen would choose us in the end, the fiend in me made damn sure every move was meticulously calculated to ensure there was no other outcome.

For her, I will always be that devil.

From the moment I witnessed her wield her pain like a fury from the underworld, I understood I could have never been the one to offer her that complete solace, no matter how much I desired to be.

It was her who had to bring her course full circle.

I was merely an instrument in her design.

But I could look into her beautiful eyes of storm clouds and showering stars and accept her darkness. I could devour every last drop of guilt and shame that wanted to lock her in purgatory. I could become the demon of her nightmares, the monster of her shadowy abyss, and kill ruthlessly for her. This dark seed was already planted in my nature, but she gave it purpose.

My only risk of damnation was if I didn't get the girl.

I lean against the deeply veined bark of a tree and spin my ring, thoughts chasing the symbols that still linger amid this marshland like the dwindling light peeking through the branches of black willows.

Halen is down in the ravine visiting her memories. I give her this time every year to be alone with her thoughts.

She's become a highly sought-after criminologist the feds and other agencies request for the highest profile cases. Once she moved out of the shadows, accepting her unorthodox and even dangerous methods to profile the killers she hunts, she's become renowned in her own right.

As for me, I never returned to my full-time position at the college. Rather, I opted to elevate my assistant professor, Ryder, to take over my course load so I could accept a research grant to write a book. While I've funded most of the research and trips myself, having it partially funded through the university faculty grant will give the project an air of credibility in academia for those who need that shit.

The book itself delves into the awakening I underwent during my sabbatical years ago in Egypt—the one that plunged me into the depths, where I uncovered a dark secret that the ancients hid from us all.

This awakening, I have no doubt, will rock the academic realm.

But damn, chaos is coded in my DNA. Let's raise some fucking hell.

Hermes was the trickster god, after all. *Wink.*

So now, Halen and I divide our time between investigating crime scenes and traveling for the book. And in the moments between, we fuck, and fight, and love, and feed our desires.

We do have particular tastes—and an insatiable appetite.

When we're hungry, we eat.

We've become quite adept at feeding our cravings.

And I still feel her when her emotions soar. Like they are now. A mix of elation and turmoil that makes me curious as to what my little muse is thinking about down in that ravine.

While I believe she's come to a place of acceptance

with her loss, at times I still sense the melancholy that grips her around the same time every year as her wreck.

Halen has never spoken of her miscarriage. There are scars outward and inward that haunt her, and the loss of her pregnancy is one of those. We did once have an unspoken conversation as to where we stood on contraceptives, when I tossed out the birth control pills her doctor prescribed her, and she smiled that devious sprite smile at me. Then we fucked like animals for hours afterward.

We're not trying, but we're not *not* trying. As time goes on, and she doesn't become pregnant, we're faced with the reality that it may not be in the stars for us.

My desire was born in her eyes, the eyes I want to pass down to that beautiful piece of us we can create together, but we are complete whether or not this happens. It would only add to our completeness, not steal from it otherwise.

Then there are other rare moments when I feel her fear, when I see it crest in her eyes as she looks at me, the fear of my deteriorating mental state. In this world, there's a fine line between genius and mental illness.

Though I've never thought about it in a clinical sense, this is the only fear I wish I could alleviate within Halen. One misstep on the tightrope could mean the difference between creating a *magnum opus* and a permanent address at a psych ward.

So every day I strive to keep my vow to her, that she will never lose me. She's the reason I remain in this world at all. She's my answer to the manic episodes, the sleepless nights. The havoc that threatens to tear through my mind is quelled by her touch alone.

To obtain the desire of our heart, a sacrifice has to be made. There is always a trade.

My eyes were wide open when I made mine.

It wasn't a difficult choice. It wasn't a choice at all. Love lures us into a madness where escape feels like a cruel punishment.

One day, if the demons become too much of a threat, she knows how to make it stop.

And I will welcome her lovely damnation.

For now, when those restless instances do occur, I remind myself I'm just a speck of dust floating in the cosmos being observed by my seer. There's an ironic comfort in knowing our crude, base material still has eons to go before it's perfected into gold.

Then I kiss my muse, swallow the lovely sounds she gifts only to me, and plot our next life, where I get to seduce her all over again.

The magick in chaos is part stubborn belief in our will to be realized, and part the mechanics of the elements around us on a quantum level. For all that we know, there are infinite unknowns.

It's what we cannot see that bends and shapes us, the darkest matter of the universe swims in our cells, a chaotic dance of form like the motions of the stars. The light is warped, but it's how we know it's there.

We reunite with our twin flame over and over through the course until we reach the highest form of harmony. But before we see the light, it's going to get dark, and it's what we do in those darkest moments that define us.

Muse to the devil. Goddess of the moon. She captures

me in her beautiful flickers of light. That's where I'll always find her, there in the flicker.

I look down at my hand, spin my ring.

Halen feels me just the same, can always sense my hunger. When the need to surrender to the primal violence dominates my atoms, when the ravenous bloodlust demands to be satiated, my lovely, wicked muse speaks to me of omens and death, whispers of blood and retribution.

She feeds me in my dark abyss.

Halen

I trace my finger over the symbol of the philosopher's stone engraved into the clay wall. I make two trips a year when I visit my parents' gravesite, and then return to Hollow's Row to visit the ravine.

This is where Devyn found her brother and buried him beneath the bones of their rend sacrifices. This is where she marked his grave with a symbol of their journey to deify themselves, to escape their disease together.

When the task force had the deer carcasses removed, most of Colter's remains were discovered. His remains have since been relocated to one of the town's cemeteries. Despite this, I feel Devyn would still consider this his place of rest.

During the case, Devyn chose to tell me about her brother when we were here together. I've wondered if she did so at the time because Riddick was nearby, to appear as if she was trying to steer me away from the society theory, or if there was some other, personal reason.

Even though this chasm has been cleared of all the death, the faint scent of decay remains, like the scene has been imprinted with her mourning. I often see her in my mind in those last seconds together on the crest of the dam, when I gave her my diamond pendant.

Despite my logical disposition, I still feel a connection to her, even though I know it's impossible that she's alive. I've since conducted more in-depth research into Huntington's Disease.

Even though I have search engine alerts set with her name and details, and scour databases every couple of months searching for a death certificate for any Jane Does that fit her description, it's only a matter of time before her body is found and identified.

So I suppose I'm really here visiting her, as I choose to believe that in some way, she left a part of herself here with her brother. That this is her place of rest, too.

I'm still unsure if I was meant to find and help Devyn, or if she was meant to help me see that this world is not black and white. To live in the gray is to experience life as it was meant. Passionately, fearlessly. Even recklessly. And there can be peace, a form of escape for the things we cannot control, for the sorrow that will otherwise destroy us.

I hope she found hers in the end.

Inhaling a deep breath, I place the pink gladioli beneath the symbol. "I hope I'll see you again," I say to the open air, even though I have difficulty believing in such a possibility.

As I turn and start toward the other side of the ravine, I think back to my first memory of following Emmons into the marsh, seeing the eyes woven to the trees, and his visceral anger. It was fear I sensed in him, but its source wasn't what I initially presumed.

Emmons was fearful over what Devyn had done, drawing attention to them by going rogue with her own rituals. His fear drove him to extreme measures in the days that followed.

In psychology, we're taught that fear is the weakest emotion, that its purpose is to be transmuted into its opposite, positive emotion which encourages the healing process. While I do agree, I also believe fear is the most powerful motivator on a destructive path.

It aims to overpower, manipulate, and destroy.

It's how we deal with our fear that determines what our outcome will be.

Uncovering these fears in suspects has become the basis for my profiling technique, and it's helped me close six cold cases.

Kallum and I departed the current case to make this trip, and already the pull to return to the scene is compelling me back there. Just last week, the case escalated and was upgraded to serial killer status, the media giving the unknown subject a moniker: The Acolyte.

The suspect suffers from erotomania, and has an especially brutal kill method.

In order to connect with this offender, I'll have to immerse myself in their delusion. Which I admit, does induce a deep level of fear. Once the door has been

331

opened, there's no sealing it off. Entering into another person's world of obsession is dangerous.

But Kallum is always there to catch me if I fall too far.

As I trek back toward the path of boulders, I stumble over a loose rock. "Shit."

I look down and catch sight of something buried beneath a patch of thickly grouped bloodroot. My heart vaults as I shove my tote bag to my backside and hunch down, clearing aside the white lobed flowers to reveal what's hidden beneath.

At first, I think I've finally discovered what happened to my Hollow's Row notebook. While working the ravine one day, I set my journal down and forgot it there after Emmons took a fall. I returned later to look, and even asked the other members of the task force if it was recovered.

It never turned up.

But as I lift the notebook out of the flowers, adrenaline speeds my pulse. After two years, the condition should be worn and damaged from the elements—yet it looks like it was placed here just recently.

I glance around the ravine as a murder of crows takes flight above the ridge. The flapping beat of their wings holds me captive in a crushing vise of apprehension until I force myself to look down at what lie on the rocky earth beneath.

My fingers caress the soft beige yarn. Then, with a tremor gripping my hands, I hold up the small quilt, my eyes tracking the intricate stitchwork of the baby blanket.

A hot ache forms in my throat as I instinctively touch my belly.

Logically, I know it's not possible. Devyn isn't alive, she can't be, and yet I'm holding a blanket knit with her signature pattern.

A mix of uncertainty and comfort envelops me as I touch the delicate stitches, my thoughts trying to decipher the meaning.

Regardless that my doctor assured me it was possible after my operation, I haven't been able to conceive. Some days it's an afterthought that doesn't impact my life. Other days, it's like suffering that painful loss all over again.

My fingers splay over my belly as I blink away the moisture. Then I push the blanket onto my lap and part the notebook open. I flip through the pages, a sense of nostalgia overcoming me as I scan my research notes.

There are no additions, nothing has been altered—then I pause at a highlighted section of text.

...in darkness, she found it filled with light. It was joined with it, since it had become divine according to her, and it lives in her. It also brought them out from darkness into light, from grief to joy, from sickness to health, from death to life.

A tear slips free, and I swipe at my cheek, the ache burning in the center of my chest.

The passage was taken from a translated text on the secret of the alchemists' philosopher's stone.

And I didn't highlight the passage.

"Devyn," I whisper, my voice shaky, my heart and mind violently battling for dominance.

Rationally speaking, I'm logical enough to admit that it's our vanity that wants to denounce the inexplicable and declare the things we cannot explain as impossible. That it's the most logical, rational explanation to accept we're simply incapable of understanding the workings of the universe.

"I hear the music," I whisper to the elements, my hand cradled to my belly.

I clutch the soft blanket, a sprig of hope growing, before I clear the tears and tuck both the notebook and blanket away in my crossbody tote. Then I start up the ravine.

Kallum appears at the top of the ridge, and heat gathers beneath my skin at the strikingly sinful sight of him. I swear, it should be illegal to be so fucking sexy.

He meets me at the halfway mark and extends his hand, pulling me up beside him and keeping his fingers laced through mine until we reach the top.

Beneath the weeping limbs of the giant willow, he cups my face and kisses me, tasting the salt on my lips. "I want to spend the rest of the day just tasting you."

I link my arms around his neck and push onto my toes to be closer to him. "Are you finding that too much of a challenge, professor?"

"Don't tempt me, Dr. St. James." His groan makes me shiver, then his features contort as he pulls out his phone and shows me a text from Hernandez, who has recently become a part of our team after the last case we worked together. "A fourth victim was just recovered."

The strike of a drum resounds within me as a wild flame ignites, whispering to the huntress like a seductive lure to chase the darkness.

My wrists locked against his neck, I spin the ring around my finger as I look deep into Kallum's beautiful, clashing eyes. He created the Harbinger for me, to save me when I was lost, and when we destroyed all the evidence, we retired the killer to a cold case.

But a cold case is never officially closed.

"I think it's the Acolyte that needs a challenge," I say, sensually stroking the back of his neck.

Kallum's nostrils flare, and a muscle flexes along his jaw as he swallows. Sometimes, I can only glimpse of the killer banked beneath his charisma and deceptive beauty as he keeps the Harbinger at bay. But then there are other times, like now, when he lowers the mask, and I'm confronted with the devil in all his fiendish, diabolical glory.

He licks his lips and catches the white strands of my hair between his fingers. "We can do whatever we want," he says, his tone suggestive.

"We can," I agree as I bring a hand between us and slip my fingers down the sculpted ridges of his chest. "But first...maybe we can get lost for a few hours," I say, earning another rough groan from him.

"Fuck, sweetness." A devious glint flashes amid the flinty shadows of his eyes before his lips crash against mine.

He hauls me up against his strong body and carries me toward the hood of the car, where he doesn't waste time stripping me of my clothes.

As he removes my shirt, I glimpse the fresh tattoo on my forearm, the verse that reads: *The alchemy of the soul is transforming pain into creative genius.*

I once told Kallum that he was the philosopher I

wanted branded on my body, and now I have his words inked into the scar tissue.

Out of all the beautiful things he's said, I chose this because of what it means to me, of what it reminds me. When Kallum said this our first day on the case, at the time, his blurt felt random, but I can now see how his mind drew the conclusion.

Kallum took my pain, all of my anguish and heartsickness, all the broken pieces of me, and transformed the darkest parts of my soul into a ghastly masterpiece.

During those early moments, I was too consumed with the case, and honestly, with him, to see the signs clearly. I questioned Kallum's mental health many times throughout the course of the case, wondering if it was a performance.

Trying to diagnose Kallum Locke is like trying to fathom quantum theory—a topic he insists on sadistically torturing me with. One of the leading psychiatrists in the country was unable to establish a diagnosis, when he told me that I'd have to do so myself.

Dr. Torres said that Kallum's violent tendencies were made worse by his obsession, but it's in his obsession where the treatment lies.

Just as Kallum looks to synchronistic symbolism to guide him, I've been linking the signs. Like how on that very first day Kallum was displaying the marks of psychosis and an affective disorder.

At that point, he had spent six months apart from me. As we grew closer during the case, those moments of delusion and chaotic bursts of mania happened less frequently.

I touch my ring, thinking about the *ouroboros*. To the

ancients, *pharmakon* was both poison and cure. The snake's venom is where we derive its antidote. In the same way, as Kallum's obsession is the root of his psychosis, it's also what keeps him tethered to sanity.

The remedy to the mental illness is in the ailment itself, the very heart of the problem, his obsession with his muse.

And I'll always be with him to counterbalance the frenzy with grounding logic and reason.

Because I don't just crave his maddening, fiery passion —I need it. I need him. I am so utterly, fervently in love with Kallum that it can frighten me, the fear I have of losing him. When I think about those terrifying, endless seconds on the dam with Emmons, where I thought Kallum was gone, and the violent force that tore through me as a result...

I am the fucking abyss.

And I refuse to lose him to any monster, outward or within. The demons that threaten to annihilate his mind will discover how dark my shadow can become, how fiercely I will fight to protect the man who is branded into my flesh and my soul.

All the philosophers had their elements. Heraclitus, fire. Thales, water. If there can be only one element argued to belong to Kallum Locke, a chaoist at heart, it would have to be aether.

The *prima materia*, the dark matter of the universe. The chaos of the soul.

As he deepens the kiss, his hand settles over my belly. Being consumed by him, I unlink my arms from around his neck and touch the crescent concealed beneath his crisp dress shirt.

In another lifetime, maybe we wouldn't have had to wade through hell to be together, and Kallum wouldn't have to walk a tightrope over an abyss of insanity, or I'd have no fear of falling too far into the void.

Our love story is bittersweet, saturated with heartache and loss, sacrifice and all that we strive to give to each other.

But as Kallum said, our story can be beautiful here, too. Because we have pain, we can have pleasure. Because of the darkness, there is light. There is so much loveliness beneath the shadows when we let our eyes adapt to the darkness.

As he fills me wholly, completely, leaving no room for those fears in this moment, I know that whatever the universe has in store for us beyond this point we'll face it together.

A thousand love stories told through the ages and one moral endures:

The darkest love kindles the brightest hope.

We could be a romance, or a tragedy. But that depends on where you pause the story.

In life, there is no such thing as a happily ever after. There's a sad moment. Pain. Struggle. Then a brief moment of pleasure and contentment. Maybe even happiness. But the credits don't roll. The story keeps going. So there's more sadness, more pain. More struggles and pleasure.

Until the story just…

Stops.

EPILOGUE

WHAT IF

KALLUM

The brightest little pixie laugh captures my attention to stop me in my tracks.

Sheltered under the eaves of the quad, I remove my hand from my pocket and touch my chest at the sudden, foreign ache. I then turn in search for the source—and there she is, the most exquisite creature I've ever laid eyes on.

Wittgenstein wrote: *Whereof one cannot speak, thereof one must remain silent.*

He spoke on this in reference to negative theology, when what we experience is too ineffable to define, only a fool would make an attempt to put it into words.

And I would have to be a fool to try to define this rapturous rush that overpowers me.

As I make a study of her from my secluded corner, the chorus from *Media Vita in Morte Sumus* spills into my head, and suddenly, I know without fail I'm a devil who's stumbled into heaven.

She throws her head back and laughs, and I'm slammed with a cyclone of emotions—all of them, every goddamn emotion she has ever felt and will ever feel crashes into me.

It feels like a heart attack.

Yet it's the bittersweet melancholy steeped in honeysuckle and clove, an ache so euphoric it nearly drops me to my knees, that holds me bound, fearful of walking away from her.

I don't just want to take my next breath, I crave it like a wasteland craves rain.

This angel has washed up on my shores of despair, and my heart beats for the first fucking time. God, it's painful, but I've never felt so fucking alive.

Her long waves pulled back into a low ponytail, she nibbles her lip. Tucks the escaping strand of white behind her ear. So docile, yet so fucking sexy, I have the uncontrollable desire to devour her all at once—every last sinful drop.

As if she senses my predatory gaze, she looks my way and our eyes connect. I'm speared right through my sternum by the prettiest shade of hazel. Her mouth parts as I offer her a lopsided smile, and it only lasts a moment, but I swear I feel her delicious shiver roll through me.

She returns her attention to the man and woman, and I make an educated guess that these are her parents. The woman shares a hereditary trait; the same vein of white streaked through her dark hair.

I watch as the couple walk off, leaving my prey all alone.

Taking one determined step toward her, I immediately halt when I spot the diamond ring on her finger. She's twisting the band, her expression shifting from a captivating smile to a tight frown.

I feel as if I'm standing on the precipice of an abyss, destiny hinged on a single choice.

Fuck it.

I push through the barrier, cutting a direct path to my muse.

The sun sets behind the campus, the rays of faded orange and pink cast her in an aethereal glow as I stalk toward her, my gaze tapered to a pinpoint on my prey.

I sink my hands into the depths of my pockets as I approach, slowly, so I'm not tempted to touch her. "You're an intriguing little thing."

Her hazel eyes narrow, but there's a faint curl to her lips. "I must be. I've noticed you studying me like some cryptic artifact, Professor Locke."

Amused, I grin and cock my head. "So my reputation proceeds me."

"It does," she says, crossing her arms. "The renowned professor of all things occult and esoteric philosophy." Her smile stretches. "But also, I've heard more than one person refer to you as the bad-boy of academia."

My smile turns devilish. "I suppose it depends on who you talk to. But please, it's Kallum."

She licks her lips, and my gaze drops to her mouth as I suppress a groan. "Well, it's nice to officially meet you,

Kallum. Maybe next time you can show us around your department."

I look past her to the couple retreating from the courtyard. "How about now?" I might regret this—I'm not usually up for impressing parents—but my instincts are screaming not to let her leave.

"Now?" She arches a delicate eyebrow.

"Right now."

She bites the corner of her lip. "Thank you for the offer, but I have a job to get back to."

"*Hmm.* That's hardly any fun."

"Those are the rules, professor."

"Rules are definitely no fun." I drop my tone to a dangerous decibel as my gaze settles on the ring circling her finger, the challenge in my gaze unmistakable.

A defiant spark flickers in her eyes, then she swipes the lock of white from her vision. The desire to tuck that defiant streak behind her ear hits me fierce and hot.

I might be on my way to hell for this, but fuck, I'll descend those fiery crags for this angel.

If she needs a villain to steal her away, I can be that ruthless bastard.

"All right," she finally says, accepting my challenge. "Just…give me a minute."

"I'll wait for you."

I'd wait a millennia for her—but the crippling fear she won't return unexpectedly assaults me, and I call out, "You didn't give me your name."

A sly smile twists her sultry mouth. "I know."

While students filter past in a rush to escape the grounds, I wait patiently, more patiently than I've ever waited for anything in my miserable, selfish existence, until she mercifully returns.

My advance is intercepted by the man who shares similar features as her. I extend my hand. "Professor Kallum Locke," I say in introduction. "I head up the occult sciences department."

"Oh, of course." He accepts the handshake. "Dean Masters sings your praises every year we visit. Darrin St. James. This is my wife Silvia, and my daughter Halen."

I nod to the woman. "Lovely to meet you." Then I give my undivided attention to Halen, echoing her name like a song. "Like the band Van Halen?" I arch an eyebrow, purposely popping the dimple in my cheek.

She's affected, inhaling a fortifying breath before she nods. "Like the band," she confirms, and fucking hell, I'm tempted to steal her away just so I can keep her sweet voice all to myself. "It's this whole romantic meet-cute between my parents."

Darrin chuckles. "We met at a concert," he supplies. "Silvia was wearing this white dress, standing out like an angel and immediately ruining me for anyone else." He gives his wife an affectionate glance. "We were both in attendance here for three years before that night. I guess the fates finally pushed us together."

While he's telling their story, my focus is on Halen, the way she beams at these two people with pride and love. It's such a foreign experience for me, I'm entranced.

"It's our anniversary," Silvia says in follow up. "We return to the university every year just to reminisce. But honestly, we really should be getting back, sweetheart."

"Please, let me show you around the new wing first," I

offer. "College traffic is terrible right now. Too many reckless drivers on the roads. Trust me."

This seems to sway them, and Silvia nods in agreement.

And I am an utter gentlemen as I give the St. James's a tour. Even as we gravitate toward the other side of campus and I'm scheming how to keep little Halen longer. Forever.

I've concluded her ring is an engagement ring. I don't have to know this man to know he's not good enough for her. Hell, I'm not good enough—but I will damn sure try to be what she needs.

"You haven't mentioned what you do yet," I say to her.

"I'm a crime-scene analyst," she says. "I investigate violent crime scenes to build profiles on offenders."

I hike an eyebrow as I try to envision this beautiful sprite of a woman amid all that chaos and darkness. "That's fascinating, and dark."

A curious crease forms between her brows. "Um, yes. Some people find it scary." She twists her ring.

"Some people can't understand the draw to chase the darker side." And if I have to, I will become that darkness she chases.

She swallows, her slender throat working. "I'm sure you're tired of hearing this, but your eyes are distracting."

A smile ghosts my lips. My clever sprite is changing the topic. "Should I take that as a compliment?"

She peeks up at me as we continue to walk. "I have no doubt that you will despite my intent."

I wet my lips, tasting her on the air. "Oh no, intent is everything."

The evening has deepened to shades of navy and space, cloaking us in the dark to instill a sense of seclusion. The grounds are still as I slow my pace, forcing us to fall a distance behind her parents.

"Thank you for doing this for them," Halen says, drawing her arms around her waist.

"Sure," I say, slowing my steps further, "but just to be clear, I did this for me, simply in the hopes to get you alone."

She laughs. "You have no shame."

"None." I send her a sly smile, invoking another shiver. "You're trembling."

"I'm not used to the weather."

"Here." I remove my suit blazer and drape it over her shoulders before we wander toward the parking lot.

She hugs the jacket tighter around her, and seeing her in my clothes wreaks havoc on my mental state. I know the jacket will carry her delectable scent, and I'm tortured in preparation for tomorrow's lectures.

"You know, I recently read one of your papers," she says casually.

This surprises me, and I bury my hands in my pockets. "Which one?"

"Something on quantum mysticism that compares shamanism to the many-worlds theory." She shakes her head. "It made my head hurt, actually."

My smile twitches, and I remove a hand to run it over my mouth. "Feynman said, anyone who claims to understand quantum theory is either lying or crazy."

She glances up at me. "And which one are you?"

A strange feeling washes over me, a sense we've done this before. "I'd think that's for the profiler to decide." I send her a wink, earning a sweet blush. "But now you have to settle my ego and tell me your thoughts."

Halen stops walking and turns toward me. "Honestly? I'm a hardcore realist. I want to argue against all of it. But...I don't know. I always try to question everything, even what my mind tells me is impossible."

"That's a non-answer," I accuse delicately.

She senses she's been caught. "Okay then. I think quantum theory is witchcraft." She shrugs, and my jacket engulfs her adorably.

I can't help it, I laugh. "You're not too far off, sweetness." She inhales a sharp breath as I step right in front of her. "Here, let me offer a demonstration."

I capture her hair and pull it over her shoulder, then slowly drag the band down the length of her soft tresses, admiring the way the dark layers spill over her shoulder.

"Are you this hands-on during all of your lectures, professor?" Her tone is playful, but I note the breathy tremble just beneath.

"Never," I say truthfully. "You're the first to inspire me."

An electric current charges the air between us, loaded with too much chemical attraction to ignore.

I hold the elastic band up. "Before I saw you, your hair could have been pulled back or loose. I'm not aware of the style until I observe you, then one of the possibilities becomes true, and the other collapses. This is an oversimplification of the Copenhagen interpretation. Now" —I run my fingers through her hair, relishing in the way she shivers at my touch—"with the many worlds theory, no collapse occurs. Your hair is in many styles all at once. It's not pulled back or loose; it's both at the same time."

She tips her head back farther. "But as the observer, you're now entangled with my hair, professor."

Goddamn, the way she says *professor* does something dangerous to me. The deviant urge to wrap her hair around my fist and entangle myself so deeply inside her burns through me with vicious need.

"Exactly, and this is where our shaman finds himself," I say. "If we accept that many worlds exist, where nearly every choice, every possibility exists simultaneously, then we can pose a question of what would happen to the shaman's mind, a single consciousness, if he obtained entry to these worlds."

Halen laughs. "See, my head hurts just trying to fathom it."

"We're not meant to," I assure her. "As the shaman becomes entangled with the many worlds, this induces a state of mystical ecstasy. To those who view him from the outside, it looks like madness. But let's consider it's the *what if* paradox. All worlds have a possible highest experience, and he's attempting to experience them all at once, in search of the divine."

Halen considers this a moment. "But if you spend a lifetime in search of the highest experience, then you never get to truly live the one experience. Maybe I'm simply too logical, but to me, that's madness."

As she says this, I swear, she's stolen the breath right from my lungs. "I find you remarkable, Miss St. James."

She glances down at her ring before she meets my eyes

again. "It's Dr. St. James."

I run my tongue across the ridge of my teeth. "Noted."

She drags in an unsteady breath. "Thank you for that stimulating lecture," she says, defusing the gathering tension. "Oh, and also for the use of your jacket. Here—"

"Wait—" She freezes as I reach out and capture a small moth that's entangled its wings in her hair. Her breath stills, and I'm desperate to taste her lips, to hear her release that breath in a throaty moan.

My mouth hovers close to hers, a dare, a promise.

A goddamn inevitability.

She watches as I release the insect to the night, and it flutters toward the illuminated lamppost above us. When I return my focus to her, I accept the jacket and slip my arms into the sleeves, savoring her scent.

The parking lot is silent, the whole world has ceased to exist in her presence. Absently, she spins her ring, and a devious part of me wants to slip it off her finger, to primally claim her right this instant.

From my periphery, I catch sight of Wellington stumbling away from his parked car. He's obviously inebriated, and I think I've finally had enough of our petty squabbles and decide to report him. Halen could've been driving on the same street as him, and that thought comes with a snap of quick rage.

She looks back at her parents as they reach their car, then says, "I should go, too." She takes a step away from me, then another. As I watch her retreating farther from me, a hollowness carves out my chest.

"Little Halen," I call out, and she turns around.

Making my boldest move yet, I stalk toward her and

take hold of her hand. "I don't want there to be a *what if* for us."

She looks down at our entwined fingers, the inked sigils I've tattooed into my skin. I don't want to let her go.

"I have to see you again," I tell her.

She slips her hand free of mine. "Then I guess you're going to have to find me, professor."

I close the distance, so close I sense her stop breathing. "Across time and space, heaven and hell, this life and the next in any world"—I reach out and tuck the tempting streak of white behind her ear—"I will find you, Halen St. James."

Author's Note:

Saying thank you for reading my work just doesn't feel like enough. Lovely reader, this was a labor of love and madness, and there were many days where I feared this would be the book that broke me.

So firstly, thank you for being here, for reading my words, for giving me a reason to breathe. Every author has a love-hate relationship with writing, and while there were days where I feared I might quit, the desire to tell Halen and Kallum's story, to give readers an escape, kept me writing.

Secondly, I wanted to reiterate that this is a work of fiction. The philosophies throughout this series are not scholarly references. As Kallum said in book two, he cherrypicked the details, which I have very much done here in order to create a backdrop for their story. Kallum's opinions of philosophers and teachings are not my own (his ego has no rival), and he's cunning enough to know how to bend and twist these philosophies to further his personal agenda (which he did to the extreme).

If you're interested in learning more (and from direct resources) about occultism, chaos magick, Dionysian Mysteries, Nietzsche, Carl Jung, Shadow Self, Cleopatra the Alchemist, or any other piece of history, theology, and mythology within, I urge you to delve into your own research, and enjoy the journey down the beautiful, magical rabbit hole.

Thirdly, there were themes and symbolism throughout this series that I wanted to touch on more closely.

Kallum's deeper reason for why he referred to Halen as his moon goddess. Alchemy has been layered through this series, and to me, personally, alchemy is everything and anything, but here is a direct link to where you can find this quote from below, which gives deeper insight to the sun and moon references: https://www.rcpe.ac.uk/her-itage/alchemy-college-collections

"The Sun and Moon are major symbols in alchemy. They represent the two most precious metals, gold (Sun) and silver (Moon). They also represent sulphur and mercury and are often depicted as a couple bound together in marriage or as the Mother and Father of the Philosophers' Stone."

Halen often used fire to describe Kallum's eyes and his nature, referring to his volatile temperament as the sun or a star going supernova. In contrast, Halen was Kallum's albedo, the silver moon condition in alchemy for reaching the purest, divine state.

And then we have the marsh trees of Hollow's Row. As the story begins with Halen seeing the trees, I wanted to end with Kallum's thoughts on them so we come full circle.

When Halen first introduces us to the marshland of Hollow's Row, she says, "I don't like the trees." This is symbolic foreshadowing of her character that we can't possibly know at this early point, but deepens her character. While Halen is an intellectual in her own right, she doesn't have an eidetic memory, and can't call on her knowledge in the way Kallum so readily does, which is why she keeps a journal of her research. When she first glimpses the trees, somewhere in the dark waters of her unconscious she makes a chilling connection to them.

In Dante's Inferno, the seventh circle of hell, the circle of violence, there exists one of three levels that is reserved for those who attempt and complete suicide. The souls are transformed into ghastly, gnarled trees where the harpies devour the leaves, causing them pain.

For Halen, it's a reflection of her shadow, her turmoil, and her battle for the will to live.

Kallum says in his final chapter: "Like the gnarled trees of the marsh, without her, I would have become one of them, twisted and decrepit, trapped in the seventh circle of hell by my own violence."

For Kallum, the symbolism has always been more clear. He confessed in book one his contemplation of this act before he found Halen, and he felt a connection to Dante, as in much the same way Dante traversed the circles of hell to save his beloved, Kallum traversed through his personal and metaphorical hell to save his.

I feel it's important to clearly state that, if you or anyone that you know is battling thoughts of self-harm or suicide, please reach out to someone for help. There are resources, such as 988 Suicide and Crisis Lifeline: dial 988 or go to https://988lifeline.org/

Lastly, I have never faced a more challenging character arc than Professor Kallum Locke. From taking him from the start as a potential villain, to a hero, to a villain, and then an antihero, all while trying to make us fall further in love with him...writing him is as exhausting as reading him sometimes, I promise. But I truly hope that you have fallen in love with Kallum, and Halen, and their story.

I could probably write a whole other book on just the research and references, but no one wants that ha (I know I get wordy; I spend most of my days yelling at walls for this reason; I wish that was a joke), and at some point, it's time to leave Hollow's Row (for my sanity; I wish this was a joke also), but I did leave a little place open for the continuation of their story...if and when my brain has recovered enough to embark on that project. There is the vague mention of the Acolyte, and resurrecting the Harbinger. This was a compromise I had to make with Kallum in order to be allowed to finish the book.

Again, thank you, so much, for reading their story, and

for reading my note, and for taking the journey with me through the book of my heart. You will never know what it means to me, from the bottom of my dark, dark heart.

Read madly,

Trish

Where do we go from here?

If you want a little more Halen and Kallum, as in deleted scenes, potential tie-in novellas (yes, Kallum is trying to negotiate this from me), the audiobook release, and updates on any future special editions, please join my VIP newsletter list on my website at TrishaWolfe.com

If you want to dive down the rabbit hole of my backlist with more intense plots, characters, and thrilling twists, keep flipping the pages to see my preferred reading order.

Also, here is a special gift to readers: receive a FREE bonus story featuring London and Grayson from the **Darkly, Madly Duet** .

We weren't born the day we took our first breath. We were born the moment we stole it. ~Grayson Sullivan, *Born, Darkly*

Meet Grayson Sullivan, AKA The Angel of Maine serial killer, and Dr. London Noble, the psychologist who falls for her patient, as they're drawn into a dark and twisted web. The ultimate cat and mouse game for dark romance lovers.

TRISHA WOLFE READING ORDER

All Trisha's series are written to read on their own and pull you in, but here is her preferred reading order to introduce worlds and characters that cross over in each series.

Broken Bonds Series

With Visions of Red

With Ties that Bind

Derision

Darkly, Madly Duet

Born, Darkly

Born, Madly

A Necrosis of the Mind Duet

Cruel

Malady

Hollow's Row Series

Lovely Bad Things

Lovely Violent Things

Lovely Wicked Things

Dark Mafia Romance

Marriage & Malice

Devil in Ruin

ABOUT THE AUTHOR

From an early age, Trisha Wolfe dreamed up fictional worlds and characters and was accused of talking to herself. Today, she lives in South Carolina with her family and writes full time, using her fictional worlds as an excuse to continue talking to herself. Get updates on future releases at TrishaWolfe.com

Want to be the first to hear about new book releases, special promotions, and signing events for all Trisha Wolfe books? Sign up for Trisha Wolfe's VIP list on her website.

Connect with Trisha Wolfe on social media on these platforms: Facebook Group | Instagram | TikTok

Made in United States
Troutdale, OR
02/09/2024

17543245R00206